Warwick

The Man behind the Wars of the Roses

Tony Riches

Tony Riches is a full time writer and lives with his wife in Pembrokeshire, West Wales UK. For more information about Tony's other published work please see:

www.tonyriches.co.uk

To my Mum,
who taught me to read.

Acknowledgements

I would like to thank my wife, Liz, for all her help and advice and support with the editing of this book.

I also thank Calvin Hedley and all the historians and historical fiction authors who have guided and inspired my interest in fifteenth century England.

A famous knight and excellent greatly spoken of through the most part of Christendom he had all England at his leading and was dread and dowhyted [feared] through many lands. And though forward fortune him deceived at his end yet his knightly acts had been so excellent that his noble and famous name could never be put out of laudable memory.

John Rous, Chaplain to the Earls of Warwick, 1477

Foreword

Writers from William Shakespeare to best-selling modern authors have tried to show what sort of man Richard Neville, Earl of Warwick, also known of as the 'Kingmaker', must have been, with quite different results. Sometimes he is portrayed as the skilled political manipulator behind the throne, shaping events for his own advantage. Others describe him as the 'last of the barons', ruling his fiefdom like an uncrowned king.

Little is known about his early life, although we have many references to him in records of the time. People who observed events during his lifetime might have embellished their accounts, according to their political perspective. These stories eventually found their way into popular ballads and poetry, so many myths and legends developed about him.

Richard Neville's importance also meant others learned of his exploits through newsletters and handbills, pinned on church doors, used as source material by later chroniclers, who in turn will have been writing from a particular point of view. Even accounts of his life by modern historians and biographers fail to agree on key issues.

What is clear is that Richard Neville was one of the most important men in fifteenth century England. He owned extensive lands in Wales and was responsible for many years for controlling the border with Scotland. His story is one of adventure, power and influence at the heart of one of the most dangerous times in the history of England.

Chapter 1 - Autumn 1428

He held his breath and strained to listen in the long silence, knowing whatever happened would change his life. The piercing scream echoed again through the castle, then stopped. The silence worried him more than the screaming. It started again, louder and more anguished. It stopped when she called out his name.

'Richard!'

He made a fist and squeezed until his nails dug into his palm. The sharp pain helped take his mind off the negative thoughts that tortured him. Richard stood up from the chair that had been left for him and paced the candlelit passageway. The thump of his heavy boots echoed despite clean rushes on the hard stone floor. He could do nothing to help her.

Another nerve tingling scream reverberated down the passageway. Richard stopped pacing and cursed the heavy oak door of the one room in his castle barred to him. A memory flooded into his mind. His wife had screamed like this before. Their first child, Joan, had a difficult birth five years ago. He sent for a priest when the bleeding after little Cecily, his favourite, nearly killed her two years later. It didn't get any easier.

She called for him again, begging this time. 'Please. Richard?' Her voice wavered and he feared she was weakening.

The waiting would soon be over, one way or another. He forced the thought of what might happen from his mind. Women were supposed to have their mother or sisters to help them. Alice's mother was dead. She was an only child. It would bring bad luck if a man were to enter the birthing-room, so he could only pace the long, dark hallway and wait. He thought of himself as a patient man, able to put up with most things. This waiting was the worst he could remember.

He cast his mind back to the day he first saw her, eight years ago. Alice was an heiress, an attractive and spirited girl, barely fourteen years old when he married her. She looked beautiful on their wedding day, her long, dark hair under a shimmering veil of white gossamer silk. Her voice sounded clear and confident as she made her vows and pledged her life to him. As a younger son he would not inherit, so his marriage sealed his fortune.

Alice's father, Sir Thomas Montacute, was now dead. Her condition meant she couldn't travel to the funeral, so Richard made the long journey south without her. That had been barely three weeks ago. Sir Thomas survived the battle of Agincourt, only to be killed by a shard of glass when a French cannonball smashed through his window during the siege of Orleans. Alice, his only legitimate heir, inherited her father's title, his lands and his fortune, all now Richard's by right of his wife.

He was becoming a man of great importance, soon to be acknowledged as Earl of Salisbury and Baron Montacute. Their new wealth would bring new challenges from those who would dispute his rights to the vast estates. As well as others of the Neville line, there was the long-standing and bitter dispute with the Percy family, who would steal his northern lands, given the chance. They resented the expansion of the Neville estates in areas that had been theirs before they were disgraced by the ill-fated revolt of Sir Henry 'Hotspur' Percy, who sided with the Welsh against the king and paid for it with his life. Even as he pictured the rampant blue lion of the Percy flag he remembered they would have to find an amicable truce, a promise he'd made to his sister Eleanor, now the wife of Sir Henry Percy.

Although he would now have the income from the Montacute inheritance as well as from his lands and properties in the north, he wanted more for his family. He would see his daughters married well. He desperately needed a son. If this baby proved to be another daughter it would mean waiting at least another year, if not longer.

He had been brought up to know they were watched over by a vengeful God, who punished men for their sins and could condemn their souls to eternal damnation. As he had grown older, Richard struggled with his faith, a secret he shared with no one, not even Alice. He liked things you could see with your own eyes, feel and touch. All the same, he wanted to believe. Richard dropped to his knees on the cold stone floor and put his hands together.

'Please, Lord, let me have a strong, healthy son.' Almost as an afterthought, he whispered, 'Dear God, keep his mother safe to care for him.'

If he had a son he would teach him more than simply how to wield a sword. He would need to understand the politics of the court and parliament. The king was eight years old and under the care of the Lord Protector, Duke Humphrey of Gloucester. Richard had respect for the duke, who had fought at Agincourt with King Henry.

Richard had also seen how the real power at court and council was wielded by Cardinal Henry Beaufort. The cardinal grew fat like a leech in a bloodletting by lending money to those who could not afford to repay him, turning their minds against the Duke of Gloucester's slender grip on authority. He put words in the mouth of the boy king, all in the name of the church.

His son must understand how to outwit those who would deceive him. He must never trust the clergy. Richard would teach him caution in his choice of friends, to be careful where he placed his trust.

Richard could bear the silence no longer. He held his breath and listened at the door to the birthing-room. Made of thick oak, the heavy door was studded with black iron nails. He could hear nothing. In frustration he knocked on it, a loud rap that echoed in the empty corridor. He stood back. The door to the birthing-room opened and he braced himself for the news.

The midwife opened the door and stepped out into the corridor. A shrewd, practical woman, she wore the robes of a nun. He stared into her surprisingly blue eyes, trying to see any clue to the truth of Alice's condition. This woman held his future in her hands. He had chosen her well. The best he could afford, she had a reassuring confidence and knowledge of her trade.

'How is my wife?' He tried to hide the impatience he knew could be heard in his voice.

'She will live, with God's grace, my lord.' The midwife moved back towards the door, concern on her kindly face.

'The baby?' His mind raced with the life and death decisions he knew she may have to ask him to make.

'The baby will be here soon, my lord.'

'Is there anything you can give her, so she will suffer less?'

The midwife shook her head. 'Nature will take its course. The worst will soon be over.'

'I want you to tell my wife something for me. Tell her I love her.'

The midwife smiled. 'Of course, my lord.'

She closed the door to the mysterious birthing-room behind her. Richard sat down heavily on the chair at the end of the passageway, his head in his hands, to wait. His mind raced with mixed emotions. To his shame, he knew this had been the first time he'd told Alice he loved her for many years. He hoped his words would comfort her and promised himself he would tell her more often.

Although it had not been a love match Alice had always been a devoted wife to him. She had taught him much and helped make him the man he was now. She seemed to understand his bluff northern ways, his passion for the hunt and even his clumsy lovemaking. He had grown to love her now. Again he found himself wondering if he would lose her. It would be hard bringing up the girls without a mother. If they lost the baby there would still be hope, another chance for a son.

A sharp, unmistakable cry of a newborn baby shook him from his sad reverie. The door opened wide, flooding the dimly lit corridor with light. The midwife carried a linen wrapped bundle and placed it in his arms. Richard looked down and saw bright eyes staring back at him. He loosened the tight swaddling and a tiny hand pulled free, with perfectly formed little fingers, already grasping for whatever was in reach.

Alice called to him from the birthing-room. 'A boy!' He could hear the happiness in her voice.

'Richard.' He called back to her. 'We will call him Richard!' He held the baby as if he was the most precious thing in the world. 'Richard Neville.'

Chapter 2 - Summer 1439

The rambling castle of Sheriff Hutton near York, built by John Neville, third Baron Neville de Raby, had been improved over the years as the family grew and Richard's father prospered. One of the ground-floor rooms had become a library and many of the books were family heirlooms. Others belonged to Richard's mother, who rarely returned from York or London without an addition to her collection and brought many of her father's books to Sheriff Hutton. Some of the most ancient of these were in Latin, his booty from English victories in Normandy.

His mother taught Richard to read. She read aloud to him in English and French, long into the dark evenings until the candle burned to a flickering stub. As he grew older his mother would sit with him while he learned the skill of making sense of each word. She would gently prompt him when he was stuck on a word, encouraging his questions and showing him how to translate each sentence and understand the deeper meaning.

From all her precious collection of rare books and manuscripts, Richard's favourite was the *Livre de Chevalerie*. The old book's brown parchment pages, full of colourful images of jousting and lavish banquets, allowed him to enter a world of chivalry and knighthood. He read from it in the evenings at Sheriff Hutton and imagined himself as the great knight Sir Geoffroi de Charny, equally praised for skill at leading campaigns and honoured for his chivalry and courtly ways.

As the eldest son he could look forward to an easy life as a noble baron. There would always be servants to tend to his every need. Richard had been brought up to know that one day he would inherit the northern estates of Sheriff Hutton and Middleham Castle. Now he had been told he would also one day inherit the vast estates in the south.

The library also served as a scriptorium and study and was where the boys would be found each morning, improving their writing, French and Latin. Richard's father placed great importance on their learning and took a close interest in their progress. He had made a strict rule that they were only allowed out in the sunshine once they had completed the work set for them, to the satisfaction of their tutor.

Richard took his sharp knife and trimmed the nib of his new quill as he had been shown. He was writing a letter to his father, who had been absent most of the summer with his duties as Warden of the West March. He knew the Warden was an important position, responsible for safeguarding the country from invasion by the Scots, with pay of a thousand pounds a year. Although Richard's father made light of it, he overheard his mother once saying that securing the wide expanse of the northern border was dangerous and often thankless work.

Dipping the quill into the pot of thick black ox-gall ink, Richard carefully formed a swirling letter R then spelled out the rest of his name at the end of the letter. He sat back, pleased with the result and allowed it to dry before showing it to the old priest who had the task of teaching them. The priest wore the traditional cappa clausa, a grey, hooded cape over a long woollen tunic with a heavy leather belt. A hard man to please, he studied Richard's parchment with an appraising eye.

'How old are you, Richard?' His deep voice carried the hint of a northern accent.

'I will be eleven at the end of November.'

'Well, Richard, if you keep up your studies I believe we can make a scholar of you.'

He felt a frisson of pride at the priest's words, although the confusion about his future plans was troubling.

'I am to become a knight. It is my brother George who will be a scholar.' Richard frowned at the misunderstanding, then realised the priest had made a jest at his expense. He was learning more than skill with a pen and languages from the old man.

He looked across to where George was diligently copying a Latin text in his already neat hand. George had his mother's serene nature and, although not eight years old, had been destined for the church ever since Richard could remember. Richard could hardly think of anything worse than to turn your back on the glory of knighthood, to never marry or have sons and live a life of devotion to the church.

His other brother John was looking out of the window at something which had caught his interest. John was a gifted student and was able to read without apparent effort, although he rarely read a book unless he had to. Tall for his nine years, he already had their father's heavy build, as well as his bluff manner. Sometimes he would argue with Richard. The two years between them always put John at a disadvantage, which only served to make him even more resentful and competitive.

Not present in the library was their third brother Thomas, still treated as the baby although he was now two years old, or their six sisters, who were schooled with Anne by nuns from the convent near York. Anne was

Richard's wife, chosen by his father. At the same time, his father arranged a generous dowry to secure a second marriage. Richard's older sister Cecily had married Anne's brother Henry, heir to the earldom of Warwick, binding together the names of de Beauchamp and Neville.

Richard's first memory of Anne was hazy. Her father was the Lord of Abergavenny and for some reason that was where they were married. It seemed a long time ago, although he clearly remembered the excitement of that day. The people of the bustling Welsh town came out of their houses like a swarm of bees, cheering as his grand procession rode through their narrow streets with twenty mounted guardsmen front and back. For the first time Richard had realised he was someone of importance, different from the people who called out his name.

His mother had explained the ceremony to him and helped him rehearse his words. He dressed in the finest velvet with a flowing cape over his shoulders and a gold chain around his neck. He remembered Anne wore a long dress of white silk that rustled as she walked. She carried a bouquet of white roses and their wedding was blessed by a red-faced bishop wearing a tall mitre. The speeches and feasting seemed to go on forever. It all had no meaning for him, as he had only been seven years old.

There had been talk of Richard following the tradition of going to live at Warwick Castle with Anne's family. Her father, the Earl of Warwick, was a renowned soldier knight who personally taught the king to use a sword and would have been the ideal tutor for Richard. Anne's father's untimely death at Rouen earlier that year was soon followed by that of her mother, so young Henry was now the new Earl of Warwick. His sister became a duchess and Anne was sent to live with them at Sheriff Hutton.

Richard would never admit he sometimes felt intimidated by Anne, who at two year's older than him seemed so worldly wise. At least his father had chosen him an attractive girl from a noble family. She could play the lute and sing tunefully, embroidered his initials on his shirts and often came to watch him practice sword fighting. They were more like brother and sister than husband and wife. It seemed strange to Richard they would one day be required to produce an heir to the Neville fortune.

The discordant clang of the noon bell in the high tower shook Richard from his reverie. The boys were excused by the priest and raced each other down long, echoing corridors to the refectory, John easily winning with his powerful stride. Family meals were formal affairs in the great hall, presided over by his father at the head of the long oak table. Today was a simpler fare, freshly baked bread and slices of cold salted pork, washed down with weak small ale that tasted of bitter hops.

Even though there were only kitchen staff to witness it, the strict routine of each day had been drummed into them. As the eldest Richard saw the routine was followed as their father would wish and had to say grace before they ate. He waited until they were seated, heads bowed and hands clasped together.

'Benedic, Domine, nos et dona tua, quae de largitate tua sumus sumpturi.' He checked to see his brothers were still praying before he continued. 'Per Christum Dominum nostrum. Amen.'

His brothers chorused, 'Amen.'

They ate hungrily, knowing there was a long wait until their evening meal. John was always first to finish and always ready to take the leftovers from his brothers' plates. John waved his knife at Richard across the table, pretending to use it as a sword.

'The sergeant told me there's no fencing today.'

Richard scowled at his brother disapprovingly. 'Remember your manners, John.'

The afternoons were usually spent riding in the woods and practising swordsmanship with his fencing master, a dour Yorkshireman. Known only to the boys as the sergeant, he had fought as the king's Sergeant-at-Arms in France and had permission from Richard's father to be as heavy handed with the boys as he saw fit. Richard had learned to work hard and always show the man respect or suffer the consequences.

John dropped his knife with a clatter on the table. 'It's because you are going to learn to joust today.'

Richard finished eating. 'Yes.'

John looked interested. 'Are you going to use the quintain?' There was a note of challenge in his voice.

The quintain was a clever device which pivoted when hit with a lance, bringing a weighted sack to strike the unwary jouster in the neck. John was catching up fast. The sergeant had started pitting them against each other, goading Richard not to be shown up by his younger brother. Although the practice swords were made of wood, they were heavy and could deliver a painful blow. Richard had bruises and more than a few scars to show for his time spent acquiring his skill with a sword.

'I have to master the target first, before he will let me try the quintain.'

George had been observing the exchange. 'We've been allowed to come and watch.' He wiped a piece of bread around his plate, which now appeared as clean as if it had never been used.

Richard frowned. He wanted to learn how to ride with a lance before his father returned from the northern border and would have liked the chance to practice without his brothers watching. Worse still he guessed that John would encourage Anne and his sisters to join him when they returned from the convent.

A young serving girl came from the kitchens to clear their plates and Richard went to the stables to collect his horse. He enjoyed spending time in the stables, learning how to care for horses. He also learned other things from the stable lads, particularly when they forgot he was there. The duke promised Richard he could have his own destrier when he could prove worthy of it. In the meantime Richard had to contend with his own mild mannered horse. He liked to ride every day, when the northern weather allowed.

Despite the summer heat, Richard put on a padded brigandine, the most basic form of armour, fitted with leather straps to hold it securely in place. On his head was a woollen hat to cushion the inside of the heavy steel helmet he would be wearing. He led his horse from the stables, followed by the stable boy who carried his helmet and was to act as his squire. They arrived at the tiltyard, a wide level field to the side of the castle. There was a solid wooden fence down the centre of the field, the list, in the middle of which the sergeant was fixing a shield shaped target on the end of a long pole.

The tiltyard was overlooked by high stands with oak bench seating for spectators. On a tournament day these were filled with nobles and their ladies and decorated with their colourful banners and shields. Today there was no decoration, although Richard wished his brothers and sisters were not taking their seats to watch his first lesson.

He saw Anne was also there and raised a hand in acknowledgement as she waved to him.

The sergeant greeted him with uncharacteristic cheerfulness, which put Richard on his guard. A stocky man with straggling grey hair and beard, the sergeant had an open faced sallet helmet on his head and wore an old padded jack, studded with rivets, as well as a sword on his belt. Richard always thought the sergeant seemed ready to go off to fight at short notice.

Today the sergeant carried a long wooden practice lance, shorter and lighter than the one Richard would use in a real joust. Painted blue and white, it was tipped with a coronal, a crown shaped metal cap designed to allow the lance to catch and hold, making it easier to unhorse an opponent or break a lance on him.

'Well, my lord, are you ready to impress the ladies and gentleman?' There was a note of sarcasm in his voice and amusement in his deep set eyes.

Richard knew how he should answer. This was the first time he had been allowed to ride on the hallowed ground of the tiltyard, normally out of bounds to the boys. 'I am ready for your instruction, Sergeant.'

The sergeant examined Richard's horse, running a critical hand over its flank.

'A tolerant horse will carry you down the list, even if you sit like a sack of grain.' He turned and gave Richard a black-toothed grin. 'Until he learns you have little control over him and he can do whatever he wants!'

Richard had witnessed the grand tourney as a spectator, carefully studying how the jousters rode and fought. 'I know I must ride without using my reins.'

'Why is that, do you think?' He looked at Richard with his bushy eyebrows raised.

'I need my hands free for the lance?'

'Only one hand. You have to release the reins to protect the horse from the impact, or you will be disqualified. The same goes for failing to control your horse during the pass. If he stops or veers away from the list, you are marked down for a balk. If you are knocked off you mustn't be holding on to a bridle.' He shook his head at some distant memory. 'I've seen men pull their horse down on top of them.'

He gestured for Richard to mount his horse and led it to the run up position. 'Use your leg pressure. If he starts going left or right, you need to press with the opposite leg. Understand?'

Richard was growing impatient. He had practiced riding at a canter without reins. 'Yes, Sergeant.'

The sergeant looked around. 'Where is your helmet?'

Richard gestured to the stable lad who was acting as his squire. The boy approached and handed him the steel helmet. He put it on. It felt heavy on his head and he leaned forward to see, as the eye slot was high to avoid the danger of splinters.

The sergeant handed him the long wooden lance. 'Not too fast now.'

He watched as Richard experimentally raised and lowered the lance. Although well balanced, it was heavier than he expected and difficult to control, as a small movement of his arm made the tip of the lance swing through a wide arc.

The sergeant stood back. 'Aim for the target.' He pointed. 'Keep your lance high and don't let it touch the ground or hit the list when you're riding. Either could break the lance.' He grinned at Richard. 'Or it could pitch you off your horse.'

Richard kept his grip tight, silently praying his horse would understand what was expected. He trotted to the run up and took a deep breath, then cantered down the list, carefully lowering his lance. He was barely able to see the target and missed it completely. Raising his lance, he turned for a second pass. Once again, the unwieldy lance wavered and missed the target. He didn't look towards the stands, where his brother was probably enjoying the spectacle.

The sergeant walked up to Richard and grabbed his horse's bridle. 'Hold your lance firmly. Couch it under your arm as tight as you can.' He patted Richard's arm. 'Don't try to adjust your aim as you approach.'

Richard felt sweat trickling down his neck. The helmet rubbed painfully on his neck as he rode. He leaned forward so he could see right down the list to where the target was fixed, tantalisingly out of reach. This time he turned his head and saw Anne and his brother John were watching, although his sisters seemed to have lost interest.

He braced the long lance as firmly as he could and cantered again towards the target. There was a clang of wood against metal as his lance struck the target and knocked it to the ground. Richard pulled up at the turning area and trotted back, raising a hand to his watchers on the stands. He heard their cheer and applause. For the first time he had a taste of what it would feel like to be a knight. One day he would risk his life in a joust against a more experienced rider. Richard couldn't wait for his father to return.

Chapter 3 - Autumn 1442

A shaft of bright November sunlight shone through the trees on a large pig hanging by its back legs from a thick rope tied to a branch of the oak. Stunned by an expert hammer blow, the pig didn't struggle, unaware of its fate. Richard Neville watched as the butcher ended its life with a single stroke of his knife. Blood sprayed from the gash across its throat onto the earth in a bright red arc and the animal made one last shudder.

The new sword slid easily from its scabbard and felt powerful in Richard's hand. It was his fourteenth birthday present, the most expensive thing he had ever owned. The sharp blade was perfectly balanced with a heavy silver pommel that could be used as a club in hand-to-hand fighting. He glanced across at his father, who nodded in approval. That was important. The sword was a gift from him. Richard knew his duty as the eldest son and heir to the Neville fortunes. His father had given him the same name, the same penetrating blue grey eyes and dark curly hair, the same determined ambition.

The blade swished through the air and bit deep into the side of the pig, cutting through flesh and bone. Richard felt momentarily sickened as he realised in an instant why his father wanted him to do this. He had developed broad shoulders from daily use of the heavy wooden practice swords which strengthened his arm and developed his skill. Now he realised they were a pale shadow of the shocking reality of real sword fighting.

He knew one day this would be for real. Their northern lands were under constant threat and he must be ready when called to fight at his father's side. His father was also his teacher and had dark tales of how decent men died because they were too slow to kill. His life could depend on not hesitating to take the life of another man.

The pig swang on the rope as he withdrew his sword. He glanced once at his father then lunged, timing it perfectly and spearing the pig with the sharp point. The watching men cheered and applauded as he had to twist and wrench the blade to retrieve his weapon.

'Well done, Richard!' His father shouted across the clearing, his deep voice carrying the accent of the northern families.

Richard wiped the sharp blade and returned his sword to the leather scabbard on his belt. He liked the weight of it at his waist. His badge of rank and status, the new sword also marked him as a grown man. From now on he would demand respect from those who had known him as a boy.

'Thank you, Father, although I feel I had a little advantage this time.' His mother was also his teacher. He had learned from her the power of self-deprecation to imply a confidence he didn't always feel. He also inherited her charm, which made him seem wiser than his years. She taught him well and he was grateful as he watched others brag. Knowing when to remain a silent observer was as important to him as any weapon.

His father looked back at the dangling carcass and the clearing echoed to his deep laugh. Richard saw a twinkle in his eye and knew his father was proud of him. He fixed that moment in his memory and knew it would serve him well in the years to come. He knew he must also remember the terrible power of his sword. Somewhere at the back of his mind was a fearful premonition of a well-trained swordsman fighting back with even greater savagery. He pushed the thought away yet knew the image would return to haunt his dreams.

A young groom handed Richard the reins of his horse and he mounted the saddle. He was glad he had practised while wearing his sword so it didn't get in the way when his father was watching. Riding behind his father through the ancient oaks, Richard noticed how the leaves were turning the golden brown of autumn. He wondered how long it would be before he would use the sword to defend Sheriff Hutton, his birthright.

He grew up playing in these woods and knew every inch of the grounds around the castle. It had once been part of the Royal Forest of Galtres, reserved by Norman kings for their favourite sport of hunting deer, as well as to provide an income from oak timber. Much of the old forest was now gone.

Richard's father was proud of his lineage and determined to prepare him to manage his future inheritance well. He remembered how often his parents had told him the story of their rapid rise in the world. Although they were both from old families, they were not notably wealthy when they first married. His paternal grandmother was the granddaughter of King Edward III, so Richard was often reminded he came from a long line of Plantagenet kings and had royal blood in his veins.

He spurred his horse and matched his pace alongside his father, then glanced across, trying to judge if the moment was right. He still found it hard to guess his father's mood. He had passed the first test of his coming of age day. He was less certain of how his father would react to the next and decided this was the time to find out.

'I have a question for you, Father.' He hesitated, not wishing to spoil his father's mood. 'It's about Lady Anne.'

His father stared straight ahead. Richard considered repeating himself, unsure if he had been heard. His father had a habit of pretending not to hear things when it suited him. He also had a reputation for being firm, yet always fair, particularly when it came to matters concerning his eldest son.

'You have my blessing, Richard. After all, you are husband and wife in the sight of God.'

'Thank you, Father.'

His father had a smile in his eyes. 'You know what you must do now?'

He wondered if this was another test. 'What's that?'

'You need a son to inherit all I leave to you.'

'I will, Father.' He filled with pride at the thought. 'I'll call him Richard!'

His father seemed pleased. 'You must find him the best marriage you can. Nothing is more important.'

'You have my word.'

He knew life would never be the same from this moment. He was a man, with a rich and well-educated wife from a noble background. He would one day inherit his father's ever growing estates and become the most important Earl in the North. Soon he would have a son and would work to find him a wife worthy of the Neville name, as his father had for him.

He thought about Anne as he rode. Over the past four years they had become close companions, despite being chaperoned at all times. She had grown from a pretty young girl into a beautiful young woman. She was now sixteen, two years older than him, although he was taller so their age difference wasn't obvious. She had recently been helping him to improve his French.

In return, he had been teaching her the finer points of chess, under the ever watchful eye of their chaperone, an old widow who always dressed in mourning black. Now they would be able to talk about the future and where they would choose to live. His father had inherited several suitable properties, although the castle was more than large enough to house them all.

They would also talk about when to start a family. Thinking of this reminded him of the time they had escaped their dour chaperone. He had taken Anne to one of his favourite places, a secluded woodland glade on the far side of the family estate. He remembered it had been a perfect spring morning and the first time he had been truly alone with her. She had surprised him with a long and passionate kiss as soon as they were certain they could not be seen.

Richard's father had failed to explain to him the details of the facts of life and, although he had observed farm animals, he was unsure of exactly what to do. Fortunately, Anne's late mother, Countess Isabel, had educated her fully in the secrets of lovemaking. She spread his cape on the ground and made him lie with her. Then Anne started to remove her clothes.

A shout of alarm from the men broke through his thoughts. Something was wrong. Richard and his father both reined their horses and twisted round in the saddle.

'What is it, man?' His father's deep voice echoed across the woodland clearing to the men riding behind. As well as their groom and the butcher who had slaughtered the pig, there were half a dozen soldiers of the earl's bodyguard.

'Poachers, my lord. We saw them through the trees.' One of the soldiers pointed into the forest.

'Well, don't just stand there, after them!'

The men spurred their horses and disappeared into the trees. Richard followed his father after them, ducking a low branch as his horse gathered speed. He had been riding with the hunt since he was old enough, although this was the first time he had hunted men. There were shouts ahead and he knew they must be catching up with the poachers. The punishment for poaching was a death sentence.

His father was riding ahead of him and pulled up sharply. He saw a dark brown shape in the fallen leaves to one side of the overgrown track they were following. Richard spurred his horse and was soon at his father's side, leaning over in his saddle to see. A fully grown red deer lay dead.

His father pointed to the feathered stub of a crossbow bolt sticking from its neck. 'A clean shot.'

Richard heard the note of admiration in his father's voice and examined the deer more closely. Its dark blood was staining the ground, proof it had been recently killed where it lay. 'A mature doe. We're in the middle of the breeding season so it might have been with fawn?' He had grown up knowing about the red deer, which were important as a mark of his father's status, as well as a source of venison for the table.

His father agreed. 'I'd guess these are no ordinary poachers. Could be trained fighting men.'

Richard knew of stories of bands of former soldiers roaming the country, living off the land as best they could now the war in France seemed to be coming to an end. He'd also heard tales of violent robbery and even murder and scanned the trees for any sign of movement. A skilled crossbowman could shoot from three hundred paces with deadly accuracy.

His heart raced as he realised the danger they were in. His father's men were still pursuing the poachers and had left them alone in the woods. Richard's hand moved to the hilt of his new sword. It felt reassuring to know that at least he could now defend himself, although it would be no use against a man with a crossbow.

'Come on, we're losing them!' His father set off at a gallop after the men.

Richard followed close behind, riding as fast as he could. They were pressing deeper into the woods now and the path was becoming overgrown, with fallen logs and low bushes that could easily trip a horse. The excitement of the chase made him forget the danger of a hidden assassin. He spurred his mount still faster, without a care, enjoying spending time with his father, defending their lands from poachers and thieves.

The men had stopped a short way ahead and looked back uncertainly as Richard and his father approached. There was no sign of any poachers, so it seemed their quarry had escaped.

Richard's father wasn't pleased. 'You let them get away?'

'Sorry, my lord. We nearly caught one of them.' The man glanced around at the others for support. 'He must know these woods well. He just vanished.'

'They've simply gone to ground somewhere.' Richard's father pointed to where the bushes grew more thickly. 'Keep searching. I'll not have poachers on my land.'

They waited while the men spread out and began looking deeper into the forest, calling for the poachers to give themselves up. Richard didn't think this was likely. The poachers could be hiding anywhere, perhaps even watching them right now. Once again, he was reminded of the danger of their situation.

His father turned to him. 'It seems this will take some time, Richard. You should head back to the castle and be ready to greet our guests. They will be arriving soon.'

Richard was torn between wanting to return home to tell Anne his news and curiosity about whether they would catch the poachers. The guests had been invited to his birthday banquet, which his mother had been planning for a month. He squinted into the low sun, setting earlier every day now. He knew they would have little hope of finding the poachers once the light started failing.

He didn't want to seem indecisive. 'I wish you well with your hunt, Father. You are right, mother will demand an explanation if I am late.'

His father called two of the soldiers back and ordered them to escort Richard home. He turned to Richard. 'I can't have you getting lost in the woods, today of all days!'

'I know the way back well enough.'

'Well, I can spare two men. Be off with you.'

Richard knew better than to argue. He had to obey without question. As he said farewell and rode back towards the castle, he wondered if his father had set him another test. He was pleased to note that the two guards rode one each side, slightly behind him, already showing him more respect than he was accustomed to. His mother had taught him that respect was hard won and easily lost. For the first time he found himself understanding what she meant.

The late autumn sun was now dipping below the horizon, casting long shadows through the trees. Richard peered into the dark undergrowth as they rode, alert for any sign of movement. They had not gone far when a faint sound made him look into the trees to his right. It sounded like the stifled cough of someone hiding out of sight. He stopped and held up his hand to listen, as he knew he could be wrong. The guards realised what he was doing and remained silent. Another muffled cough sounded and the guards reacted swiftly.

Leaping from their horses, they approached the source of the coughing from opposite directions and disappeared into the trees. There was the sound of a scuffle and someone swore. Another voice cried out in pain. Richard wondered if he should draw his sword when they re-emerged, holding a roughly dressed man between them. They dragged him in front of Richard and forced him to kneel.

One of the guards, a burly man, had twisted the young poacher's arm behind his back and held him securely. The other guard held up a crossbow for Richard to see. The weapon was certain proof of the man's guilt if it were needed. The three men looked up at Richard and waited to hear what he wished them to do.

He gestured the man with the crossbow to pass it to him. 'Go quickly and fetch my father.' Richard's voice sounded more confident than he felt. He watched the guard mount his horse and ride back the way they had come. He studied the crossbow with interest, testing the strength of its bowstring. He saw it had a simple stirrup to help draw the string back more easily. He looked down at the man kneeling on the ground. He had never seen a poacher before and was curious.

'What is your name?'

The man remained silent, his eyes cast to the ground, as if to avoid even looking at Richard.

'Speak up, or you'll be the worse for it!' The guard twisted his arm harder until the man winced with the pain.

'Tully, my lord. Luke Tulley.' His accent marked him as a local man.

'You know the punishment for poaching deer?'

The man named Tulley remained silent and looked away. Richard could see he did.

'Which way did the others go?'

Tulley seemed puzzled. 'Others?'

'You are here alone?'

'I am, my lord.'

Richard sensed a note of truth in the man's voice. 'Where did you learn your skill with this crossbow?' He held the deadly weapon in the air.

'It's easy, my lord.' He looked up at Richard for the first time. His dark, deep set eyes revealed an unexpected confidence and humour for a man in his position.

Richard looked more closely at the man in front of him. His unshaven beard made him seem older than he was and something about him suggested he had seen more than a few adventures. He remembered how his father had been impressed by the way the deer had been shot. There was a likeable intelligence about the man and Richard felt pity for him. He had to die, that was the law.

The heavy thud of hooves sounded behind them and Richard's father arrived with the other men. They surrounded the poacher, although there was no way for him to escape the guard's firm grip.

'Well done, Richard.'

'Thank you, Father. He tells me he's here alone.' Richard felt a frisson of pride at his achievement. His father rarely complimented him, so when he did it carried extra weight.

His father turned to the kneeling man. 'You are charged with the crime of poaching. Is there anything you wish to say before sentence is passed?'

'I am guilty as you say.' He looked up with hope in his dark eyes. 'I ask for your mercy, my lord.'

'I should have you hanged.' Richard's father looked across at him. 'However, you are lucky. It is my son's birthday.' He turned to the butcher, who had been watching events with interest. 'Cut off his ears.'

Tully looked horrified and tried to struggle free. Two guards held him down while the butcher took out his knife and inspected the blade for sharpness. Richard wanted to look away. He knew poachers must be taught a lesson. An idea occurred to him as the butcher leaned forward.

'Stop!'

The men all looked round in surprise.

His father was puzzled. 'What is it, Richard?'

'I will take this man as my bondsman. He will pay for his crime with service to our household.'

His father was expressionless for a moment. Even Tully stopped his struggling while they all waited for his decision.

'A noble gesture, Richard.' His father turned to Tully. 'My son has saved your ears. Be sure to repay him well.'

Tully looked at him with clear relief. 'I will, my lord.'

They rode back to the castle, the freshly killed deer slung over the back of one of the horses. Richard looked back and could see Tully behind the butcher's old horse, struggling to keep up with the weight of the heavy pig's carcase he had been made to help carry. Tully saw Richard looking back at him and raised a hand in acknowledgement, nearly losing his grip.

Richard felt relieved his father had supported him. For a moment he regretted his action and realised he would look foolish in front of the men. He wondered if they would see his decision as a sign of weakness. He had learned some important lessons this day and hopefully gained a useful servant. Now he looked forward to the banquet and seeing Anne. They had much to discuss.

Chapter 4 - Spring 1445

Life at Middleham Castle settled into a routine that suited Richard. Much about the place had changed since he moved there with Anne from Sheriff Hutton three years ago, after the death of his grandmother, Joan Beaufort, Countess of Westmorland. The grandest rooms were within the solid old Norman keep, built to last forever, a memorial to men whose names were long forgotten.

A towering rectangular stone wall enclosed the entire wide expanse of the castle ward, used to house the castle guards and every type of useful industry from blacksmiths' furnaces to a bakery, ready if they ever had to withstand a long siege. Over the years the ward had filled with an assortment of wooden outbuildings, stables and workshops. His father allowed Richard to arrange the demolition of a long row of these to build their new apartments within the castle walls.

For months the outer ward had echoed to the rhythmic hammering of chisels on stone, men shouting orders and wood being sawn. Clever arrangements of ropes and pulleys enabled heavy stones and wooden beams made from entire trees to be lifted into place. Richard supervised the building personally, learning from the master masons and even climbing high up the rickety wooden scaffolding to inspect their workmanship.

Anne had taken responsibility for the furnishing and decoration of their new home. She hung the walls with colourful tapestries which had been owned by her family. Pride of place was given to a magnificent tapestry her father had specially commissioned of his victory against the Welsh, when he captured the banner of the Welsh Prince Owain Glyndwr. The tattered flag with its red and gold lions had graced the hall of her father's house when she was a girl. Her brother Henry now owned the banner and had given the grand tapestry to Anne as a housewarming present, a reminder of her childhood.

They still regularly made the fifty mile journey to Sheriff Hutton and would stay there on feast days and through the hunting season. Richard travelled away increasingly often, helping his father patrol the border with Scotland, checking on their guards and learning how to deal with minor disputes over land and property. Anne would sometimes travel with him and they would lodge at one of the northern outposts, although Middleham Castle was where they always returned to.

The king's messenger arrived unexpectedly one morning, causing great excitement amongst the staff. Richard studied the letter closely. It was a summons, written on the best quality vellum and bearing the royal seal, an image of King Henry as a knight on horseback, brandishing his sword. Richard had been invited to attend the coronation of the new queen, Margaret of Anjou. He was also to be made a Knight of the Realm.

The news triggered a flurry of activity, as there were preparations to be made for the four-day ride and their stay in London. Richard spent long hours with his father, who had been made a knight in the service of the previous King Henry when he was only a little older than Richard. He had become a Knight of the Garter under the Regency Council, and considered himself something of an expert on the responsibilities of knighthood.

The long journey to London was made easier by bright spring sunshine as the Neville family entourage made its way south. Their route was notorious for outlaws, who would waylay and rob travellers, holding any of importance for ransom, so their party was escorted by twenty mounted guards. Richard followed, with Anne riding at his side, then his father and mother. Luke Tully followed behind him, with the groom leading Richard's black destrier, chosen to ride in the tournament. Tully had grown into a loyal and valued companion. Richard never treated him like a servant and now he had officially become a squire. Dressed in new clothes in the Neville colours he looked pleased with his role.

Their servants followed behind, with the heavy wagons loaded with luggage and supplies, as well as Richard's valuable jousting armour. They were glad of the chance to see the city of London and the coronation pageants. Many of them had never left Yorkshire before and for some this was the journey of a lifetime. The servants who were to remain at Middleham formed two rows, their numbers swelled by people from the village who had come to see the procession leave for London.

Once they were on the road Richard decided to pass the time by learning more about the king from Anne. Her father had been made responsible for the young King's education, so she had known him since he was a child. He glanced across at her. Anne wore a blue velvet riding cloak over her dress, with a fashionable hat covering her dark hair. She was comfortable on a horse and had laughed when he suggested she might prefer to make the long journey to London in a carriage.

'What sort of man is King Henry?'

Anne thought for a moment as she rode. 'I haven't seen him for years.'

'You said you used to visit him often?'

'Yes. Father thought it would be beneficial for us both.' She rode closer to Richard so their conversation would not be overheard. 'Father would take me with him to Windsor Castle. Henry was five years older than me. I remember he was always the king, even when he was a boy.'

'He was spoilt?'

'Perhaps a little,' she smiled at him, 'My father told me he always found him to be an attentive student.'

'Did you see much of his mother?'

'She was kind to me.'

'My mother told me about attending her coronation in Westminster Abbey with my father.'

'Henry spent a lot of time with his mother. I was only a young girl. I remember Queen Catherine teaching us songs.'

Anne started singing in French, hesitantly at first, then more confidently as she remembered the words. She had a beautiful singing voice, which carried well. The French influence on the throne was to be renewed and Richard wondered how his life would be changed by the crowning of a new French Queen. One day he would be telling his own children about attending her coronation.

The thought troubled him, a dark cloud on his otherwise sunny horizon. They had been trying for a child for three years, yet there was still no sign of one. His father had always made it clear his duty was to produce a son to inherit their name and fortune. To fail would mean shame and dishonour. He wondered if his wife was barren and he didn't know what to do. Anne had consulted with midwives and once even tried a special potion from a herbalist in York, with no success. Now the questioning finger of doubt was being pointed at him.

They reached Sheffield Castle, their first stop on the long journey, just before nightfall. The old castle was a grim, dark place and their room was poorly furnished. It didn't matter as they were tired and fell asleep in minutes. Leicester Castle was their destination on the evening of the second day and their last stop before London was the great castle at Northampton, where they enjoyed a banquet with their host. The finest French wine flowed freely and musicians played long into the night in honour of the new queen's coronation.

On the final day's ride, the road was crowded with people travelling to London. Only when they arrived on the outskirts of the city did they realise the scale of the coronation celebrations. Flags and banners were everywhere and people had already started impromptu parties by the side of the road. Richard found his way through the crowded streets to the centre of Westminster, while his father took Anne with their luggage to a large mansion owned by one of his distant cousins.

Tully rode at Richard's side, enjoying the attention of the crowds, which parted to make way for them. A pretty girl in the crowd called out to him and he shouted something back at her, laughing. He had yet to settle down with a woman of his choosing and was popular with the available ladies of Middleham. Although he had no personal wealth, his promotion to squire meant he had become a man with prospects.

Richard found the sheer number of people overwhelming and was unhappy to see how they emptied slops into the street. He was glad to be on horseback as his expensive new leather boots were already spattered with mud. The people of London seemed immune to the stench which was made worse by the warm spring weather. Westminster was busy with the shouts of street vendors taking advantage of the crowds, selling everything from spiced ale to posies of bright orange marguerites, in honour of the new queen.

Richard's knighting ceremony began with the vigil, which his father explained was a time to be spent in prayer and contemplation of his new duties as a knight. One of the royal chapels was decorated with the banners of his Neville ancestors and his polished armour and sword lay on the altar. A white-haired priest wearing a heavy silver crucifix waited while Richard knelt and said a prayer of thanks in front of the altar. The priest then took Richard's sword and held it reverently in the air while he said the blessing.

Richard listened as the priest recited his well-rehearsed speech about how the sword would be used to defend the church against the cruelty of pagans and Richard would become the terror and dread of his enemies. After a hundred years of war with France there were many who would challenge King Henry's right to the throne.

He thought of his uncle, Richard of York. He could argue a rightful claim and was waiting for his chance, although the cost could be the end of the delicate peace. Richard knew the real dangers for the Nevilles were much closer to home. The Percy family would take their lands by force if they saw the opportunity. As a knight he would have to help his father deal with the ever present threat from their neighbours.

The elderly priest reverently placed Richard's sword back on the altar and quietly withdrew, closing the heavy wooden door behind him with a dull thud and leaving Richard alone for his long vigil. The ancient stone chapel was cool and peaceful after the noise of the city streets. He said a prayer for his family, although he had never been devoutly religious and soon found his mind wandering.

Richard remembered how he had discovered Anne standing patiently while two seamstresses worked on the expensive, long-sleeved, gold brocade dress she would wear at the coronation. She was determined to dress in the latest French fashion and had been pleased when he said he had never seen her looking more beautiful. Anne asked the seamstresses to leave and locked the door behind them, leaving no mystery of her intentions. She carefully removed the new dress while Richard watched.

He wondered if they had finally made a son and his nagging concern at the back of his mind returned. His father had said nothing about their lack of a child, yet he surely would soon. Richard forced himself to think about how his life would change when he was a knight. His father had told him about life at the court of the last King Henry who was always absent, fighting a noble war in France. Men were rewarded with high office for fighting at his side or, like his father, helping to keep the Scots from crossing the northern border. Richard wondered if he would be able to dedicate himself to keeping the fragile truce with France. A peace brokered by the crowning of a new French Queen.

When his long vigil was over Richard bathed in water so cold it took his breath away. He shaved his beard and had his hair neatly trimmed short before being dressed in a new shirt of crisp white linen, a symbol of knightly purity. He put on new black hose and shoes, then the bright scarlet robe, which was supposed to represent the blood he would shed as a knight. As he dressed in the ceremonial robe Richard wondered how long it might be before he would use his sword against another man.

An usher led Richard into a stateroom, brightly lit with dozens of flickering candles. There in front of him was King Henry, regarding him without any sign of recognition. The king was pale and thin, and could easily have been mistaken for one of the courtiers except for his ermine edged robe and the gold chain around his neck. Richard had been expecting the king to be sitting on a throne, wearing his crown. Instead, he was standing, flanked by his ministers. William de La Pole, the Earl of Suffolk, studied Richard as if trying to assess his value then whispered something to the king, who remained impassive.

Richard smiled as he saw Anne waiting to take her part in the ceremony at the side of his proud father. She looked strikingly beautiful in her new dress of deep red velvet, set off with a gold necklace studded with sparkling rubies. Anne caught his eye and smiled back. She seemed completely at home in such grand surroundings, as if she had never known anything different.

One of the older knights, a stocky man with a barrel chest and a white beard, had the duty of introducing him to the king. He cleared his throat and approached the king reverently.

'A candidate deemed worthy of elevation to the order of chivalry has been summoned, Your Grace.'

Richard knelt before the king, as his father had told him he should do. Four of the older knights laboriously read the sermon of the duties of a knight. Richard waited in silence while each spoke in turn, the same words said to his father and grandfather. The whole ceremony had hardly changed since the order of mounted nobles of Roman times.

The king studied Richard with new interest, as if seeing him for the first time. 'For what purpose do you wish to join the order?'

Richard replied as he had been instructed, for the first time looking King Henry directly in the eye. 'I desire to be a knight that I might serve my God, my King and my lady wife,' he paused to cast a glance to where Anne was watching, 'to the best of my abilities.'

This was the sign for Anne to come forward. She removed his scarlet robe and helped him put on a long-sleeved blue velvet houpelande, lined with white linen. Four knights each solemnly came forward and presented Richard with his white belt, chain of gold, spurs and sword.

The king solemnly placed the flat of his sword on Richard's shoulder. 'In the name of God, St. Michael, and St George, I create thee knight.' He placed the sword to Richard's other shoulder. 'Be thou valiant, fearless and loyal.'

Richard swore an oath to defend King Henry, braving death to preserve his brethren. His voice carried well and as he spoke he looked around at the faces of those present. Anne had returned to his father's side and Richard felt a surge of pride as he saw them. He was a knight of the realm at the age of seventeen. A whole new life at the royal court was now open to him.

Soldiers in the livery of the king's guard armed with sharply pointed halberds made a wide cordon in front of Westminster Abbey, holding back the cheering crowds as Richard and Anne arrived. There was a real sense of occasion as they joined the long row of nobles lining each side of the entrance to the Abbey. There were so many Richard realised every lord and lady of note must have been summoned to witness the coronation.

The new queen's escort arrived, mounted on horseback, colourfully dressed with scarlet costumes for the officers and blue tunics with gold embroidered sleeves for the guards. The clattering hooves of over a hundred horses on the cobbled streets drowned conversation amongst the waiting crowds, then a cacophony of trumpets announced the arrival of the young wife of the king.

She rode in a golden coach drawn by two horses caparisoned with white damask glittering with gold. As soon as Richard saw Margaret of Anjou he sensed disappointment. Her auburn hair flowed over her shoulders and the bright spring sunshine flashed on her gold coronet, studded with large white pearls. She looked like a queen, yet through all the pageantry Richard could see she was a nervous young woman, little more than a year younger than himself, playing the role of the new queen as she had been instructed to.

As she came closer he saw her face was set in a fixed smile. There was a shout from the crowd and her eyes darted around, as if on the lookout for a hidden assassin. Richard realised he was looking at an uncertain future for the throne of England and also saw opportunity. Queen Margaret would have no shortage of advisors and supporters, yet she would always need people she could rely on.

Margaret stepped from her coach and was escorted by a procession of royal guards, expensively dressed noblewomen and senior clergymen. She turned her head in Richard's direction as she passed the spot where he was standing with Anne and his father. Their eyes met

only for the briefest moment. Richard realised he had
been mistaken. There was a glint of triumph in her eye.
She was missing no detail of her coronation day. Margaret
of Anjou held his gaze for one second and was gone,
leaving Richard in no doubt he should not underestimate
the new queen, even though she was only fifteen years
old.

Richard and Anne followed the procession, behind his
mother and father, through the high arched doorway into
the Abbey and took their places. They watched as
Margaret of Anjou made her way up the nave to music
played by minstrels provided by her proud father, Rene,
Duke of Anjou and King of Naples, with the Duke of
Milan, two of the many heads of state in attendance to
witness the crowning ceremony.

The one head of state conspicuously absent was King
Henry. Richard had heard that the king was likely to be
watching the ceremony from a secret vantage-point. He
scanned the high vaulted galleries of the Abbey and
realised there were many places for people to hide if they
wished. It seemed odd to him that the king was not
present, although his father had explained the tradition
went back since before records began.

When Margaret reached the altar, she knelt in prayer
then prostrated herself to show her humility. The
Archbishop of Canterbury led her behind the red velvet
curtains for the anointing and placed St Edward's crown
on her head, the same crown that has been used since the
coronation of William the Conqueror nearly four hundred
years earlier.

As the new queen made her slow procession back past
the watching nobles, Richard studied those closest to her
and noted Sir William de la Pole, the Marquis of Suffolk,

who he had seen whispering to the king at his coronation, was proudly carrying the queen's sceptre.

Richard was curious and whispered to his father. 'How does Suffolk have such a role?'

His father was also watching de la Pole. 'Watch and learn, Richard. This is the man who brokered the marriage of Margaret to the king.' He looked disapproving. 'And he has established his wife as the new queen's closest companion.'

Richard looked more closely at William de la Pole. 'A useful man to know.'

His father frowned. 'Or a dangerous enemy.'

Richard pondered those words as he watched the next pair of riders prepare for the joust. The spacious courtyard of Westminster Abbey was transformed for the event, overlooked by high wooden stands specially erected to seat the royal hosts and invited guests. The brightly painted tilt rail was thirty yards long, with turning areas nearly as long again at each end. These were surrounded by the clusters of colourful tents where the jousters waited and prepared with their squires.

From one of these tents Richard saw the queen sitting high in the centre of the grandstand with King Henry to one side and her father to the other. He knew the queen's father was passionate about the sport of jousting and had brought some of the finest jousters in France across to London for the celebration contest, which was to run for three days. The French riders and their supporters were there in great numbers, their banners and pennants flying in the light breeze like alongside the more familiar colours of the English noble families.

Riding in the joust had been on Richard's mind ever since his father first told him he had been entered in the rolls. He had become expert at tilting at the quatrain, a deceptively simple target which would swing violently when struck, bringing a weighted sack around to hit the unwary. Jousting was dangerous and unpredictable. A horse could falter or a lance could miss its mark at the moment of impact. Good men had been known to die at the joust, like John Hastings, the Earl of Pembroke, who had been Richard's age when he was killed.

The prospect of being unhorsed on his first ride in such a public gathering troubled Richard. He could not afford to fail in front of the king and his new queen. As he entered the banquet the previous night the queen hardly glanced in his direction. She was the centre of attention, dressed entirely in cloth of gold sparkling with jewels. Because of the joust he had to remain sober, despite the fine wine flowing freely. Most of the riders were much more experienced than him, so Richard knew he would need more than a little luck and would have to keep his wits about him.

Somewhere in the stands were Anne and his parents, although he couldn't see them from his position at the far end of the square. Before they parted Richard's father had turned to him.

'You will remember what I told you?'

'Of course, Father.' Even as he answered Richard wondered if he would be able to hold his nerve when it mattered. He had a habit of raising his lance a little early, giving his opponent the chance to attack rather than defend. He didn't want to disappoint Anne. Her father had been one of the finest jousters in the country and had even tried to teach the king. Anne often came to watch him at jousting practice and was a skilled horsewoman herself.

Luke Tully interrupted his thoughts. 'Time to be putting your armour on now, my lord.' He had been polishing the new breastplate until it shone.

Richard held the breastplate in place while Tully fastened the leather straps to the silver buckles on his backplate. The elbow and knee caps on the vambraces to protect his arms and cuisses on his legs had to be loose enough to give him freedom of movement. As Tully expertly adjusted the straps holding the armour in place Richard spotted his groom waiting in the shadows with Samson. His horse was also wearing plates to protect his head and chest and was resplendent in the Neville colours.

Richard tried on his jousting helmet to make sure of a comfortable fit. He'd worn it many times in practice and had extra padding fitted inside, although he found it cut down his field of view more than he would have liked.

Tully lifted the visor. 'How does it feel?'

'Hot and heavy!' Richard shook his head to check the helmet wasn't loose.

Tully pulled a face. 'Rather you than me, my lord!'

'Help me take it off. I'll leave it until I'm mounted.'

Tully carefully removed the helmet and offered Richard a cup of bitter ale. Richard drank it gratefully and peered out through the flap in the tent. The next riders were about to take their turn. He watched as they made a measuring pass, saluting one another, then gave the sign they were ready. Their horses launched into a fast gallop and in an instant there was the clash of lances striking armour. Richard strained to see from his position, although the cheer from the crowd told him what he needed to know.

His own turn soon came. As there were so many knights in the list each rider was only having two passes. His groom led Samson to the tent and Tully helped Richard into the saddle. He patted the richly decorated horse affectionately.

'Samson will do you proud, my lord.'

Richard looked down to the other end of the tilt rail where his opponent was also making ready. He had been drawn against one of the French riders who seemed about his own age. Richard silently thanked God he hadn't been pitted against one of the battle hardened chevaliers he had seen strutting around the banqueting hall.

'What do you make of the Frenchman, Tully?'

'His horse has seen better days.'

Richard looked again at his rival's steed. He couldn't make any judgement about the Frenchman's horse, caparisoned with a brightly coloured cape, richly decorated with gold fleurs-de-lis reaching almost to the ground. He realised Tully was trying to be encouraging.

'Hand me my helm, Tully.' Richard put it on, then his new steel plated gauntlets, and waited for the marshal's command. The marshal was an officious looking Frenchman, from the Duke of Anjou's retinue. Richard wondered if he would be truly impartial.

'Servez lances!' The marshal's strongly accented voice echoed through the courtyard of Westminster.

Tully handed Richard his lance. Lighter than he had been used to, the final three feet at the tip were painted white, made to shatter if he could strike the target on his opponent's armour. The lance felt well balanced as he braced it under his arm and raised and lowered it experimentally.

'A volonte!' The marshal signalled for the riders to show they were ready.

Richard raised his lance and moved Samson closer towards the tilt rail. Silence fell over the watching crowd. He was already feeling hot inside the helmet and had to turn his head to see if he could find Anne or his father. The narrow slot over his eyes obscured his view.

Taking a deep breath and leaning forward as he had been trained, Richard urged the heavy horse into a gallop as they had practiced together so many times at Middleham Castle. Samson lunged forward with all his strength. Both horses covered the short distance in seconds and he felt the bone-jarring shock of the impact through his armour as the Frenchman's lance shattered on contact.

Richard began to slide from his saddle with the momentum of the blow. He remembered his father's warning about the point of no return and threw his lance to the side as he'd been trained to do, heaving with all his strength to pull himself back upright. He didn't even know if he had scored a hit on the Frenchman. Richard pulled up and turned to where Tully was waiting with a fresh lance.

'Did I get a clean strike?'

'You did, my lord. Well done.'

Richard took the new lance and held it firmly, sighting down the long straight line of the tilt rail. This was his last chance. The Frenchman at the other end made the sign he was ready and the crowd fell silent again. Both horses charged and this time the Frenchman missed. Richard's lance hit him square on, bending with the force and lifting him almost out of his saddle.

Time seemed to pass in slow motion. The Frenchman's lance clattered to the ground as he started falling backwards. His gauntleted hands grabbed helplessly at the air as he fell, his armour clattering on the hard cobble-stones of the courtyard. The crowd gasped, many standing to have a better view.

Richard pulled up and turned to watch as the marshal made his ruling. He gave the sign for a win and Richard felt a sudden mixture of elation and relief. He passed what was left of his lance to a grinning Tully and pushed up his visor to survey the cheering crowd. He still couldn't spot Anne or his parents, although he saw the queen. She was standing now. There was no sign of a smile as she raised a hand in acknowledgement of his victory over the Frenchman.

Chapter 5 - Winter 1448

Thick blue ice formed on the moat at Middleham Castle and heavy snow showers turned the bleak Yorkshire landscape white during one of the coldest winters anyone could remember. Guards were always posted on lookout duty despite the freezing weather, more to warn of approaching visitors than through the danger of attack. The sentries were glad to have something to relieve their boredom as they watched a lone rider picking his way down the slippery track leading from the village.

As he came closer one of the guards shouted down to him. He called back that he'd travelled a great distance with an important message from Duchess Cecily of Warwick. His tired horse was taken to the stables and the messenger was led to see Richard, who had already been told of his arrival. The man made no excuses for his dishevelled appearance and damp clothes. He simply produced a folded parchment, neatly sealed with red wax.

Richard thanked the messenger, handing him a silver coin and sent him to the kitchens for something to eat. He also sent for Anne and studied the seal on the letter while he waited for her to arrive. The seal was the bear and ragged staff of the house of Warwick. Anne's brother Henry had died in a hunting accident two years before, leaving Richard's older sister Cecily to look after their daughter, who had inherited the title.

Richard had grown a dark beard which he kept neatly trimmed. He stroked it as he wondered what his sister was asking for. He made a quick calculation. The little girl would be about five years old now. He guessed Cecily needed his help to find her daughter a suitable husband. His father had arranged their marriages when they were not much older and paid a significant dowry to secure the deal. Cecily was a wealthy woman and would be thinking of the future. Perhaps she was intending to remarry. Richard frowned at the thought.

Anne arrived with her maid, who began lighting candles from a long taper she carried. The last of the winter sun soon fell below the horizon and the room was growing darker. They waited until the maid had finished and left, then Anne watched as Richard carefully broke the seal and spread the parchment out on the table so they could both read it. They both gasped in amazement. Cecily's only daughter, their young niece, was dead from a fever.

'She was so full of life when we last saw her!' Anne wiped a tear from her eye and reread the neatly handwritten letter. 'Poor Cecily.'

Richard put his arm around Anne's shoulder and held her close. 'It is the worst tragedy for my sister, her only child.'

'We must do what we can to help her.'

Richard pointed to the letter. 'You realise what she is saying, Anne? You are the new Countess of Warwick.'

Anne thought for a moment, sadness still in her eyes. 'And you the Earl of Warwick. This changes everything, doesn't it?'

'I must send a message to my father. Annie was his favourite granddaughter.'

'Your mother, as well.' She put a comforting hand on Richard's shoulder. 'You must tell her.'

'Yes, of course. Will you find her for me? I need to think about this.'

Anne went to look for his mother while Richard paced the room, wondering if he should ride to the north to find his father. Rumours of fighting at the border with Scotland had reached them and Richard's father had taken a small army of men to investigate. That was over two weeks ago and nothing had been heard from him since. Richard had said nothing to Anne or his mother, although he was concerned. His father would be quite a prize for the Scottish raiders if they could capture him. He decided to go in search of him, taking enough men for safety and travelling light for speed.

Richard galloped as fast as he dared in the darkness towards the flickering orange glow lighting up the night skyline. The acrid smell of smoke reached him on the light breeze. They had been taken by surprise again, despite the extra guards and sentries. It had taken over a month to find his father. Instead of returning home as planned, he was now supporting his father's forces at the West March, as the king had appointed him and his father joint wardenship two years before.

Richard galloped towards the flames, followed by his men. He had been riding out to patrol the border many times with his father. He had yet to be involved in any fighting, although they had seen a few remote farmsteads which had been destroyed, allegedly by the Percy family.

By the time they reached the village Richard could see they were too late to do anything to help. He looked down the muddy track that ran through the village. A row of simple crofts built from local stone led to an open area that was probably used on market days. A dog ran towards him, barking as he approached, startling his horse. He calmed him with soothing words and rode towards the scene of the fire.

A dejected family with several small children stood by the ruin that had been their home. The roof was completely gone and the walls had fallen down. Only the blackened stones of the hearth still stood. He saw the few possessions they had tried to save were in a charred heap.

Richard dismounted and walked over to speak to them.

'I'm sorry we didn't get here quicker.' He glanced back at the still smouldering building. 'I will send men to help rebuild your house.'

He reached into his purse and gave the family a few silver coins which they accepted gratefully. He realised his gift was probably more money than they had seen in their lives.

More people emerged from their houses and several young men of the village watched Richard with interest. He turned to them. 'Did any of you see who did this?'

One of the men stepped forward. 'Percy supporters, my lord.'

'Not the Scots?'

'No, my lord.' The man seemed as if he knew more than he was saying.

Richard was wondering what to do when there was a shout from the other side of the village.

'The grain store! They've set fire to the grain store!'

The villagers kept their precious grain harvest in a large wooden barn, set back from the single track that ran through the houses. A burning arrow was sticking from the dry thatch of the roof and the flames were already spreading. Richard saw fresh sparks spitting into the dark sky as the fire took hold. There was no way to see where the arrow had come from. Richard guessed the villagers were right.

Even as he watched, a second burning arrow flashed through the night and thudded into the roof of the barn close to the first. Whoever fired the arrows couldn't be far away. His father had told him the Percy family recruited experienced archers who had fought in France. They were probably already making their escape.

'Over there, to the right!' One of his men shouted and pointed into the trees.

Richard hesitated for a second. He had to make sure they saved the grain. He turned to Tully, who was close behind him.

'Take some men and see if you can find anyone. Take them alive if you can!'

Tully selected some soldiers before leaping back onto his horse.

'Good luck to you!' He shouted after them as they galloped off.

Richard was glad to have someone he could trust. If there was any chance of catching whoever was responsible Tully would do it. In the three years since he was appointed as Richard's squire Tully had become Richard's right-hand man. Most importantly, Tully had won the respect of the men and earned his place at Richard's side through his skill and actions in the border fighting.

'Quickly, we need water!' He shouted to the remaining soldiers, who rushed into the nearest houses looking for anything they could use. Some started work at the village well, hauling up buckets as fast as they could, while others filled theirs from the large horse trough close to the grain store. The villagers realised what they needed to do and formed a human chain, passing buckets along the line from the well to the barn, handing back empty buckets for refilling. They struggled to throw the water high enough to reach the roof of the barn. When it reached the flames there was a hiss of steam.

Richard looked at the smoke billowing from the entrance to the barn. 'We need to work faster!' He shouted.

There were now dozens of villagers working with Richard's men. They soon emptied the horse trough. The well was old and they were taking too long to raise enough water. The flames were now lighting up the night, fanned by the breeze. Bitter tasting smoke made their eyes water as they struggled to put out the blaze. Richard could feel the heat on his face.

'It's no use, my lord.' One of the villagers said the words they all knew were true.

Richard could hear the precious grain beginning to crackle and spit in the blistering heat. He refused to give up.

'Open the doors.' He looked into the soot-blackened faces of the villagers. 'We'll save what we can!'

They followed his order. Two young men threw open the huge barn doors and everyone with buckets began desperately filling them with grain. The chain of people passing buckets were now adding to a growing heap of grain a safe distance from the barn.

Richard watched as they worked in the darkness and then made a decision. 'That's enough!' He beckoned for them to stand clear. 'We can't risk any more.'

The villagers stood in despair as they saw the rest of their precious grain being lost to the flames. It had been a good harvest and there would have been enough to see them all through until the spring. Now they would go hungry.

Richard noticed one of the women from the village looking at him. Although her dress was made of the same coarse wool they all wore, something about her caught his attention. He walked towards her, away from the flames and heat of the barn, now burning out of control. As he came closer she ducked back inside the small doorway of her house, then came back out with a pewter tankard of ale, which she handed to Richard. His throat was parched from the smoke and exertion and the ale was refreshing and potent.

'Thank you.' He studied the woman more closely. She was more attractive and younger than he had first thought. Her long dark hair was loose over her shoulders and her eyes sparkled in the light from the fire.

'What is your name?'

'Megan, my lord.' Her voice had the soft accent of the northern villagers.

'Do you know who I am?'

'I do, my lord.' She held his gaze.

There was a shout behind him and Richard's hand swiftly moved to the hilt of his sword before he recognised the sound of Tully's voice. He drained the tankard and handed it back to Megan. They both watched as Tully and his men rode into the village, one of the horses carrying a man with his hands bound with rope.

'You've caught one then?'

Tully seemed pleased with himself. 'Wasn't easy, my lord.'

'Was he carrying a bow?'

Tully shook his head. 'Not when we caught up with him.'

Richard cursed. It would have been the proof he needed. 'Bring him here.'

The prisoner was dragged from his horse and made to kneel in front of Richard.

Richard frowned at him. 'Are you responsible for these fires?'

The man refused to look at him and made no move to answer.

Richard tried again. 'Are you working for the Percy family?'

The man looked down at the ground at the mention of the Percy name. It was going to be hard to persuade him to talk. At least Tully had captured him alive. He would give them the evidence they needed, eventually. Richard noticed the young girl named Megan was watching to see what he would do.

'Untie him.'

One of Tully's men stepped forward and loosened the rope binding the kneeling man's wrists.

Richard looked down into the man's eyes. The man seemed in fear of his life.

'I want to see your hands. It should be easy enough to tell if you were an archer.'

The man moved like a striking adder, so fast no one could stop him. Snatching a knife from one of the men who was supposed to be guarding him, he grabbed Megan and held the blade to her throat.

'Stand back!'

Richard instinctively drew his sword. He saw the desperate look in the man's eyes. 'Let the girl go. I'll see to it you have a fair trial.'

The man gave a humourless laugh. 'Get back! All of you!' His eyes darted around as he tried to decide his best route of escape.

There was a crash of splintering wood as the burning barn finally collapsed in a shower of sparks, new flames shooting high into the night sky. The man dropped his knife and fell backwards, both hands clutching at his throat. Megan pulled away from him and looked in shock at the crossbow bolt sticking through the man's neck. It had penetrated right up to the feathered flight at such close range.

Richard glanced back to where Tully stood. 'You could have hit the girl!'

Tully slung his crossbow back over his shoulder. 'I saw my chance.' He looked across at Megan. 'In case you are wondering, that was the first time I've killed a man.'

She seemed pale and shocked but as far as he could tell she was unharmed.

Richard returned his sword to its scabbard and turned to her. 'Have you any more ale?'

Megan led him into her house. Richard looked around the sparsely furnished room, taking in the details of her life. The wooden shutters over the small windows were closed, so the only light was from the red glow of the fire in the stone hearth. A spinning wheel stood next to balls of yarn and a sack of new wool. Bunches of lavender and other dried herbs hung from the solid wooden ceiling beams, giving off their delicate scent. A thick sheepskin rug on the earthen floor added a little comfort and he could see a bed covered with woollen throws. The aroma of freshly baked bread made him feel hungry, as it had been a while since he had eaten.

Megan closed the door behind him and slid a heavy piece of wood into place to lock it from the inside. The significance of her action answered the question that had been in Richard's mind since he first saw her. She threw another log on the hot coals in the fireplace and it immediately burst into bright flames, taking the coolness from the small room. She poured him another tankard of ale. It tasted warm and had a bitter tang of hops Richard found refreshing.

'You live here alone?' He looked at her appraisingly.

'Yes.' She seemed to be considering whether to tell him something.

She moved closer to him and they looked into each other's eyes. Richard felt the powerful connection he sensed when he first saw her. His mother taught him to believe some things happen because they are meant to. He believed her now. He put down the tankard and unfastened the silver buckle on his sword belt. Carefully removing it, he laid the sword to one side.

Megan put her arms around him. She held him close and they stood in silence. The fire crackled as the flames discovered sap in the burning log. Richard felt the soft warmth of her body and sensed her respond as he gently caressed her back.

She whispered in his ear. 'I want you.'

Richard stroked her long hair. It felt like silk as it ran through his fingers. He kissed the soft skin of her neck, then found her lips and kissed her again, longer this time. He felt intoxicated by her wild energy and realised he had been hoping for this from the moment he first saw her. There was no question he was abusing his power over her though. If anything she had a strange power over him.

She took his hand without speaking and led him to the wooden chair by the fireside. Gesturing for him to sit, she knelt at his feet and pulled off one of his black leather riding boots. She gave him a mischievous look as she threw it to one side, before pulling at the second. Richard wore a padded velvet doublet, laced at the front. Megan worked out how to undo the fastening and took it from him, then pulled his heavy cotton undershirt over his head. She ran her hands through the dark hair on his bare chest, tracing the scar he had gained learning to fight with a sword. He liked the feel of her slender fingers as she caressed the hard muscles of his torso.

Richard turned her round and untied the back of her woollen dress. She was naked underneath. He reached inside and caressed the smoothness of her back before pulling the top down to expose her breasts. Her skin was pale where it hadn't seen the sun and contrasted with the brown of her neck and arms.

She pulled away from him and led him to the bed, gently pushing him down so he lay on his back looking up at her. She gently pulled off the rest of his clothes and her eyes flashed in the candlelight as she loosened her dress and let it fall to the floor. He pulled her towards him and kissed her again, longer this time, feeling dizzy with desire. Her touch told him what she wanted him to do.

Chapter 6 - Spring 1451

Richard and his men rode hard from Middleham Castle in the glorious spring sunshine, the hooves of their horses thundering as they galloped north. He travelled light for speed, with a dozen of his best mounted archers and his squire Luke Tully. He felt the familiar sense of exhilaration and anticipation as the Northumberland village came into view. Richard visited Megan as often as his duties on the northern border allowed; although this time he had to wait much longer than usual. As well as the tour of his new estates in South Wales, he was spending more time in the Great Council of Westminster.

The people of the remote village had been cautiously wary of him until he won their respect by helping with rebuilding the barn. He brought in expert stone masons and carpenters, who made sure the barn was built to last, with proper foundations and a slate roof to replace the ruined thatch. He also paid for a new tavern to be built on the outskirts of the village where his men could stay in some comfort.

The tavern had now become the focal point for the remote village, a meeting place and also where business was done with people from neighbouring villages. They rode up to the stables at the rear of the tavern now and dismounted. Richard patted his horse on the neck and handed the reins to Luke Tully.

'How long are we staying, my lord?'

'The men deserve a rest.' Richard stared up at the sun, trying to judge the time. 'It's less than a day's ride. We will stay here tomorrow and be ready to leave early the following morning.'

He glanced up the stony lane to where he could see Megan's cottage in the distance. 'You can stock up with provisions.' He smiled at Tully, glad to have someone he could trust. 'You know where you can find me if I'm needed.'

Tully grinned. 'We'll be here if you need us, my lord.'

Richard walked up the lane through the middle of the village, nodding to people who recognised him. Chickens wandered freely, searching for spilt grain on the path and a tethered goat, with udders ready for milking, watched him approach. The door to Megan's cottage was propped open to let the fresh air in. He ducked under the low lintel and went inside. Megan was making bread on the oak table. Her long, dark hair was tied back and she wore a white cotton apron. An earthenware vase of yellow daffodils brightened the small room. Megan looked up in happy surprise as he entered.

'Richard!' She wiped flour from her hands on her apron and hugged him. 'You should have sent a messenger ahead. I would have been ready for you.'

'I rode here as fast as any messenger could.' He unbuckled his belt and placed his sword in the corner of the room, then took her in his arms and looked into her eyes. 'I've missed you, Megan.'

She hugged him tightly. 'It has been such a long time. You will see a difference in Margaret.'

Richard crossed the room to the wooden cot to see his daughter. He had chosen to live in Megan's simple cottage whenever he visited, so no one seemed surprised when it became obvious she was expecting his baby. He had worried about Megan as her time came near. Fortunately she had no problems delivering a strong and healthy baby. They named her Margaret, in honour of the queen who had made such a powerful impression on Richard despite her young age.

Now little Margaret looked up at him with her mother's eyes and smiled broadly at him. She was his greatest secret.

'Can I pick her up?'

'Yes, of course.'

Richard carefully lifted his daughter from her cot. She felt heavier than he expected. He noticed she was wearing a thin cotton smock and wished he had thought to bring new clothes for her. He'd given Megan money for the care of their child and guessed she must be saving it, as there was no sign of it having been spent on anything in the cottage.

'She's going to be a strong girl.'

'I can't believe her first birthday is coming round so soon.'

He laughed as his daughter tightly gripped one of his fingers with her tiny hand. 'I wish I could spend more time here.' He sat in one of the wooden chairs at the table with Margaret on his knee and watched as Megan finished her bread making. She kneaded the dough expertly, turning it and adding a little more flour before kneading it again.

Megan glanced up at them as she worked and smiled at the sight of the two of them together. 'How long are you here for?'

'I can stay tomorrow. Then I have to ride to Alnwick.'

'You're going to the castle?'

'This village is too close to the Percy lands. It's time I talked to them.'

'Have you heard something?' She looked at him questioningly. 'There's been no trouble since the fire.'

'I've been worried about your safety.' He needed to share his concern. 'You know they pay spies to report on our activities. It can only be a matter of time before they learn of our daughter.'

Megan stopped kneading the dough. 'Are we in danger?'

'My father has been exchanging letters with Sir Henry Percy. I think they are both ready for a truce.'

Megan covered the dough with a muslin cloth and placed it on the hearth to rise. 'Why isn't your father going to Alnwick in person?'

'He was going to. I persuaded him to let me deal with this, so I could see you.'

'Do you trust Sir Henry Percy?'

'I'm not sure.' Richard frowned. 'He is married to my aunt Eleanor, one of my father's sisters, so he is family in a way. The marriage was supposed to bring the families together.' He looked at her. 'I don't have any choice, Megan. Even if I left a dozen men here full time to protect you, they could send a hundred whenever they wanted.'

She poured him a tankard of dark ale. 'You must be hungry?' Without waiting for his answer Megan carved him thick slices from a cured ham and cut some of the rough bread she had baked earlier that morning. Although he was used to fine food in London, Richard preferred the simpler tastes of Northumberland and the freshness of butter melting on still warm bread.

After they had eaten he told her about his long and difficult journey to Wales, where he had to protect the rights to his inheritance. He owned property in twenty counties but almost none of it came without problems. Richard knew it would take years to sort it all out. It seemed there was a claimant for every acre of land and each stone of every building.

Megan wanted to know all about Wales, which she seemed to regard as a land impossibly far away and full of mystery. She had never been out of Northumberland. When he offered to set her up in a fine house in London, she turned him down immediately, even though as far as he knew there was nothing other than her birth to keep her in the north. He found her lack of education endearing and was unsurprised at how little she knew of the people or geography of Wales.

Later they lay together in the darkness. Margaret was fast asleep, tired out. Megan held Richard close and asked the question he knew was going to come.

'Have you told her?'

'I was going to.' He looked at her, trying to judge her reaction. 'Then she told me she is with child. We have waited a long time, Megan. I hope it is a son.'

She said nothing. Although the darkness meant he couldn't see her eyes, he could sense her sadness.

Richard broke the silence. 'I started thinking about what she would do.'

Megan sat up and he saw the outline of her body silhouetted in the moonlight from the small window. She had yet to fully regain her figure after Margaret was born and her once girlish breasts were now full and heavy from feeding their daughter.

'What could she do?' Her voice was softer this time and she sounded worried.

'She could make me promise to stop seeing you.'

'How can she?'

He struggled to answer. 'I am married to her, Megan. Although I was too young to even know what I was saying when I made my marriage vows, I am bound to her. If she makes me give my word, I have to honour it.'

Megan lay back next to him. 'You know how much I love you, Richard?'

'Of course I do.' He held her close. 'I love you too.'

She kissed him. 'Sometimes I wish you were simply a tenant farmer, instead of an earl. Then you could live here all the time.'

Richard laughed at the thought. 'I would be so happy living here with you.' He gently traced the smooth curve of her exposed breast with his finger, stopping as he reached the gold ring and a sapphire pendant she had on a silver chain around her neck. He had given the ring to her when Margaret was born. Megan stubbornly refused to wear it on her hand but he took some consolation from seeing she always wore it around her neck.

Megan was fiercely independent and took great pride in her self-sufficiency, refusing to accept any money for herself, only reluctantly taking his gold coins for their daughter. He admired her for it and wondered if she had any idea of the value of the precious sapphire. It had cost him a small fortune and had been made into a pendant by one of the finest silversmiths in London.

'You know I have duties and responsibilities?' He looked into her dark eyes. 'One day my visits will have to end.'

She hugged him, 'I know. I have always known.' She kissed him again, more passionately this time. 'Let's make the most of the time we have together.'

Richard reflected on that conversation as he rode to Alnwick. They had enjoyed an idyllic day together. He'd seen his daughter take a few faltering steps, nearly falling over then looking pleased with herself as she found her balance. He repaired the wooden shutters on the windows of the cottage which suffered in the winter storms and wouldn't close properly. It felt good to live the simple life of a villager, even if only for one day. It saddened him to know his double life could not continue for much longer. His father would probably understand but Anne would almost certainly insist on him swearing to end the affair.

Their daughter woke them in the night with her crying and he had watched as Megan comforted her. Despite her northern toughness he admired so much, there was a softer side to Megan and he heard her sobbing when she thought he was sleeping. Although she was smiling as she waved him goodbye, when he turned in his saddle for a last look, she was wiping a tear from her eye.

'The castle is ahead, my lord.' Tully interrupted his thoughts.

Richard saw the high turrets emerging through the trees in the distance. He turned to his men. 'Remember we are here to agree a truce. You need to be vigilant. No drinking and definitely no fighting, understood?'

His men followed him down the long straight road approaching the castle, which controlled an important crossing over the river. A flock of noisy seagulls wheeled overhead, their shrill cries reminding him they were not far from the coast. The castle was an impressive sight. Even grander than Middleham Castle and more imposing, the banner of the Percy family flew proudly from the highest tower of their stronghold, a rampant blue lion on a golden field.

Sir Henry Percy, Earl of Northumberland, was waiting with a small group of men to greet them in person.

Richard guessed he must have been alerted of their arrival by his sentries, as he could see men stationed along the battlements, watching them carefully. He realised they were as wary of him as he was of them. Sir Henry seemed older than Richard expected, with his hair and beard a silver grey and a stout figure from his enjoyment of fine living.

'Sir Richard! Or should I address you as Earl Warwick?' His booming northern voice sounded condescending to Richard.

'Good day, Sir Henry.' Richard rode up to where Sir Henry Percy was waiting and dismounted, signalling for his men to do the same.

'You've grown since I last saw you, Richard.' He grinned, revealing several missing teeth. 'In importance as well as height.'

'You could say that, Sir Henry. The Percy family has also done well.'

'Yes, we have indeed. We have done better than we could have hoped.' He admired Richard's imposing black stallion. 'A fine hunter, by the look of him?'

'He's served me well, Sir Henry.' He patted his horse on the neck. 'Well suited for the long distances I have to ride these days.'

'I'll have your men shown to the stables.' Sir Henry gestured to one of the servants in his group. 'You must come and meet your aunt Eleanor. I don't believe you've seen her since you were a boy?'

'I remember her well, Sir Henry.' Richard followed them into the immense baronial hall of the castle, richly decorated with tapestries and a collection of huge antlers. Armed guards followed them into the room at a discreet distance and he realised Sir Henry was taking no chances. He was aware of how he had skilfully separated him from his own bodyguard, although there was nothing he could do about it without risking offence.

Richard's aunt was waiting to greet him and he kissed her hand. She was a tall woman, dressed in a long-sleeved emerald gown and wearing a veil of fine lace that made it hard for him to judge her mood. Younger women, also expensively dressed with tall hennin hats, who he guessed were her daughters, stood to each side of her.

'I'd hardly have recognised you, Richard.' She paused and looked at him more closely. 'You've grown into a fine young man.' Her voice was soft and sounded well educated, reminding him of his mother. She turned to the woman on her left, an attractively younger version of herself, who was accompanied by a knight Richard thought he recognised. 'This is your cousin Lady Katherine and her husband Sir Edmund Grey.'

Richard kissed his cousin's hand. 'It is a pleasure to meet you Lady Katherine.' He knew she was the same age as himself. He saw sharp intelligence in her eyes and was reminded he was under the closest scrutiny. He turned to her husband and greeted him with a smile. 'Honoured, Sir Edmund. I believe I have seen you at court?'

'Indeed you have, Earl Warwick, also at the council in Westminster.'

Richard realised he could be useful ally in the Percy stronghold. He turned to the other woman, a tall girl who fidgeted nervously as she waited. Richard studied her more closely and guessed she was about fifteen, although she could pass for older.

His aunt introduced her. 'And this is your cousin Anne.'

'I am so pleased to meet you at last, Lady Anne.' Richard kissed her hand and noticed how she blushed at the compliment. Of all of them, Anne was the one who looked most like his sisters. He had expected the meeting to be difficult but was glad he had come in person, as he doubted his father would have been bothered to describe the situation to him adequately.

The thought of his father reminded him and he turned to Sir Henry. 'My father sends his regards, Sir Henry.'

'Tell him we will visit Middleham in the summer. We plan to stay in York and it is too long since I last saw your father and the Countess.'

'I will, Sir Henry. He will be pleased to see you.'

Richard was also pleased. Many years had passed since the two of them had met and this would mark his visit to the Percy stronghold as a success. He was going to be too busy sorting out the lands he had inherited to spend much time travelling to the far north to deal with family problems.

Sir Henry gave him a tour of the castle and proudly showed him the battered shield thought to have belonged to his great grandfather, Sir Henry 'Hotspur' Percy, who died fighting King Henry IV. He had been waiting for the right moment to raise the reason for his visit and it seemed appropriate to discuss it now as they stood in front of the historic shield.

'The king is displeased with the feuding between our families, Sir Henry.'

'Yes, he has written to me.'

Richard studied the old shield, the symbol of the Percy determination to fight, even against overwhelming odds, for what they thought was right. Plate armour had made shields like that virtually obsolete, so it belonged to a bygone era. He decided Sir Henry would appreciate directness.

'I came here to agree a truce.' He looked at the earl, who had been on the council overseeing the care of the king when he was an infant. 'It would reflect well on us all if you can agree to end the feud between us.'

Sir Henry sighed. 'You have my word, Richard. I'll do what I can.'

'And your sons?'

Sir Henry didn't answer. He stared at the ancient shield.

'Can you ask them to honour a truce?'

Sir Henry's mood changed. 'I cannot, sir, be held accountable for the actions of my sons!' His raised voice took Richard by surprise.

'Let us hope then, sir, they share my wish to see an honourable peace between our families.'

Sir Henry seemed to have recovered his composure. 'Yes.' He looked at Richard. 'I'll drink to that.'

The tone of his voice made it clear the discussion was over. He led Richard to see the new cannon he had personally commissioned from the forge master. The powerful weapon was the grandest Richard had ever seen and would need several men to load the heavy oversized cannon balls. He was certain he was being shown it for a reason.

Later that evening they sat down to a fine banquet in the great hall of the castle. Sir Henry was determined to leave a good impression. Richard sat to his right, next to his cousin Katherine, who looked beautiful in a rich blue velvet gown set off with a diamond necklace which flashed in the candlelight as she moved.

The table was set with fine silver and porcelain and skilled musicians played tunefully in a gallery. The centrepiece of the banquet was a large wild boar with long white tusks, roasted whole. The feast included every type of game bird and a wide range of exotic delicacies. This was so different from the bleak picture of life in the castle he had imagined from his father's account of his visit there long ago. He wondered if it had been planned for his benefit.

Whenever his goblet was empty a servant appeared to refill it with strong red wine. Richard knew he must keep a clear head, although the warmth of the wine improved his mood.

He turned to his cousin. 'Lady Katherine, how are your brothers Henry and Thomas?'

'Henry spends much of his time in London and my brother Thomas is busy safeguarding the Scottish border.' She placed her hand softly on his arm. 'I am glad you and your father are seeking peace with our family, Earl Warwick, although I fear my brothers would not agree.'

Richard sensed amusement in her eyes and was conscious of her hand still resting on his arm. She was an attractive woman and he found the physical contact unexpectedly arousing. He glanced to see if her husband was watching. He seemed to be in deep conversation with his younger cousin Anne, who was seated to his right. In a flash of insight he realised Lady Katherine had contrived to be seated next to him at the banquet.

He tried to compose himself and answer her. 'Why is that?'

'I think you know the answer.' She looked at him appraisingly. 'I will tell you anyway. For my brother Henry it is a matter of honour. He is to inherit all of this.' She looked around the great hall as if seeing it for the first time. 'Thomas inherits nothing. He has little to lose in remaining a thorn in the side of the Neville family, who have done so much harm to us in the past.'

Autumn leaves were falling by the time Anne's baby was due. Richard had an entire wing of Warwick Castle specially furnished for her confinement and they moved there from Middleham as summer drew to a close. His mother made the journey south to be with her at the birth and Richard engaged the best midwives and physicians from the royal court. She was radiantly healthy and he had no concerns about the birth, only that it had to be a boy.

He took no chances, making Anne start her confinement early and ensuring no one with any kind of illness was allowed near her. He had waited seven long years for this moment. His father would be so proud to have an heir at last. Richard had seen what could happen when there was no male line to inherit. Titles and estates could be swept away. Everything his father had worked for could be lost if he failed to have a son. There had been so many false hopes he'd begun to wonder if Anne was capable of conceiving a child. At least he knew he was capable of fathering one.

She was sitting in a chair by the window in her room. Her long, auburn hair, normally tied back and covered, was combed down in the way she knew Richard liked. It reminded him for a moment of the young girl he first knew. His eyes went to her bulging belly. Although she was wearing a loose silk gown it did little to conceal her condition.

Anne turned to Richard as he came into the room. 'The midwife saw me this morning and said I am near my time.'

'Good.' He looked at her bulging dress. 'I'll be glad when this waiting is over.'

'So will I, Richard.' She looked out of the window at the last of the summer sun. 'I am tired of this room. I miss our rides together.' She turned to him. 'I even miss the noise and dirt of the city.'

He took her hand and saw a look of concern in her eyes. 'What's the matter?'

'I hope you won't be too disappointed if it is a girl?'

They had discussed it many times since Anne first discovered she was with child. They both knew this could be their only chance, although there was no point in making things worse for her.

'I'll be happy once I know you and the baby are both well.' He was used to avoiding the question.

'I know you will call him Richard if it is a boy. We've never discussed girls' names?'

Richard had not even allowed himself to think about a daughter. He was still holding her hand and gave it a gentle squeeze.

'Did you have a name in mind?'

'Isabel.' Anne's mood brightened again. 'If it is a girl, I should like to name her after my mother.'

Chapter 7 - Summer 1453

After two years of relative peace between the families, Richard arrived at Middleham Castle to find his brother's wedding celebrations overtaken by preparations for a battle. Hundreds of heavily armed soldiers were camped in the outer fields and horses occupied every available stable in the inner ward. The normally peaceful castle echoed to the ringing sound of blacksmiths' hammers and men shouting orders.

He was summoned back from business in Wales by a worryingly urgent message from his father, demanding his immediate return. The timing was not ideal. He had been once again defending his estates in Wales against a challenge from Edmund Beaufort, the Duke of Somerset, who had used his influence with the king to be granted lands which were rightfully his. Richard hadn't hesitated though, as his father would not have called him home without good reason.

Anne was to follow the next day in her carriage with their daughter, so that he could travel more quickly. It had been a disappointment to him when their first child had not been a son, although there was plenty of time for more children and he loved Isabel. She looked older than her two years. Her dark hair had grown longer and she wore fashionable little dresses made for her by Anne's own seamstress.

Richard's mother invited him into her private rooms. They felt refreshingly cool after the summer heat and the thick walls silenced the noise outside. His mother looked tired and preoccupied with everything going on at the castle. She gave him a welcoming hug. The delicate scent of rose water, her favourite perfume, reminded him of when she had held him close as a child.

'It's good to see you, Richard. We didn't expect you to get here so soon.'

He unbuckled his sword and sat down heavily in a comfortable chair, loosening his tunic and rubbing his eyes. It had been hot on the road and he was tired from his journey. 'I rode through the night with a few of my guards. The rest of my men will be here in a few days with Anne and Isabel. There wasn't time to send a rider ahead.'

He had a lot of questions and knew his mother would have most of the answers. He often thought they were alike. Nothing of importance escaped her attention, particularly when it concerned her family. She also had a gift for encouraging people to take her into their confidence. Richard found himself wishing she could have travelled with him to Wales. His mother would have known what Edmund Beaufort was up to.

Richard was concerned. 'Where is father? Is he here?'

'He went to the village with your brother Thomas to recruit more men. They should be back before nightfall.'

'His message said you were ambushed. What happened?'

'We were on our way back to Sheriff Hutton. They blocked our path and surrounded the whole wedding party.' His mother frowned at him as she remembered something. 'You should have come to your brother's wedding, Richard. You know Thomas was offended by your absence?'

'I'm sorry. There was urgent business I had to take care of.'

'You are an important man now, Richard. You must remember people will judge you, not only by your actions.' She looked at him intently. 'They also judge you by what you choose not to do.'

He could tell by the tone of her voice she wasn't talking about missing his brother's wedding.

'What is it?'

She looked at him and he noticed a twinkle in her eyes.

'I know about Megan, Richard. I also know about Margaret.'

'How?' He had kept his secret well, or at least he thought so, until now.

'Megan came to see me. She brought little Margaret with her.' His mother smiled. 'She is a beautiful woman, Richard. And Margaret is a clever little girl.'

Richard felt a surge of pride despite himself. 'She must be five now. She is a lot like you.'

'Margaret is my granddaughter.'

'Why did Megan come to see you?'

'She doesn't want her daughter to grow up and marry some village boy. She wants Margaret to become a lady, to have an education.'

Richard understood. He did his best to see Megan and little Margaret as often as he could, yet it would never be enough. Worse still, his duties in the council made it hard to find time to visit and Margaret was growing up without him. He often found himself thinking how different life would be if he had been able to marry Megan.

'What am I supposed to do? Tell Anne I have a secret daughter and I want her to come and live with us?'

'That's exactly what you are going to do, Richard.' His mother spoke firmly, as if he was a young boy again.

Richard silently cursed. Anne had been right. It had changed everything when they were confirmed as Earl and Countess of Warwick. Almost overnight he became one of the richest landowners in the country. He had also become one of the highest ranking nobles in the country, with all the duties and responsibilities that came with the title.

He could easily have settled for a role in the court or council and enjoyed his new wealth. It had never been in his nature to take the easy option. Richard had been brought up with a clear sense of duty, so was doing everything in his power to deal with those who wished to dispute his right to every acre of land. There was no need to keep Margaret a secret. People would respect his honesty and forget his indiscretion, or so he hoped.

'You are right as always, mother.' He gave her a hug. 'It would be a weight off my mind to not have to keep Megan a secret any more. You can help Margaret to grow up a lady. I will have to speak to Anne and will try to explain to my brother Thomas.'

'Thank you, Richard. I know they will both understand.'

'I hope you're right.' He looked at her questioningly. 'Now I need to know about the ambush. What did they do?'

'Your father ordered them to make way and let us pass in peace.' She shook her head at the memory. 'They ignored him. I was worried, as they had a lot of armed men and I could tell some of them had been drinking. They had definitely planned to ambush us.'

'Are you certain they were Thomas Percy's men?'

His mother frowned as she tried to recall the details. 'Most of them were wearing his colours. I saw the Percy banner and your father said both Thomas and Richard Percy were there, urging the men on. They were keeping their distance, though.'

Richard shook his head. 'What were they trying to achieve?'

His mother looked at him. 'You know this was simply a matter of time?'

Richard did. His brother's marriage to Lord Cromwell's heir, Maude Stanhope, would further increase the Neville estates at the expense of the Percy family. Thomas Percy was an outspoken young man and had publicly criticised the Nevilles. This time he had gone too far. Fortunately his brother Thomas made sure they travelled with a well-armed escort.

'How has father taken all this?'

'As you would expect, your father is furious. I worry he'll take the law into his own hands.'

Richard could see his mother was concerned. They both knew the old feud with the Percy family could one day put them all in danger. He'd worked hard to avoid direct conflict and now his brother's marriage seemed to be taking them to the brink of civil war. If all the soldiers camped outside were anything to go by, his father meant business.

'Father knows better than anyone. Unless he can prove he is acting in self-defence, there is no way he can justify attacking the Percy family.' Richard shook his head. 'That might have been the way things were done in the old days. Now it's a lot more complicated.'

His mother looked at him, her expression serious as she handed him a letter bearing the king's seal. 'Your father received this. You should read it, Richard.'

He took the letter and studied it carefully. The stern reminder from the Royal Council stated that, as Commissioner of the Peace and Member of the Royal Council, his duty was to keep the peace and uphold the law. If he failed to stop what they called riotous gatherings and large assemblies all his titles would be forfeit. Richard knew his mother was anxious for him to tell her what it meant.

He looked at her. 'It all makes sense now. What did Percy's men actually do when you found you were ambushed?'

She thought for a moment. 'They shouted rude insults, called us names.'

Richard shook his head. 'Why do you think that was, Mother?'

She immediately saw his point. 'They wanted us to react, to attack them first!'

'I believe this is a plot by Father's enemies on the council to have a reason to see him removed.'

'Why?'

'I was in Wales to stop Edmund Beaufort, Duke of Somerset, from taking the lands that are rightfully mine. He has a lot of influence at court. I fear he has chosen to side with the Percy family.'

'Now I see why you have to stop him.' She put her hands on Richard's shoulders as she had when he was a boy and looked into his eyes. 'You must help your father see what's going on, talk him out of it.'

Richard laughed at the idea. 'That's the problem. Father has been around the council much more than I have. He knows what this is all about.'

'What do you think we should do?'

'I think I have an answer to that. If it's not already too late.'

The banqueting hall at Middleham Castle had been decorated for the wedding celebrations yet the talk now was all of tactics. Richard sat at his father's side. The ladies had retired after their meal. His brother Thomas's new wife Maud had hardly spoken all evening and he supposed she was wondering what she had let herself in for. She seemed pretty enough and Anne would find her pleasant company, so his brother had done well, all things considered.

As well as Thomas and John, his brother George had also joined them from Oxford where he was studying for the priesthood. Richard's father had told him one day he hoped his son George could rise high in the church, perhaps to even become a Cardinal of Rome. Now twenty-one, George was tall and handsome and had inherited his mother's skill of silent observation. Richard glanced across at him now and George acknowledged him with an almost imperceptible nod of his head.

Richard's father dismissed the servants. He closed the heavy oak doors behind them and poured himself another goblet of wine. Richard looked across the table to where his three brothers sat. Their faces looked grim in the flickering candlelight. They all knew he had been summoned home to Middleham to help them come up with a plan for dealing with the Percy family.

'How many men do you think they can muster?'

Thomas answered. 'It's hard to be sure. I think there could have been as many as a thousand when we were ambushed.' He looked across at his father. 'Thomas Percy's been busy recruiting more men in York since then, handing out his livery to anyone who will take his money. He could have double that number now.'

Richard was surprised. 'That's illegal. Some would even say an act of treason!' He saw the significance of his words was not lost on them.

His father pushed back his chair and loosened his tunic. 'I warned the council the Percy family's actions were disloyal. The king wasn't minded to do anything about it. I was able to persuade them to order Sir Thomas Percy and his men to help defend the Duchy of Guyenne. As you know, he simply ignored the command.'

Richard remembered. This was not the first time he'd heard the story. A weak king was one thing, although for him to back the Percy family was cause for concern. 'Now Guyenne is now lost to the French, so he could be accused of treason?'

His father scowled. 'There was a time he'd have been thrown in the Tower for that, waiting to lose his head.'

Richard turned to look at his brother John. 'Weren't you also summoned to go to Guyenne?'

His brother looked flustered and clearly didn't want to answer in front of his father, so Richard turned to Thomas. 'I'm sorry your wedding has turned into such a complicated situation. I hope you understand why I needed to be in Wales? Edmund Beaufort is doing his best to make trouble for me and I won't let him get away with it.'

Richard's father poured himself another generous goblet of wine. 'We were more than a match for them, Richard, even without your men. A typical Percy bluff. They didn't dare to take us on.'

'Now our family name is at stake.' Richard leaned forward in his chair and looked across the table at his brother John. 'And you've already started defending our honour. I've heard you were going to hang some of Percy's tenants?'

John now looked defensive. 'A threat. I wouldn't have actually hung anyone. They were hiding Thomas Percy, or at least they knew where he was. '

Richard shook his head. 'That kind of thing doesn't help our position, John. What about that business at

Catton House? It sounded like a drunken brawl. Did you have to smash all his windows?'

'Richard Percy's men came after our bailiff at Staincliffe while he was in church. We think they have him held prisoner somewhere, that's if they haven't murdered him already.'

'Are you sure of that?'

Once again John was silent and Richard realised he mustn't be too hard on his brother. He was falling right into the Percy's clever trap. They knew exactly how to provoke John into giving him all the proof they needed to turn people against the Nevilles and into Percy supporters.

George spoke for the first time. 'We can't allow ourselves to be drawn into a fight. What we need is a truce.'

His brothers looked at him in surprise. There was assertiveness in his voice that silenced them. George had always been the quiet one yet now he spoke like a man who should be listened to.

His father nodded. 'You are right, George. A truce would make things much easier for me at the Royal Council. The question is how?'

Richard answered. 'We'll have to muster as many men as they have, more if we can. I'll need time.' He did a quick mental calculation. 'I can call on five or six thousand men. I will have to pay them well. At least we don't need to go around the streets of York recruiting drunks and beggars to our cause.'

Thomas sat up in his chair and looked interested. 'Then what?'

Richard's father answered for him. 'We make a show of strength, so we can talk and remind them we, at least, honour our truce.'

John finally spoke. 'So your plan is that we are simply going to let them off, after all they've said and done to damage our family name?'

Richard shook his head. 'No.' He stood up and walked over to the door, opening it to make sure no one was listening, then closed it and returned to his seat. 'What I'm going to tell you is a great secret. You understand our lives could depend on keeping it so?'

They all looked at him, waiting to see what he was going to say.

'I have a trusted man in the household of Edmund Beaufort, Duke of Somerset. I pay him well to keep me informed of the duke's plans and he knows to learn what he can of the goings on at court. Through him I've recently learned the king is gravely ill. He has fallen into a strange stupor from which his physicians fear he might never recover.' He looked at their faces, enjoying the power his knowledge gave him for a moment. 'The queen hopes to keep it secret for as long as she can, of course. It would never do if the people knew they had a madman on the throne.'

There was a long silence as the implication of Richard's news sank in.

Richard's father was the first to speak. 'Who is going to act as Protector?'

'Well, certainly not the Duke of Somerset, if there is anything I can do about it!'

Thomas was curious. 'Who then?'

Richard poured more wine into his goblet and raised it in the air. 'I would like to propose our uncle. Richard Plantagenet, the Duke of York, as Protector of England.'

Richard rode at his father's side as they arrived at Sandy Hutton. Both were on imposing black war horses and dressed in full battle armour, wearing the Neville colours. There were more men than any of them could have hoped, as in addition to the sizeable army of retainers who had marched from the Warwick estates, his father's allies had turned out in force to support the Neville family. His sister Alice's husband, Baron Henry Fitzhugh and his brother-in-law, Baron John le Scrope of Bolton, had swelled their numbers close to ten thousand, more than they expected the Percy family could ever hope to muster.

The site for the muster had been chosen after much discussion. Close to York and within easy reach of their castle at Sheriff Hutton, yet far enough from the Percy stronghold at Topcliffe to avoid the risk of direct confrontation. On rising ground and surrounded by open fields, it would be impossible for them to be approached from any direction undetected. They were fortunate with the long hot summer, as the ground was baked hard and dry. Sandy Hutton was so named because of the sandy soil, which made it easy to build defensive ditches and plant sharpened stakes. Richard hoped none of it would be needed. At least it kept the men occupied.

Although his father was in overall command, Richard had taken care of the detailed planning, which was more of a challenge than he expected. He had plenty of experience of looking after smaller numbers of men as Warden of West March and the principles were the same, although the scale of this was entirely different. He had needed to arrange for a second army of cooks and bakers to make sure there was enough food for so many hungry soldiers. An entire field had been set aside as a makeshift kitchen, with stoves and open fires already burning.

He had sworn his brothers to secrecy about their real plans, making each responsible for the conduct of their own retainers. The chain of command meant they had good communication, despite the enormous numbers of soldiers. Richard had also taken the precaution of posting scouts to report back on the movements of the Percy family. As expected, they were rallying, with all their supporters and retainers marching to meet at Topcliffe. The latest news had proved he was right to summon men all the way from Warwick, as Baron Clifford had been sighted leading a sizeable army of men towards the Percy stronghold.

The sound of a horn called the men to muster. Richard and his father rode over to where his brothers were talking with the barons. Richard had never thought about it before. His trained eye could tell immediately that neither of his brothers had ever been involved in any real fighting, although both of them were wearing full suits of shiny new armour.

Richard looked out across the fields. They were empty for as far as he could see to the distant woodlands and that was how he wanted it to stay. He was sure their numbers and position had also been reported by Percy supporters. He was less certain about whether they would have the nerve to march from Topcliffe and attack such a large army. This was a show of strength so they had made no secret of their location, openly parading along the main roads to the cheers of the local people.

He turned to his brothers. 'We have sent a message to Sir Henry Percy proposing a meeting in York to discuss the reinstatement of the truce between our families. The Archbishop of York has agreed to oversee our talks and I will accompany father. The two of you have to keep these men busy with drill and make sure they stay sober and ready if we need them. Remember they are here to keep the peace, not to fight.'

John looked at the army of men and back at Richard. 'We could be attacked while you are in York.'

Richard's father replied. 'If we are attacked, we can fight back but you must be certain before you give the order. The men are not to march from here. If the Percy family want a fight they will have to come to us.'

Richard agreed. 'You will have plenty of time to see them coming. Keep lookouts posted to be sure. If there is any trouble send a fast rider to York to let us know.' He turned to John, aware of the need to restore their relationship. 'I'd be grateful if you will take personal command of my Warwick infantry, John. They are experienced men. The best of them have recently returned from France, so will be useful if there is any trouble.'

John thanked him and went to inspect his new troops. Richard made a mental note to arrange for both his brothers to have some military experience at the Scottish border. He had always been the one to ride at his father's side. Someone else had to look after the family name now he was away at Warwick Castle and Wales so much. It could make the difference between life and death for them at some point in the future.

Tully joined Richard and his father with an escort of twenty hand-picked men for the short ride to York. There was no guarantee Sir Henry Percy or his brother Thomas would even come to the meeting. At least his father would then be able to show the Royal Council he had acted honourably and in the spirit of their letter. As they rode off he took one last look at the thousands of men preparing for battle. Whatever the outcome of the next few days, he knew it marked a turning-point in his life.

Chapter 8 - Spring 1454

Richard felt in high spirits as he rode with Tully through the noise and dirt of the London streets to Westminster. Ahead rode fifty armed cavalrymen, with fifty more following behind, wearing the bright scarlet Warwick livery and his badge of the bear and ragged staff. They were an impressive sight and people moved out of their path and stopped to watch as they passed. Some cheered, as Richard's support of his uncle was popular with many, although he was well aware London was still a dangerous place.

Every noble within the city travelled with a bodyguard of armed retainers, a sign of the lingering fear of unrest. Even the church had paid for soldiers guarding places of worship, both as a precaution against opportunist looters and as a safeguard to protect the clergy.

As they neared the more heavily populated streets a shout rang out from the crowd as someone recognised his badge.

'A Warwick! A Warwick!'

The call was picked up by others in the crowd, who joined in chanting and cheering enthusiastically.

'A Warwick! A Warwick!'

Richard appreciated the show of loyalty and turned to Tully. 'I suspect your hand in this?'

Tully shook his head. 'Not me, my lord.' He raised a hand to wave to the crowd and leaned across in the saddle so Richard could hear. 'Good to see we have some supporters though.'

Their procession reached the Palace of Westminster. The towering shapes of Westminster Abbey and the great hall came into view. Richard recalled that same journey they had made when he was knighted by the king. So much had happened since that memorable day. He was now a leading and influential member of the Royal Council and owned one of the finest mansion houses in the heart of the city. Through Anne's inheritance he had more castles and estates than any other man alive.

His private army of several thousand men included hundreds of the best archers in the country, armed with deadly longbows and experience of using them in many battles in France. Instead of the soft deerskin jackets padded with tow archers usually wore, Richard equipped every man with a sallet helmet and a brigandine coat, with protective metal plates, which kept them warm in winter and provided more protection.

Luke Tully had formed a personal guard from the best of Richard's soldiers. These loyal hand-picked soldiers were trained to use the crossbow with deadly accuracy. Every man had his own plate armour, which they called their harness. Wherever Richard went these men were never far behind.

Tully had also become a man of some wealth. He took care of himself and had the lithe physique of a fighting man. Richard had helped him invest his pay wisely and presented him with an expensive suit of heavy, well-fitting mail armour, as well as a fine sword and dagger. As Richard's squire and companion he had learned to blend unnoticed into the background, to be Richard's eyes and ears, always vigilant and observant. Richard had rewarded him generously for his loyal service and relied on him for his personal security.

Richard's gamble with the fortunes of his family in the fields north of York had paid off handsomely. Sir Henry Percy was forced to honour the uneasy truce while his father emerged with his reputation as a peacemaker and upholder of the law enhanced, now appointed by the Royal Council as Chancellor of England. None of the Nevilles had forgotten the insult to their name. Slowly and surely the power and influence of the Percy family was being reduced.

The king remained in his strange stupor at Windsor with the queen. Richard's informants told him the royal physicians had no clue of how to cure his illness and he had yet to acknowledge his own son. It suited Richard that people were saying Edmund Beaufort was the father of the infant Prince. Although he had publicly drawn attention to this allegation, secretly he refused to believe it.

He recalled his reaction to the look Queen Margaret had given him at her coronation. He regretted her poor choice in siding with the self-serving Beaufort, which put them in opposing camps. Whatever anyone said about her, Margaret of Anjou was an intriguing woman with great courage. Richard remembered that her motto was 'humble and loyal.' He would have enjoyed acting as her guide and confidante, to earn her loyalty. It now seemed that was not to be.

Richard's long standing feud over his lands in South Wales with Edmund Beaufort had ended in triumph. He had finally regained his coveted Lordship of Glamorgan, which the king had foolishly granted to Beaufort. He had taken Anne and Isabel to visit his castle in Cardiff, a growing town in a strategic position on the Bristol Channel. Although planned as a private celebration of his victory, their visit had turned almost into a royal progress, with what seemed like the entire population of the town turning out to cheer their arrival. Even now he could hardly believe he had won.

Edmund Beaufort's reputation was in ruins. The duke had other things on his mind now Richard of York was Protector and Defender of the Realm of England, as well as the Chief Councillor. He also had plenty of time to consider them, safely locked up as he was in the Tower of London, awaiting trial by his peers, who held him responsible for the losses in France.

They arrived at the grand palace of Westminster and Richard found his way down the narrow corridors to join his father in his uncle's private apartments. Tully and half a dozen men of Richard's personal guard were stationed outside the door to ensure their conversation would not be overheard. London was full of spies and there were still many supporters of the court faction in Westminster.

The high ceilinged room was flooded with light from massive, leaded glass windows. Richard noted how the falcon and gilded fetterlock badge of Richard of York had already been colourfully re-created in the stained glass of the central panel. The impressive window was his uncle's way of making his mark on the place and showing he was going to be around for a long time.

'Welcome, Richard,' his uncle crossed the room to greet him and shook him warmly by the hand. 'Your father and I have been reminiscing about the old days in France.'

His uncle had an undeniable presence despite his stout build. Clean shaven and expensively dressed in a black tunic and fine black leather boots, he wore his heavy gold chain of office with obvious pride. Richard thought his uncle looked older now, with his deeply lined face and thinning, grey, shoulder-length hair. He had a trace of a

West Country accent and a habit of hesitating before he spoke, as if he was always evaluating what people were saying.

Richard joined them and sat down. 'I fear that France is lost for ever now, thanks to our friend Somerset.'

His uncle looked at him, his steel-blue eyes missing nothing. 'That is why we have to make sure we hang on to Calais. I plan to return there as soon as we've sorted out this mess.'

Richard was interested. He hoped for command of Calais when the time was right. 'What's going to happen to Somerset now?'

Richard's father answered. 'We have to set up a commission. It will take time. There's no hurry, Somerset's not going anywhere.'

'What if someone tries to get him released? I've heard the queen has been visiting him regularly. Can we be sure of the loyalty of the men guarding him?' It bothered Richard he was unable to tell who was more loyal to them or to the king. The guards at the Tower weren't paid a great deal and could easily be bribed, or men loyal to the queen might even be persuaded that Somerset should be set free.

His uncle shook his head. 'Don't worry about that. I'm not going to let him slip through my fingers again.' He sat back in his richly upholstered chair. Richard saw an ambitious gleam in his eye. His uncle had waited a long time to be in this position and he realised the three of them sitting round that table were now in control of England. 'Let's forget about that bastard Beaufort. I want to hear the latest news of the king.'

'Our plan seems to be working.' Richard looked at his uncle. 'I arranged for the priests to exorcise his demons as you suggested.'

'Good. It won't be long before word of that gets out.' His uncle looked pleased. 'People are superstitious. They didn't seem too concerned to learn that the king is ill. We can make sure word of this gets out now.'

His father laughed. 'They won't like the idea he has the Devil in him!'

Richard's informants in the queen's household at Windsor Castle confirmed what he already suspected. Queen Margaret was engaging every physician she could find in her desperation to restore the king's health. They were trying out all manner of treatments on him. They purged him, shaved his head, bled him and made him drink potions of all kinds. It would have been easy to arrange for his medicine to be poisoned. The problem was the finger of suspicion would immediately point to Richard of York. His uncle's plan could achieve the same result with almost no risk.

'What if the king recovers his health?'

His uncle was scornful. 'You've seen him. Even when he was well he wasn't much of a king.'

Richard agreed. 'When our deputation went to Windsor to enquire after the king's condition we couldn't get a single word or sign from him. I don't think he even knew we were there.'

His uncle looked pleased. 'I've banished Queen Margaret to Windsor. I've also cut her allowance and reduced her staff as much as I can. I'm sure the people would agree it's only right she should live within her means.'

Another thought occurred to Richard. 'What about the Prince of Wales?'

His uncle frowned at Richard's use of the new title for the king's infant son. He had been outmanoeuvred by the court faction on the Council and forced into publicly recognising the young Edward as the new heir. Queen Margaret had surprised them all by giving birth to a strong and healthy boy and at a stroke had ended any plans to claim the throne.

Richard's father had a practical way of seeing it. 'We will do what we can to prepare the country for the new king. We have at least fourteen years until he reaches his majority. That's a long time.'

✣

Warwick Castle had become Richard's family home, where he returned after visiting his estates which ranged from Yorkshire to Cornwall. Anne's father had kept it well maintained, although Richard enjoyed making it into one of the finest residences in the country. Anne had grown up there and Isabel was born in Warwick Castle. Conveniently situated in the midlands, it suited them to live within equal reach of his furthest estates in the north and as far west as Cornwall.

He also made it one of the best defended castles in the country. It had been built on a bend in the River Avon, on a sandstone cliff which provided natural defences. Richard added to these new bronze cannons and gun crews trained to use them. He also employed an army of labourers to dig the moat wider and deeper, and strengthen the walls to withstand a siege.

He regularly visited London and was now an infrequent visitor to his old home at Middleham Castle, so relied on his brothers Thomas and John to protect his interests in the north. He had paid for them both to raise and train a sizeable army of retainers, on the condition they were to remain within the law and not attack the Percy family without justifiable cause.

The ancient oak trees in Warwick forest were beginning to turn an autumnal golden brown when his brother Thomas came to visit with important news. He arrived dusty and exhausted, having raced from the north to Warwick so he could personally tell Richard what had happened.

Richard met him in the private rooms he had built as his study. He never had much time for art, although this room was dominated by an impressive and colourful tapestry of the English victory at Agincourt. It had once graced the study of Humphrey, Duke of Gloucester, brother of King Henry V and had cost Richard a great deal. He thought it money well spent, as the scene reminded him of the time when kings led by personal example.

Parchment maps of the English Channel were spread out on his heavy oak desk, half hidden under the plans for a new sailing ship he had commissioned, his latest obsession. He enjoyed his regular visits to the shipbuilders to inspect progress with its construction. On his last visit he had seen the first of the heavy oak planks of the hull being formed in a great steamer, before being fitted into position, giving him his first glimpse of her graceful lines.

He called a servant to bring them both a tankard of cool ale and watched as Thomas drank most of his straight down before Richard had even taken a sip. Richard's brother had changed a lot since they last met. He was tanned and now had a well-trimmed beard that made him look older. The fashionably ornamental dagger he used to wear on his belt was replaced by one similar to Richard's, a fighting weapon ready to use in an instant.

The greatest change Richard noted was in his brother's manner. He had always been courteous if a little restrained. Now he spoke with the confidence that comes from being in command.

Thomas placed the now empty silver tankard on the table. 'You look well. This is a fine place you have.'

'Thank you, Thomas. It's good to see you.' He noticed Thomas was looking at the nautical maps and shipwright's drawings and picked one up to show it to him. 'My new ship. She will be finished soon. I have decided to name her *Trinity*, after the great flagship of King Henry, *La Trinity Royal*.'

'A ship fit for a king?'

Richard was momentarily conscious of the huge difference in their standing, as well as their financial circumstances. 'Is that how you see it, Thomas?'

'It is how a great many people see it, Richard. You know they are talking of you as the new hope for our country.' He picked up one of the charts from the table, a detailed map of the section of the English Channel between Sandwich and Calais. It had hand written notes of depths, submerged rocks and shipwrecks. 'It looks like you are already planning her maiden voyage?'

'I've learned the skills of navigation and plan to ask for the Captaincy of Calais as soon as the time is right. The Duke of York relieved Somerset and appointed himself to the post in July. Since then he's had nothing but trouble with Somerset's garrison.'

'I'd have thought there was more than enough to keep you busy here?'

Richard shook his head. 'I have experienced men to tend to my estates and I am tired of the stench of London. Calais would be an ideal base to start building new alliances with the French.' He looked at his brother questioningly. 'I don't think you rode here to discuss my career plans?'

'We've arrested John and Thomas Percy and sent them both off to the debtor's prison in Newgate!'

'I like to think I know what's going on yet you surprise me Thomas.'

Thomas looked pleased with himself, for a moment reminding Richard of the little boy he once knew. 'We were expecting trouble from the Percy family, ever since we heard they had formed an alliance with Henry Holland, Duke of Exeter.'

'I never liked him. Holland gained more power than he deserved when he took over from his father as Constable of the Tower of London.'

Thomas nodded. 'You know our uncle nearly caught them all when they tried to take control of York.'

Richard remembered. Their uncle had been furious and sent an army to arrest Holland and the Percy conspirators. Exeter had evaded him and sought sanctuary in Westminster Abbey. York had him forcibly removed. 'If it had been up to me, Holland would have been executed for treason. Unfortunately, he is married to our uncle's daughter, Anne.'

'We were lucky. One of your spies in the Percy household came to Middleham one night and warned father of a plan to attack our house at Stamford Bridge. Thomas and Richard Percy had gathered about two hundred men.' His brother looked pleased with himself. 'We were ready for them.'

'What happened?'

'When they saw us most of their men ran for their lives. Father arrested the Percy brothers and we marched them back to Middleham Castle. They were tried in the York courthouse and fined eleven thousand two hundred pounds.'

Richard laughed. 'Father's revenge! They'll never pay, of course?'

Thomas shook his head. 'That's why they're in the debtor's prison. It's not a pleasant place. It's what they deserve. At least we won't have to keep looking over our shoulders, wondering what they're getting up to next.'

Chapter 9 - Spring 1455

None of them expected the king to recover his health so soon. Word of his sudden restoration spread like fire through a field of dry straw and almost overnight there had been a complete reversal of fortune. Queen Margaret was systematically undoing all their work. First she ordered the release of the dukes of Somerset and Exeter from their imprisonment. Then the court faction began plotting their revenge on York and his supporters.

Richard realised he would have to act swiftly to escape the retribution of his enemy Edmund Beaufort. Riders went out from Warwick Castle to summon his retainers from every part of Richard's lands. Reports of looting and unrest were reaching him from London. Although hundreds of well-armed men were soon guarding his family, Richard wondered if even that many would be enough if the people turned against him.

A messenger arrived from his father, who had returned to the relative safety of Middleham Castle. His uncle was rallying an army at Sandal Castle at Wakefield in West Yorkshire. He planned to meet them both with as many men as he could as they made their way down to London. There was no word of his brothers, although he guessed they were more capable now of looking after themselves.

Anne was waiting with the girls to wish him well on the day of his departure.

Isabel ran up to him. 'Au revoir, Papa.'

'Au revoir, ma fille.' She squealed in delight as he picked her up and held her high. 'So you speak to me in French now?'

Anne looked proud. 'I've been teaching them both a little.' She glanced at Margaret waiting patiently to say goodbye to her father. 'It will be useful for them when we go to Calais.'

Richard smiled at her. She had been incredibly understanding about Margaret. His mother had been right. He'd felt relief to have his secret out in the open. It helped that Margaret had turned into such a likeable girl. She was seven now and able to be quite a help to Anne with little Isabel.

'You seem to have forgotten. Somerset has been put back in charge of Calais.'

She returned his smile. 'I'm sure you'll find a way to deal with Somerset.'

He gently lowered his daughter to the ground and took his wife in his arms. Feeling the warmth and softness of her body through the thin silk dress she had chosen to see him off.

She held him tightly. 'I don't want to let you go.'

'You know I have to do this.'

Anne's eyes glistened with tears. 'There will be no going back if you have to fight the king.'

'No. I hope it doesn't come to that. We'll be ready if we have to.' He looked at her, then down at Isabel. 'I'm glad we chose this castle where you grew up as our home. It is a fortress and I have stationed more than enough men to ensure your safety.'

She tried to smile at him. 'Take care, Richard.'

He took one last look at them both and turned to go.

Anne called after him. 'Come back safely to us!'

'I will. I promise.'

Richard met with his father and uncle in dramatically changed circumstances. Dismissed from their important posts, they were replaced by their enemies, all favourites of the queen. They had also not been invited to a special council of peers in the Lancastrian town of Leicester, arranged to discuss providing for the safety of the king's person against his enemies. Richard, his uncle and father had instead been summoned to appear before the council at the end of May. They knew what it would mean. The stakes couldn't be higher.

They lodged for the night at the house of a loyal York supporter in Royston, a Hertfordshire market town north of London. Richard had ridden with over a thousand men marching behind him and many times that number were standing armed and ready for his call. He felt no need to act like a fugitive in his own country. Although he knew he would be easily recognised he didn't care, preferring to show his strength.

The Duke of York was pleased to see him, despite his anger at the sudden turn of events. 'One more year. That's all we needed!' He paced restlessly around the room as he spoke, the lines on his face seeming to grow even deeper. 'Now they summon us! To be locked up for putting the country to rights?'

His father's mood was also dour. 'We should have dealt with Somerset when we had the chance.' He made a chopping sign with his hand. 'Cut off the head of the snake!'

Richard disagreed. 'You did the right thing, Father. If we had executed him the queen would be having us arrested right now. We followed the letter of the law. Let's hope they do the same.'

His uncle stood and crossed to peer out of the leaded glass window, as if he half expected to see the king's guard coming to arrest them. 'I am not going to give Somerset the satisfaction of seeing me locked up, in the Tower or anywhere else. The bastard got the better of me in France and I've sworn he'll never do it again.'

Richard remained silent for a moment, thinking his position was much the same. The time had come to discuss a solution to their problems. 'We aren't the only ones who want to see Somerset pay for what he did in France. It will be fairly easy to get the people on our side.'

His uncle looked thoughtful. 'Yes. We need to hold our nerve. I think this is a time to prove how loyal we are to our King Henry.'

Richard understood his uncle's plan. 'We could all sign a letter that leaves no scope or opportunity to charge us with treason.'

'No!' His father was still angry.

Richard calmed him. 'That's what will make this plan work, Father. It's a way of showing our respect for the king and appointments in his name. We'll have to set aside our personal feelings for now.'

They agreed and the owner of the house was summoned to bring a quill, ink and parchment, as well as sealing wax. Richard wrote the letters while his uncle dictated and they all signed, then he carefully made a copy of both and they sealed them all with the York falcon and fetterlock. Confirming their absolute loyalty, the letters asked the king not to believe the false allegations made by their enemies and demanded the Duke of Somerset to be placed in their custody to face a commission of his peers and answer for his misdeeds.

A messenger was dispatched to London with the letters and their host provided a meal of hot roast beef with fine wine from Bordeaux, which happened to be his uncle Richard's favourite. The wine and their plan went some small way to restoring his mood, although Richard found himself wondering what the future held for the three of them.

He woke the next day to a perfect spring morning and found his father and uncle already preparing to ride to meet the king, who would be making his way north to Leicester. They expected he would be travelling with a sizeable guard, so should be easy enough to find. Richard took charge of mustering the men and counted over seven thousand, including a dozen heavy bronze cannons of his uncle's artillery and his own army of longbow men. He knew they would be needed before long.

Richard studied the hastily prepared barricades blocking the roads into the town of St. Albans. His uncle had taken the precaution of sending scouts ahead of them to provide some advance warning of the king's position. They had returned with troubling news. He guessed the choice of barricading themselves into the town had been the Duke of Somerset's idea, revealing his lack of military skill. The town lacked any defensive walls and the narrow streets would limit the number of men he could use to man his barricades.

They set up a temporary camp outside the town and waited, confident that their presence had been observed. More men were expected to arrive later in the day and there was still time for the king to respond to the letter confirming their loyalty. They were not prepared to wait at the barricaded gate like a servant and they had no wish to start any fighting. Better to see what the king's advisors would have him do next.

Richard's father was the first to spot the small delegation heading towards their camp from the town. They had sent several messengers to explain their terms, although none had been allowed past the barriers, so there was little hope that any messages had reached the king. Now at last there were two riders, one carrying a flag of truce. They knew the other would be one of the king's main supporters.

His father squinted into the spring sunshine, his eyesight still sharp for his age. 'I'd say that's my brother-in-law, sent to find out what we're planning.'

Richard knew Humphrey Stafford, Duke of Buckingham, and his father went back a long way, both serving under King Henry V in France. They had since had their differences, although his father had always been civil to Buckingham for his sister Anne's sake. He looked at his uncle, who scowled at the thought of having to negotiate with the man and realised the duke was a poor choice of intermediary. It had been within Stafford's power to support their case against Edmund Beaufort and help to win over the queen. Instead he had decided to side with the court faction and had since been openly critical of York's efforts to bring the country back into some order.

Buckingham was clearly unhappy with his task when he arrived. He dismounted from his horse and eyed the three of them cautiously, his voice faltering as he spoke. 'The king demands to know why you are arrayed against him.'

They regarded him in silence, then Richard's uncle replied, his deep voice booming in the still air. 'Tell the king we are his loyal liege men. All we ask is to be involved in the government of the country. We also request the king to deliver certain men into our custody, so they can have a proper trial.'

Buckingham looked surprised. It seemed this was not the answer he expected and he didn't know how to respond. 'Who would you have stand trial?'

Richard's uncle answered for them. 'The Duke of Somerset for one.'

Buckingham remained silent and scowled as he understood. He had always been loyal to the king, yet his silence suggested he wasn't a supporter of the troublesome duke, who many were now blaming for the loss of their lands in Normandy.

Richard stepped forward. 'Has the king received our letter stating our loyalty to him?'

Buckingham looked unsure. 'I've heard no mention of it.'

His father spoke next. 'In that case, Humphrey, will you take our answer to the king?'

Buckingham stepped towards his horse and climbed back the saddle. He shouted back to them. 'I think you know the king could not agree to hand over Somerset. It would be best for us all if you disperse so that the king can proceed to Leicester.'

Richard's father started to become angry at the duke's tone. 'I think it would be best for you to ride back to the king and return as soon as you can with his answer.'

Buckingham spurred his horse and sped back to the town, followed by his flag bearer. Richard was concerned the king's forces were also waiting for reinforcements to arrive. They had decided to wait for the arrival of John Mowbray, Duke of Norfolk, who was bringing more than enough men for them to have the advantage of numbers. St. Albans was a small town and Richard guessed there could hardly be more than three or four thousand men in the king's escort. It would take many more to surround the place on all sides.

Richard squinted up at the sun. He guessed noon was approaching and he felt hungry. He went back to join Tully, who he'd posted to keep watch on the town. A dog barked somewhere and the sun glinted on polished metal as one of the men at the barricade moved. Otherwise the town of St. Albans seemed deserted.

'I wonder where they all are?'

Tully looked at him. 'Who, my lord?'

'The people. There are hundreds of people in St. Albans.'

'I expect the king's men have ordered a curfew for their own safety.'

Richard frowned. 'I still would have expected to see more activity.'

'Well I've been watching for a while now.' He shaded his eyes and peered at the nearest of the barricades. 'All I've seen is a traveller heading towards the town on the London road.'

Richard looked round. 'Where is he now?'

Tully pointed back down the road. 'He went to the barricade. They must have turned him away.'

'Let me know if you see anyone else.'

Tully seemed puzzled. 'Do you think they are taking their time, waiting for reinforcements to arrive?'

'That's what worries me. As far as we know the king was travelling with knights of the council and their bodyguards.'

Tully sounded thoughtful. 'There must be people still going about their business. Innkeepers and the like. The king's men would hardly take any notice of an unarmed man walking down the street.'

'You mean we could get someone into the town? See what they're up to?'

'I could give it a try.'

Richard was surprised. 'You?'

'Who else? I used to be a poacher, remember, my lord? Better than waiting around here.'

Richard shook his head. 'I know you'd do it, Tully. I need you to watch my back if we go in fighting.'

'I have a man who will try for us, my lord.'

'Good. Tell him to take the long way around. I'd like to know if there is an unguarded way into the town.'

An hour later Tully called him to say Buckingham was returning. This time he remained on his horse and shouted to them from a safe distance. 'The king wishes you to know he will give up no man and any that oppose him will die as traitors.' He seemed to enjoy the disappointment he could see on their faces. 'The king says he will destroy all who rise against him. He has ordered that every mother's son will be hung, drawn and quartered as an example to those who would think to be disloyal to the crown.'

He seemed more confident, almost arrogant now he was sure of the king's position.

Richard's father walked up to his former friend. 'Are you sure those are his words?'

Buckingham nodded. 'I spoke to him myself and told him your demands.' He shook his head. 'I am sorry it has come to this, Richard.'

'So am I, Humphrey.'

They watched as the two horses rode back to the barricaded entrance and disappeared from sight.

Richard's uncle turned to them. 'We'll wait no longer.' He turned to Richard's father. 'You and I will lead the main force, taking one barricade each.' He looked at Richard. 'You are to be ready in reserve.'

The three of them shook hands without speaking further before going off to prepare the men. Tully had been waiting at a respectful distance and was eager to know what had been going on.

'It seems we have two choices, Tully. To leave and wait to be tried for treason, or to fight and be condemned as traitors to the king.'

Tully understood. 'So fight it is then.'

'We've drawn the short straw, I'm afraid. Held back as the reserve. I must admit I hoped it wouldn't even come to a fight.'

Tully helped Richard check the straps on his armour, the latest from Burgundy, lighter than any Richard had worn before and more flexible. He strapped on his sword and dagger and tried drawing both to make sure the straps weren't fastened too tightly. Tully wore a steel sallet, his heavy mail and a breastplate under his livery emblazoned with the Warwick bear and ragged staff. He slung his crossbow over his shoulder and strapped a full quiver of bolts to his belt, as well as his sword and dagger.

The ancient ditch around the town of St. Albans had been dug over a hundred years before and proved useless as a protection against the charge. A few of those at the front fell to arrows fired from behind the barricades. The rest scrambled over them. The narrow streets made it hard to advance in numbers, so they soon turned into a press of men and engaged in a clash of brutal fighting, stabbing and hacking at close quarters.

His own soldiers had been reinforced by the arrival of his old companion from his days on the Scottish border, the former Sheriff of Northumberland, Sir Robert Ogle. He had brought six hundred well trained men-at-arms from the Welsh Marches in support of their cause. Together with his archers, Tully's crossbowmen, his personal guard and over a thousand foot soldiers in full harness armed with swords and halberds, he felt confident they could give a good account of themselves when called to fight.

Tully's scout finally returned with the news he had found an undefended entrance into the town.

'There is a track, my lord. Through some gardens and little used, by the look of it.'

'Will it get us into the heart of the town?'

'Yes, my lord. There are soldiers outside a tavern. It looked like they were resting.'

'None of them were guarding the track?'

'No, my lord. They didn't even notice we were there.'

Richard was pleased. 'We must move fast to take the advantage.'

He made a decision. The king's forces were preoccupied with dealing with the main attack. It seemed the men at the barricades were holding their ground. They wouldn't be expecting an attack from the other side of the town.

He turned to the commander of his archers, a thick set man with a deep scar on his face, gained in the French wars. 'We are going to find a way to take them by surprise. Once we make our move I want you to follow close and have your archers ready to fire over our heads when we engage the enemy.'

'We'll be waiting for your signal, my lord.' The burly commander went off to brief his men.

Still moving on foot and with as much stealth as they were able, Richard's men rushed down the narrow lane and soon found themselves in the market-place, behind the Lancastrian defences. A small group of soldiers were building another barricade and shouted in alarm as they saw the red-coated men streaming into the streets with the banner of the bear and ragged staff flying high. Richard's men-at-arms didn't hesitate, cutting them down without mercy.

To make the most of his surprise, Richard ordered his personal guard to carry trumpets and to make as much noise as they could, startling the king's forces and making them believe they were facing a much larger army. His ploy proved to be even more effective than expected, as the trumpeting echoed around the old town, confusing their enemies and making it hard to tell the direction of the attack.

The sombre clanging of a bell responded to the trumpeting as the king's men raised the alarm. The sound was coming from the bell tower in the market square. Whoever was ringing it didn't seem to realise the bell acted like a beacon, drawing Richard's men to the centre of the town.

Tully started up a cry of 'A Warwick!, A Warwick!,' which was soon picked up by his men as they advanced into the mass of knights in full armour and soldiers in the livery of the king forming around the royal standard in the town square. Richard drew his sword and charged into the melee, shouting as loud as he could for his archers to fire. On his signal a hail of deadly arrows flew overhead. Some fell harmlessly to the cobbled streets. Most found their mark, maiming and wounding the king's men, making it impossible for them to fight.

Richard's men were on them before they could recover, slicing and stabbing with such ferocity the ground grew slippery under their feet with blood. Someone shouted that the king's lords were hiding in a tavern and several of Richard's men began smashing down the door. It gave way with a sound of splintering wood and several armoured knights rushed out and began fighting for their lives.

Richard recognised the familiar figure of Edmund Beaufort. The duke was using his sword to slash savagely into one of Richard's scarlet liveried men-at-arms when Tully raised his crossbow and sighted. The steel tipped bolt thudded into Beaufort's shoulder, easily cutting through his plate armour at such close range. He was distracted by the sudden pain and a soldier smashed him in the head with a poleaxe, throwing him to the ground to be trampled in the rush of soldiers who neither knew or cared who he was.

Richard didn't witness Beaufort's death. He was looking into the heart of the market square where he saw the unmistakable figure of the king surrounded by a guard of heavily armoured knights, including many he recognised. Some of them were bleeding from arrow wounds. The familiar figure of old Sir Henry Percy savagely hacked at the nearest man's exposed neck with his sword as Richard watched.

He shouted to his red-coated archers. 'Spare the commons! Go for the knights!'

Richard knew he would win the day if he could reach the king. A shower of deadly arrows struck many of the men guarding the king and as his men-at-arms charged forward Richard saw more soldiers in his uncle's colours of murrey and blue rush from a side street. They had overcome the barricades at last. The two forces joined and filled the market square. The knights fighting around the king showed no sign of surrender, even though many had been struck by arrows and could see they were surrounded on all sides.

He spotted his uncle in the distance and fought his way through the mass of men towards him. They fought side by side. Richard found himself remembering how he had first learned what a sword could do as he hacked and thrust his way toward the royal standard in the centre of the square. He was tiring with the exertion of it all and the helmeted knight he was fighting saw his chance, striking hard at Richard's sword hand.

The sudden jarring pain caused Richard to yell out and drop his sword and it clattered to the ground. Swiftly pulling out his dagger with his left hand, he flung himself at the heavily armoured knight and plunged it hard into the eye slot in his helmet. The man continued falling backwards, yelling in pain. Richard retrieved his dagger then grabbed his sword and turned to face the next man.

His hand was throbbing painfully as he raised his sword and wondered how much longer he would be able to fight, then recognised his new adversary. Baron Thomas Clifford, High Sheriff of Westmoreland and grandson of the infamous Sir Henry 'Hotspur' Percy. Richard knew that the baron had fought with distinction in France at the side of the former king's brother John, Duke of Bedford. He saw Clifford was bleeding from severe wounds and almost unable to fight on.

Richard shouted to him over the noise of the fighting all around them. 'Yield to me, Sir Thomas, I've no wish to see you dead!'

The baron realised the battle was lost and his sword dropped from his hand. It clattered to the cobbled street and he sank to his knees in submission, life ebbing from him. One by one the lords guarding the king began to surrender, surrendering their weapons as they realised the futility of their fight.

Some, including Humphrey Stafford, Duke of Buckingham, who had threatened Richard so recently, were able to run despite their injuries and sought sanctuary in the safety of the Abbey of St. Albans. Others were less fortunate, slaughtered before the order could be given for the killing to stop.

Richard sheathed his sword and cautiously removed his gauntlet. He had chosen to wear an open helmet for visibility. His new light armour had suffered dents and saved him from injury except for his sword hand, which had been struck hard by a blow during the fighting. He wasn't sure when it happened although it felt as if one of his fingers was broken.

Richard tried to ignore the pain in his hand as he joined his uncle, who was kneeling where the king lay wounded. Blood ran down the king's neck and he was in shock. For a moment Richard thought the king's madness had returned.

The king stared at them both. 'Why?' His eyes were roving over the twisted and broken corpses of his knights, full of horror at the sight before him as if storing the memory. 'You wound me, your anointed king?'

Richard's uncle stood. 'Someone tend the king's wound. Quickly now!'

Luke Tully picked up the royal standard from where it had fallen in the fighting and held it upright. A light breeze unfurled the flag and Richard noticed the king glance in its direction as men carried him into a nearby house out of the view of the carnage.

Richard looked out across the square recognising several of the fallen bodies.

His father joined them. 'Sir Henry Percy is dead.' He wiped the sweat running down his face. 'So is Edmund Beaufort!'

Richard shook his head. For all his faults, Sir Henry Percy had been family and he regretted that there was now no prospect of ever finding a peace between their families. He was not sorry to see the end of Edmund Beaufort. 'We must go to the king. Ask for his forgiveness.'

Chapter 10 - Spring 1456

Richard stood at the bows of his flagship and breathed the fresh salty air of the English Channel. The king had finally appointed him as Captain of Calais, nearly a year since the fateful death of the Duke of Somerset in the battle at St. Albans. Richard had been frustrated by the delay and powerless to do anything about it. The Calais garrison hadn't been paid and grew desperate, seizing wool held in Calais and selling it to buy food. They had demanded a full pardon for this, as well as all the back pay due to them before they would let Richard take up his post.

The queen was also determined to stand in his way. She misjudged the mood of the London merchants and tried to silence their complaints with special courts. They refused to recognise her authority and rioted when Lord Buckingham ordered the arrest of some of the ringleaders. The delicate peace erupted into violence on the streets and the queen fled in panic from the city with the young prince, leaving the king at Westminster.

The Duke of York had not forgotten the debt he owed to Richard for his success at St. Albans or the promise he had made to give him Calais. The king's supporters had gained a majority on the council, which made the duke's position as Protector of the Realm untenable. He resigned from his post and asked the king to grant a full pardon for the garrison in Calais. He also persuaded the king that Richard, as Captain of Calais, would make it the jewel in the English crown once more and ensure the men were paid in future from customs revenue.

As soon as Richard's appointment had the royal assent he wasted no time in leaving for Calais. As well as the status and generous salary that came with the post, Richard looked forward to the prospect of representing the crown and ruling England's last stronghold in France. He was also charged by the king to engage and maintain enough ships to intercept any invaders and protect English traders from pirates that frequented the busy waters of the Channel in search of easy pickings.

Most people in England understood the military importance of Calais, which was why it had a permanent garrison of over two thousand men, England's only standing army. Richard knew the real value of the town was commercial, one of the most important ports for the lucrative trade of exporting English wool and cloth, lead and tin to the continent. Richard had brought with him men who knew the wool trade well and promised to help him profit from the virtual monopoly the Calais traders enjoyed.

Richard also had a special mission from his uncle, the Duke of York, which was to build an alliance with Philip of Burgundy. They knew a time might come when the Lancastrians would call on Queen Margaret's powerful connections in France. If Burgundy could be persuaded to lend support to them it could help maintain the delicate balance of power. He was also keen to develop his own network of contacts and allies, as well as to take advantage of the opportunities for gathering information from merchants and travellers.

Weather permitting, Calais was still within easy reach of Warwick Castle and London, and provided a useful base from which he could build his own army and navy without fear of interference. He had inherited the garrison and a small fleet of ships, which he planned to turn into the largest private navy in the world. Although he would miss the comforts of Warwick Castle and his London Mansion, he could return home whenever he wished and intended to make a grand new home for his growing family at the castle of Calais.

Most of all, he was glad to be away from the noise and noxious smells of London and bitter politics of Lancaster and York. He had proudly carried the king's sword at the head of their triumphal return to the city after the victory at St. Albans. He should have known their enemies would soon regroup and Queen Margaret now had more influence than ever. Despite his best efforts, most of the key positions had now been filled with Margaret's favourites who began to undermine everything he stood for. With the resignation of his uncle as Protector of the Realm he knew it would be harder than ever to make his mark through the Council.

As he looked towards the distant shape of the French coast, he thought about his family. They'd had to stay behind at Warwick Castle and would join him to live in Calais when safe to do so. He'd been concerned that Calais was still a dangerous place for his children. Another daughter had been born in June. They named her Anne, after her mother. Although Richard had been bitterly disappointed still to not have a son, he'd been relieved his wife and the baby were both healthy and well.

Richard sensed someone approaching across the wooden deck behind him. He turned to see Tully, who was enjoying being back at sea and already on first name terms with most of the crew. He had changed his usual clothes for the rough navy wool of a sailor, although he still wore his silver-handled dagger at his belt. Sometimes Richard almost envied Tully's easy going life.

Tully squinted at the horizon. 'The helmsman says we should be able to make out Calais soon, my lord.'

Richard felt a sense of anticipation as he searched for the old tower at Calais in the distance. He'd waited a long time for this moment. At first, all he could see was the endless grey-green of the sea all the way to the horizon, then he could make out a dark shape on the skyline.

'Over there.' He pointed.

Tully looked again. 'I can see something. I think it's a tower?'

'Yes. It's marked on the chart as the Tour du Guet. An old watch tower they use as a beacon to warn ships in stormy weather. Captains also use the tower to navigate the entrance to the harbour.'

Tully's usual light-heartedness was replaced by a sudden seriousness. 'What sort of reception do you think we'll get there, my lord?'

Richard frowned as he remembered. 'The garrison were all appointed by the Duke of Somerset. They won't be happy to see the man who shot their lord and master.'

Tully put on an innocent face. 'Where would you have heard a thing like that, my lord?'

'I read the reports the Duke of York had from witnesses of the battle. One of the shopkeepers said he saw a man bring Somerset down with a crossbow.'

'It could have been anyone.'

'Yes, it could have.' He looked at Tully. 'Truth is I've no idea how we'll be greeted. Lord Rivers, Richard Woodville, has been Lieutenant of Calais for the past five years. Both he and the garrison commander refused to recognise my uncle's authority when he appointed himself Captain.' He looked back out towards Calais. 'Now

Somerset is dead and I am here on the orders of the king, Lord Rivers has agreed to surrender his post.'

'Who is to take his place, my lord?'

'No one. I'm going to run Calais myself.'

Their ship was met at the approach to Calais by a pilot boat rowed by a team of swarthy oarsmen who looked more like pirates than the king's men. They expertly helped the crew of Richard's ship to tie up safely alongside the stone quay. Richard stared up at the ramparts of the ancient Rysbank Tower, looming over them, dwarfing the ship and guarding the entrance to the busy harbour. Seagulls called noisily and in the distance he could hear music playing. He was almost overwhelmed by the sights and smells of the town that was to be his new home.

Richard looked out across the harbour. There were ships of every kind, all bustling with activity. An old warship was being prepared to sail, with men climbing high in the rigging. Close by a fine merchantman was teeming with gangs of men using cranes and hauling with ropes and pulleys to unload heavy bales of English wool from its cavernous hold. Fishing boats were unloading wicker baskets full to the brim with live crabs. A brightly painted Langoustiner, flying the flag of Brittany, was docking at the wharf, its crew calling out to each other in heavily accented French.

Richard was pleased to see the huge bronze cannons that defended the harbour were still in place pointing out to sea. There had been rumours that the garrison had sold off some of the precious artillery in lieu of pay. He knew it would be hard work to restore morale amongst the men. They had been treated so badly they had come close to mutiny at least four times in the past year.

Overlooking the estuary to the west was the grand Castle of Calais. He had been warned that the castle had suffered from poor maintenance in recent years. Richard planned to make it as comfortable as any he owned in England. It had once been the home of his uncle and the duke had given him useful advice about how it could be improved. He had also spent long hours sharing his experiences of Calais and the neighbouring areas of France and Burgundy with Richard. The knowledge was useful and Richard had been an attentive listener.

As he stepped from the gangplank he was greeted by the commander of the garrison, Lord Welles, accompanied by a contingent of the garrison. Richard had chosen to wear a burnished silver breastplate over his tunic, which flashed as it reflected the bright sunlight. He also had a flowing dark-red cloak over his shoulders. Tully said it made him look like a Roman Centurion, a comparison he was not unhappy with.

The effect was not wasted on Lord Welles, who seemed surprised to see the two hundred men of Richard's personal guard assembling on the quayside, resplendent in their new steel sallets, bright red livery and fully armed with halberds, swords and daggers. Once they were formed up in orderly ranks Tully raised the Warwick banner of the bear and ragged staff. Richard felt a sudden surge of pride as he watched it unfurl in the light sea breeze.

Richard had a further surprise for the commander. His long wait had given him time to equip a fleet of fast ships armed with the latest guns. He planned to keep them ready to sail at short notice and had recruited the best sailors in Portsmouth and Dover as his crews. His captains were all staunchly loyal, with long experience of sailing in the Channel. The new fleet now filled Calais harbour, decks lined with hundreds of armed men.

He turned to Lord Welles, who was looking at the ships in amazement. 'Where is the Lieutenant of Calais?'

The garrison commander pointed to the castle. 'Lord Rivers is waiting for you, Earl Warwick, in the castle. That is where the formal handover ceremony is to take place.'

Richard knew the commander had been the loyal supporter of his old adversary, Edmund Beaufort and had been the main reason for the delay in his taking post. His refusal to welcome their arrival was a deliberate snub. For all that, he was a decent man trying to do his job as well as he could.

'I understand you saw it as your duty to ensure your men were paid what was due to them.' He looked the commander in the eye. 'I'd have done the same myself.'

The commander relaxed a little. 'Thank you, Earl Warwick, these have been difficult times for us.'

'Well, it will be different from now on. I plan to restore the garrison of Calais to its former glory. I'll pay the men out of my own pocket if I have to.' Richard realised the guards at attention behind the commander were listening. He was confident his words would be shared with the whole garrison before nightfall.

As word of Richard's arrival spread through the town, crowds of people came out to see him. He was approached by an officious looking man he recognised as the Mayor of Calais by his chain of office. The Mayor introduced a delegation of merchants who managed the wool trade through the Company of the Staple, which had a legal monopoly on all wool exported from England. Richard shook hands with each of them and noted they looked genuinely relieved to see him, particularly when he introduced the men he had brought to help him develop and improve the wool trade.

The people of Calais lined the narrow, cobbled streets and cheered as Richard marched with his men behind the garrison commander to the castle, where Lord Rivers formally handed over Calais to Richard. Rivers looked much younger than his fifty years and was an experienced commander who had fought in France at the side of his uncle, Richard of York. If only he had been loyal to their cause, he would have been a real asset to Richard in Calais.

'You will need to keep a close eye on the French, Earl Warwick.' Lord Rivers studied Richard's brightly dressed guards with disdain. 'We've had a couple of serious attacks in the last few weeks.'

'My first priority is to build up the strength of the garrison. I've brought experienced men with me and intend to recruit as many more as are needed to ensure the safety of the town.'

'I commend Lord Welles to your service. He has served well for many years.'

Richard had already planned to rid Calais of the Lancastrian supporters as soon as he could. He turned to the garrison commander. 'I'm sure you are looking forward to returning to England?'

Lord Welles looked relieved. 'Yes, I am my lord. My work here is done.' He glanced at Richard Woodville as if seeking reassurance. 'There is a ship waiting in the harbour to take me and Lord Rivers home.'

With the formalities over, Richard was taken on a tour of the town. He had many questions and was rarely content with the answers he was given. Calais had been allowed to decline, despite the obvious wealth and potential he saw everywhere. He was also surprised at how cosmopolitan the town was, and although the main language he heard was English, there were merchants and traders from all over the continent talking in French, Italian and Spanish.

He called a meeting of the wealthy and influential merchants of the staple. They had enjoyed a monopoly over the export of English wool for almost a hundred years and were keen to be reassured they would be allowed to continue. Richard knew the workings of the wool trade from his northern estate managers. Now he planned to use it to fund the running of the garrison as well as the changes he needed to make in Calais. The merchants were men of business and were happy to support his planned improvements, agreeing loans so that work could start straight away.

Richard was disappointed with the condition of the castle. A sprawling, untidy place, it had been extended and added to by various owners over the years. Its elevated position gave impressive views over the shallow waters of the estuary to the sea, although he could see cracks in the walls wide enough to fit his finger in places. The once elegant wooden shutters were missing from many of the windows and the rooms were gloomy and cold. He immediately commissioned builders and craftsmen to begin restoring it to a home fit for his family to live in, opening up the marble fireplaces and painting the walls with a fresh coat of whitewash.

He chose a spacious wood-panelled room overlooking the estuary as his new study. One wall was decorated with an aggressive looking falcon and gilded fetterlock badge. No one could be in any doubt the room had once belonged to his uncle the Duke of York, before he had been forced to hand it over to the ill-fated Duke of Somerset. Richard hoped his new home would bring him better luck than either of them. He spent his first night in Calais alone, looking out to sea, with a goblet of fine French brandy and wondered what the future held for him there.

Chapter 11 - Summer 1457

Richard listened to his informant's news with a sense of growing concern. The Belgian merchant had been on a ship calling at Dieppe, where he learned that four thousand heavily armed Frenchmen were preparing to sail in a fleet of warships. Their intended destination had been a secret, although the merchant was certain they were under the command of Marshal Pierre de Breze, Grand Seneschal of Anjou and Normandy and supporter of Queen Margaret.

Since his arrival in Calais Richard expanded his own fleet of ships, buying and converting the best he could find. His plan to take control of the Channel angered the French and he had been wondering when they would do something about it. Calais was not yet an impregnable stronghold. He visited the wool trading ports of Dover and Sandwich, Lydd and Romney for supplies and raised funds for new ships. Despite all this there was still work to do on the outdated defences.

Richard had spent long hours out at sea learning how to navigate the Channel and use a lead and line to check safe depths. He had also been learning how to fight from the deck of a ship. The techniques of ramming and boarding were well tried and tested and they had found that the heavy stone cannon balls of his deck mounted guns needed to be used at close range. This meant his crews had to practice holding fire until the last moment. They practiced the art of sailing close alongside an enemy ship without them having the chance to open fire first.

He was visiting the harbour defences when he was approached by his gunnery captain, a shrewd man who was well respected. He was also one of the few captains who had chosen to remain in post after the handover.

'If I can speak frankly, my lord, we are not yet ready to intercept the French fleet, despite all the training we've done.'

Richard looked at the gunnery captain with interest. 'What do you suggest we do?'

'There's no need to risk your ships yet, my lord.' The gunnery captain had lost his right hand fighting the French and had a habit of waving the stump of his forearm in the air as he spoke. He gestured with it now towards the row of heavy cannons pointing out to sea.

'We should use our shore based artillery?'

The gunnery captain agreed. 'Your ships can remain safely in the harbour.'

'The French will have to come to us.' Richard liked the idea. 'Are you sure we have enough artillery to take on the entire French fleet?'

The captain gestured again with his stump. 'If you bring every gun you have up here we could blast them out of the water.'

For the rest of the day the place was a hive of activity, as the great bronze cannons were moved into place. Hawsers as thick as a man's arm were tied round the barrels, then huge A-frames made from whole tree trunks were used to lift them onto specially strengthened wagons for the long haul up to the gunnery battlements. Teams of oxen strained as they pulled their heavy loads and the sun set in a flame-red sky before the last of the cannons was in place.

The lookouts reported French ships on the horizon the next morning and Richard joined the gunnery captain on the battlements. He had filled the ramparts of the Rysbank Tower with the most extensive artillery defences Calais had ever seen. Great lengths of heavy chain stretched across the harbour entrance as a precaution and the outer row of ships also had their deck mounted guns trained out to sea. Rows of archers and crossbowmen took their places on the decks, quivers full of arrows and crossbow bolts.

If the French succeeded in breaking through, they were going to have to have another surprise on the road from the harbour. Richard had remembered how effective the hastily erected barricade at St. Albans had been in the narrow streets. His men had barricaded the main streets leading from the harbour and the rest of the garrison were waiting behind them to defend the town. The air was tense with anticipation. The men were in high spirits and keen to see action.

There were so many ships in the French fleet that Richard found it hard to count them. Visibility was good on the clear summer morning and from his high position he had an excellent view. To the untrained eye it looked as if the French were sailing right past. Richard knew better. His long hours at sea meant he knew what they were doing. As he expected, on some signal the French fleet turned so that the wind was with them as they headed in his direction. He guessed the navigator was probably taking a bearing on the Rysbank Tower.

The French sailed line astern, so they presented his gunners with the smallest possible target. The manoeuvre meant there was no doubt. The French had decided to teach him a lesson and, if the merchant's information was correct, could outnumber his garrison by two to one. He was grateful for the warning. If they had been caught unprepared it would have been a different battle. Richard was also glad he had decided not to face the huge fleet on the water. His men were ready and waiting.

Glancing up at the castle, he hoped his wife and daughters had taken his advice to barricade themselves into one of the rooms with heavy oak doors. He had tasked Luke Tully to oversee the men of his personal guard defending the castle. He knew Tully would much rather have been at his side, rather than guarding his family. Richard had missed them, despite his frequent visits back across the Channel to Warwick. They had sailed as soon as their rooms in the castle were ready. Anne didn't like Calais, although she had helped him win over the important families of the town, who only knew the Lancastrian version of events in England. It had been important for Richard to build the support of the townspeople as well as the men of the garrison. She had overseen their first grand banquet at the newly restored castle, which had been a great success.

Richard had earned the respect of the garrison soldiers by leading raids into the French territory to the south of Calais. His daring harassment turned the tables on the French and established him as something of a hero to the men. They respected his word that they would no longer have to worry about their pay, and the new commander of the garrison was turning them into a respectable fighting force.

His thoughts were interrupted by the gun captain shouting the order for his crews to make ready. Richard watched the team closest to him. One man swabbed out the barrel of their cannon and the loader placed a new parchment cartridge of gunpowder inside, followed by a wad of cloth and rammed it home. The heavy ball was then carefully rolled in and packed in place with some extra wadding, a tradition from experience at sea where the cannon ball could roll out in a swell. The men stood back and waited for his order. They had a dozen cannon balls waiting to be fired, as did each of the heavy guns pointing out to sea.

Richard looked down the teams of men crouching by each gun and saw they were all prepared and waiting for his signal. 'Hold your fire until I say!'

The French ships were so close now he could clearly make out the figures of sailors moving around on the decks, preparing for action. He had worried that Calais was full of French spies and his plan would have been known. Now he was certain the French captains didn't have any idea what was going to happen.

'Ready!' He raised his sword, watching the approaching ships as they began to navigate towards the harbour entrance. 'Fire!'

Matches were put to touch-holes. For a second there was an eerie silence and it seemed nothing was going to happen.

All the guns fired in an ear splitting salvo, sending several tons of cannon balls and heavy shot towards the French fleet. Great splashes in the water showed many had missed their mark, then the closest ship heeled over hard in a sudden turn. The stone balls smashed into its masts and rigging, shredding the sails and splintering wood. Richard smelt the sulphur in the gunpowder and felt the ground under his feet vibrate as his guns fired again. He could hardly see the French fleet through the drifting smoke as the guns roared continuously.

Richard raised his sword again and shouted. 'Cease fire!'

The French were turning away. The men on the ramparts watched as one by one the ships disappeared into the distance, several of them with torn sails and broken masts, with smoke drifting behind. A cheer went up from the gun crews as they realised the plan had worked. The little town of Calais had taken on the pride of France and won without a single man even leaving his post. Richard's ears were still ringing as he went over to shake the hand of the gun captain who suggested the idea.

Richard shouted to make himself heard. 'Double brandy rations for all the men!'

The cheering was picked up by the men on board the ships in the harbour, then the people in the town. The celebrations went on long into the night.

Richard stared at the young captain in disbelief. After abandoning their attempted assault on Calais, the French had sailed on to the English coast where they attacked Sandwich at dawn and burned the town to the ground. The captain's clothes were blackened with soot and he had a bandage wrapped around his hand which looked as if it had been bleeding. Richard poured them both a goblet of his best brandy and handed one to the captain, who accepted it gratefully.

'Tell me what happened?'

'We were sailing back from Dover when our lookout spotted the smoke, my lord.' He took a sip of the brandy and collected his thoughts. 'As we got closer we could see the French fleet sailing away. I ordered the crew to head for Sandwich to see if there was anything we could do.' His face looked haunted by the memory. 'We were too late.'

Richard couldn't believe what he was hearing. 'Do you know how many were killed?'

The captain shrugged his shoulders. 'I don't think we will ever know the number, my lord. I was told a lot of people fled as soon as they realised what was happening.

The town was completely destroyed. One of the men from Sandwich told me the French appeared without any warning and began killing and burning. The people did their best to defend the town.'

Richard shook his head and waited while the young captain took a sip of brandy.

'The French ran for their ships once reinforcements arrived from Dover.'

'What were they trying to achieve?' The question was as much to himself as he tried to make sense of it.

The captain seemed unsure. 'They looted anything of value. I heard they took some of the Kentish men as prisoners.'

Richard understood. 'What about the French losses.'

'I would guess that over a hundred were drowned trying to make it back to their ships, my lord. The sea was getting rough by that time. Many of their boats were swamped.' He looked at Richard. 'We were in no mood to rescue them, my lord, although we did take a few survivors prisoner.'

Richard stood. 'Well done, Captain. We might be able to exchange them to get our people freed. This is all worrying news.' He shook the captain by the hand. 'I am grateful to you for bringing it to me first.'

He watched the captain leave, then sent one of his men to find Anne and ask her to join him in his study. When Anne joined him Richard told her the captain's news, interested to learn what she would make of it.

She looked worried. 'They were under the command of a personal friend of the queen?'

Richard frowned. 'I understand the fleet was commanded by Pierre de Breze. He represented her father the Duke of Anjou in the negotiations for her marriage to the king. I have no proof she was in contact with him, of course.' He shook his head. 'I don't need any.'

Anne knew what he meant. 'People will work it out for themselves.'

'Exactly.'

'And now you will make sure that everyone blames this on the queen?'

'Of course.'

Anne sat down to consider what it all meant. 'It's a dangerous game you are playing, Richard.' She frowned at him. 'Are we ready to take on the whole of France?'

'We might have to, whatever I do or don't do. My informants tell me the queen is secretly negotiating through her family connections in France. She is trying to prepare an alliance with King Louis that will make it impossible for our supporters to ever gain the upper hand again.'

'This invasion of Sandwich will possibly change all that.'

'It seems incredible that the Queen of England could in any way condone such a thing. The people would never forgive her for it, especially the men of Kent.' He looked at Anne. 'You know Queen Margaret has been appointing her favourites to key positions in the name of the king?'

'Does that mean she will try to have you replaced, Richard?'

He saw the concern in her eyes and took her hand in his. 'Now it will be much easier to persuade the council of the need to invest in more ships. New ones, not converted old hulks. They should also now appreciate that I'm the man who should be commanding them, not the Duke of Essex.'

Richard took the opportunity of his brother John's wedding to see his parents. He arranged for John to be married by Archbishop Thomas Bourchier in Canterbury Cathedral and the entire family had made the long journey south from Middleham Castle for the occasion. Anne got on well with John's new wife Isabel, an attractive heiress of fifteen from a respected family.

More than a year had passed since he'd last seen his mother. He noticed her lustrous black hair was tinged with silvery grey. She looked at him proudly when he hugged her in greeting.

'I've missed you, Richard. It seems longer each time between your visits.'

'You must come and see us in Calais, Mother. The sea air will be invigorating for you.'

She pulled a face. 'You know I won't set foot on a ship. As for sea air, there is more than I will ever need at Whitby. I don't need to go all the way to France.'

'Calais isn't France. It's English.' He realised he'd fallen for her taunt. 'Calais is where I live now and you know it's perfectly safe. The girls are growing up and I want them to get to know their grandmother.'

His father intervened. He looked older and had put on a little weight. 'I must congratulate you, Richard. Who would have thought a son of mine would become Lord High Admiral before he was thirty?'

Richard was pleased at his father's words. 'Essex is furious, I've been told. Although he had only one ship, the *Grace Dieu*, to defend the whole coast of England, so he has brought it on himself.'

His father looked serious. 'You need to watch him though, he makes a dangerous enemy.'

'I need to watch everyone who supports the queen, which is one of the reasons I now live in Calais.'

'I heard you were granted a thousand pounds from the Duchy of Lancaster with your new position as Admiral?'

Richard nodded. 'I insisted on it as a condition of the agreement.'

'They'll never pay, you know?'

'They will, Father. One way or another, I'll make them pay.'

Richard's mother interrupted them. 'When are you going to have another child, Richard?' She looked at him questioningly. 'We're still waiting for a grandson.'

His father chided her. 'Leave the boy alone, Alice. There is plenty of time for him to have a son.'

Richard laughed it off. It secretly bothered him that Anne showed no sign of becoming pregnant again. 'I am happy for now with my beautiful daughters.'

His father looked at him. 'Have you found suitable husbands for them?'

'No, not yet. Anne is still a baby of course. Isabel is turning into a fine young lady.'

'You should discuss the matter with your uncle. The Duke of York has four healthy sons. Your daughters could do a lot worse.'

Richard needed to find out more about his uncle's plans for his sons. Edward was already taller than him and was a skilled jouster. The others were younger, although if they inherited a little of their father's courage and determination they would make worthy husbands.

As he rode back to his ship in Sandwich he thought about his father's words. The king could suffer a relapse at any time or even die from the strange illness that plagued him for so many years. His uncle had sworn he had no wish to claim the throne, and then there was the young Prince to consider. His father was right and had given him something interesting to think about.

Chapter 12 - Summer 1458

'Twenty-eight, my lord!' Luke Tully had climbed high up the rigging to count the size of the distant Spanish fleet, barely discernible through the sea mists of the early dawn. He nimbly dropped the last few feet to the deck and crossed to join Richard at the forecastle. 'No sign they've seen us yet. Looks like they're hove to, fast asleep.'

'That's a lot more than we thought.' Richard was torn. 'There is still time to make it back to Calais yet it would be a great prize.'

The Spanish fleet had been spotted the previous day, heading up the Channel. He had a warrant from the king, which gave him sole authority to ensure the safety of the seas. Victory over this fleet would establish his reputation not only in Calais. It would be the talk of the whole continent if he could pull it off. It would mean risking everything, though. If he failed the best he could hope for was to be held for ransom in some distant Castilian jail. That was if he wasn't killed.

Richard acted decisively as soon as the fleet was sighted, ordering his ships to be ready to sail at two in the morning, to catch the Spanish before dawn. His best archers and men-at-arms lined the decks as they set out from Calais with great enthusiasm and dreams of Spanish booty. Under the terms of his commission, Richard was allowed to keep any ships and share the goods he seized with his men at his own discretion.

Now he saw at least sixteen warships ahead, surrounded by a dozen smaller vessels. All flew the flag of

Castile, allies of the French and were a potential threat to the security of England. He looked back at his own fleet, which had now grown to five warships, three heavy carvels with several cannons on the decks and four pinnaces, their decks crammed with his archers and crossbowmen. His crews had gained useful experience of manoeuvring their ships in the sometimes unpredictable waters of the English Channel. A few had engaged with pirates, although most were untested in a real battle at sea.

'The wind is in our favour.' Richard studied the sails and his banner of the bear and ragged staff flying proudly from the mast. 'If we sail back to Calais now I'll always wonder how it would have turned out.'

'The men are all behind you, my lord.' Tully grinned.'

Richard glanced up at the sky and guessed they still had a couple of hours before the sunrise. 'Let's hope the Spanish are in their hammocks. Our best chance is to take them by surprise.'

'Captain!'

The captain of his flagship *Trinity* was a likeable veteran of many sea battles and had led the training of the less experienced men. He wore a heavy iron breastplate and helmet and had a sword at his belt. Richard had known him for many years and respected his judgement.

'My lord?'

'Set a course to intercept the Spanish, if you will. We need to reach them before they raise the alarm.'

'Yes, my lord.'

Richard watched the captain as he ordered his crew to set the sails and make ready their guns. He hadn't hesitated for a moment at the prospect of taking on a force twice their size. He had chosen his men well. Now he hoped he wasn't leading them to a watery grave. He scanned the Spanish ships for any sign of movement.

They were under sail in a loose formation. The early hour meant their captains and most of the crew would still be sleeping. He also knew they would be keeping a lookout and trained to be ready to defend themselves at short notice.

The horizon was showing the first glimmering light of dawn as they approached the Spanish fleet. Now the months of practice would be put to the test. Each of the warships was to choose a target and be ready to fire across the decks once close alongside. Richard hoped to capture as many of the massive Spanish warships as he could and had given orders to fire at the rigging, only trying to sink them as a last resort.

The rest of his small fleet were to take on the dangerous task of distracting the remaining Spanish ships and do their best to keep them occupied. Archers climbed high onto the yard-arms and braced their feet in loops of rope. Crossbowmen protected the gunnery crews, who had to work on the open decks, while the men-at-arms stayed out of sight in the relative safety of the holds, waiting with their hooks and ropes for the call to board the enemy ships.

'Steady now, men.' Richard felt a moment of anxiety mixed with excitement as he realised they were past the point of no return. He could see the black shapes of the cannons of their chosen ship were still unmanned. His captain had made their approach on a close reach and now eased the main to cut their speed of approach as they prepared to draw alongside.

'Fire at will!'

The cannons boomed and the flash of gunpowder lit up the early dawn. Instead of stone balls, the cannons were loaded with the round shot linked with lengths of chain, which slashed through the rigging and sails of the enemy ship so it could no longer manoeuvre. Anyone unfortunate enough to be in the path of these weapons didn't stand a chance.

Richard's advantage of surprise was short lived. Spanish crewmen poured out onto the decks, readying cannon to return fire with startling efficiency. As the alarm was raised, the entire Spanish fleet went to battle stations. His archers in the rigging and forecastle began choosing their targets with deadly accuracy, arrows thumping into the bodies of the enemy gun crews and keeping them from firing.

Tully and his hand-picked crossbowmen were standing ready to fire if any Spaniards tried to board. They were all armed with the latest windlass crossbows, designed to be redrawn faster than the old stirrup model. Richard scanned the ships to either side of him and could see they were in much the same position as himself.

'Brace yourselves!'

There was a dull booming crunch of timber as they rammed the enemy hull and men began throwing grappling hooks on ropes to pull the enemy close enough to board.

This was the moment Richard had been waiting for. 'Sound the trumpets!'

The shrill note carried well over the noise of battle and was the signal for the waiting men-at-arms to leap across to the Spanish ship. A slip would mean being crushed to death, as though the sea was calm the gap between the two ships widened and closed with the rise and fall of the swell. The Spanish were ready with swords and knives and had archers of their own. A man next to Richard yelled out as an arrow struck him hard in the chest.

Richard drew his sword and joined the rush of men onto the enemy deck. Although his men had tried to pull the two ships as close together as they could, he still had to leap over the gap of dark swirling water. There was no time to dwell on the consequences. As soon as his feet landed on the Spanish deck he was fighting for his life, hacking and slashing at the Spanish, who fought back with unexpected determination.

He felt the deck was slippery underfoot and glancing down, he realised he was standing in a pool of fresh blood. He looked up in time to see a Spanish sailor armed with a long handled battle axe, which he swung viciously. Swiftly sidestepping, Richard took a glancing blow on his shoulder. His plate armour buckled under the heavy blade and he felt searing pain. Momentarily stunned by the shock of the impact he fell to his knees and saw his attacker raise the sharp bladed axe for a second blow.

The man cried out in alarm as a bolt from a crossbow thumped into his chest, ripping through his thick leather breastplate. The Spaniard fell over backwards and crashed to the deck. Looking behind, Richard saw Tully's crossbowmen now lined the deck of their ship, firing carefully aimed shots across at the Spanish. At such short range the effect was deadly, every bolt counting, shifting the balance in their favour.

'Find the captain!' Richard yelled as they started to take control of the ship.

'Here, my lord!' One of his men-at-arms had his knife at the throat of a man too well dressed to be a common sailor. It looked as if he had put on his ornate armour in a hurry and he was protesting angrily in Spanish.

'Are you the captain of this ship? Richard shouted, trying to ignore the agonising pain from his injured shoulder.

The Spaniard stopped his protest. 'Soy el Capitan.'

Richard didn't speak any Spanish although he was confident he could make himself understood. 'Tell your men to surrender the ship or they will all die.'

The Spanish captain seemed to understand as his shouted orders soon had the Spanish crew dropping their weapons.

Richard turned to one of his garrison lieutenants. 'Lock them up in the hold and take care of this ship. We'll come back. We've work to do first.' Richard gestured to where two Spanish warships were attacking one of his carracks.

'Back to the ship, men.'

They climbed back on board and cast the captured Spanish ship adrift, heading for the next closest. One of his warships had been boarded by the Spanish and he saw his men on board were fighting bravely despite being heavily outnumbered. Many were already dead or dying so he needed to act fast.

He pointed to the Spanish warship. 'Fire at her hull. We need to try to sink her if we can!'

His gun crews had trained for months and had already loaded the heavy stone cannon balls. The deafening sound of them all firing at once was followed by the sight of several jagged holes in the side of the Spanish ship. They fired again, at closer range now. The hull planking shattered at the water line in a shower of sharp splinters and the sea began pouring in.

The cheer from the men soon died as they came under attack from the other direction. Another Spanish warship rammed them hard on the port side, sending a judder through the whole ship. Richard knew what was about to follow. He stood with his back to the forecastle, surrounded by Tully's crossbowmen. They held their fire until the first grappling hooks flew over the rail, then unleashed a salvo of bolts into the men attempting to board. The men-at-arms charged, hacking down the Spanish who had bravely jumped across the gap between the ships, fighting as soon as they landed on the deck.

Richard called to the archers.

'We'll have to burn this one, fire into the rigging!'

The archers were ready and touched a flame to their fire arrows, which flashed through the dawn light into the tarred rigging and set the sails of the Spanish ship aflame. Fires took hold with surprising speed and acrid smoke was soon billowing across the deck, making Richard cough.

'Disengage!'

The captain was already turning them away from the blazing Spanish warship and the crew watched as men desperately worked to douse the flames. Richard turned as a scream cut sharply through the noise, in time to witness one of the Spanish archers fall to his death from the burning rigging.

The whole area was now a confusing mass of ships engaged in ramming and boarding. Richard looked around, unsure which of the warships to tackle next. The sunrise was tinged with red, warning of worsening weather and the once calm sea was starting to build into a swell.

'Over there!' He caught the helmsman's eye and pointed.

They manoeuvred alongside and managed to rope the two ships together, quickly boarding to join in the hand-to-hand fighting. Richard joined Tully and his crossbowmen in the forecastle.

'Aim for the soldiers, spare the sailors.'

Tully's men were steadily working their way through hundreds of crossbow bolts, making each count, then pulling back the windlass lever and dropping another bolt into the firing mechanism. Unlike the archers, who were firing from high in the rigging, the crossbowmen shot at close range across the deck, once again with devastating effect.

The Spaniards surrendered under the onslaught, throwing up their hands and letting Richard's men collect their swords. He looked across at the dead and dying men and realised this was no victory. They had been lucky that several of the Spanish fleet had chosen to escape rather than fight. At least one had sunk and another was still burning. Although he had now captured six of the grand warships, his men were exhausted with many wounded. Worst of all, the Spanish had been able to recapture one of their ships back, along with the men he had left aboard. He wasn't going to abandon them.

Richard found the captain. 'I'm minded to see if we can parley with the Spanish commander. How do we go about it?' Richard was realising there was much more to fighting at sea than ramming and boarding.

'We should ask for an exchange of prisoners, my lord. We don't want to be taking a load of Spaniards back to Calais with us.'

It took much longer than Richard expected to agree terms and transfer the prisoners and injured men, as well as burying the less fortunate at sea. The flotilla returned to Calais in the late afternoon and Richard looked back at the ships following in his wake. Despite the loss of some good men, all his fleet were returning home. The ship's surgeon thought he had a broken collarbone which would take a long time to heal. He also had six fine Spanish warships, his reward for a hard day's fighting.

The Duke of York arrived in Calais unannounced. It had once been his home and he wanted to see what Richard had made of it. After a tour of the city he inspected the fleet in the harbour and the new defences. He now sat in Richard's grand study enjoying a goblet of his best brandy and seemed pleased with what he'd seen.

'You know the people are all talking about how you beat the Spanish? The stories are more outlandish every time they are retold.' His uncle studied him, taking in the canvas sling the ship's surgeon had made to help his wounded shoulder heal. He seemed to be reassessing Richard's potential. 'You deserve their admiration for your bloody recklessness!'

'We had a bit of luck that day. My men fought well. So did the Spanish.'

'The people needed some good news, Richard. You've given them something of their pride back and it doesn't hurt our cause at all.'

'Despite the queen's attempts to have me indicted for piracy?'

The duke looked at him sternly. 'You did push it a bit far with the Germans, Richard. You know there are some in the Council who are only waiting for an excuse.'

'How much support do we have in the council these days?'

His uncle shook his head. 'Almost none. They are all far too busy feathering their own nests.'

Richard knew exactly what he was referring to. His successes in Calais meant he had become wealthier than his uncle and father combined. A lot of his new wealth had been invested in the town of Calais, building up his private navy and paying all the extra men he had recruited. He was the richest man in England now and hardly spared a thought for their troubled King or his troublesome Queen and her self-serving advisors.

He looked at his uncle. The duke was starting to look old now and perhaps a little drunk on the fine brandy. His hair was thinning and he seemed to have lost some of the iron determination that Richard had admired. He wondered if he should raise the delicate question of what he had planned for the marriage of his four sons.

'What do you want me to do?'

'That's what I like about you, Richard. You get straight to the point.' He crossed to the table where a large map of the area surrounding Calais was spread out. 'I hear you've not been limiting your harassment to the Spanish, the Germans and the French?'

'I had to show Burgundy we are not to be underestimated. We regularly patrol the border and sometimes they like to try our patience.'

'Well, you asked what you can do. You can make an alliance with Philip of Burgundy. Meet him. Make sure we can rely on him if the queen does a deal with the French.'

Richard studied the map as if he's seen it for the first time. 'Is there anything we need to worry about?'

'The queen is raising an army. She is doing her best to finish us, Richard. Finish the House of York and all we stand for. It's what she's been planning ever since she was crowned.'

'What are you planning?' Richard realised the seriousness of what the duke was saying.

His uncle drained his goblet. 'This so-called peace can't last much longer, Richard. We're going to have to fight for what we stand for.' He looked at Richard. 'This time the fight won't be a battle like St. Albans. This time it's going to be a war, a bloody war.'

Chapter 13 - Summer 1459

Richard waited impatiently for the commission of enquiry and wondered why he had even bothered making the trip to London. He probably could have stayed in Calais and let them draw their conclusions in his absence. The problem was the queen had made no secret of her desire to have one of her loyal followers in charge of Calais. He couldn't risk playing into their hands and letting them use the incident as an excuse to remove him from his position.

The great carved door creaked as it opened enough to let the usher slip through.

'They are ready for you now, my lord.'

Richard scowled at him, then remembered the man was simply doing his job. He followed the usher into a stuffy, wood-panelled room and found himself facing the grim faced commissioners. Seated along one side of a long table, they were all men he knew from the council. None were men he would ever call his friends. There was one chair set before them, covered in green leather. He was invited to sit and hear the charge that had been made against him.

'Sir Richard Neville, Earl of Warwick and Captain of Calais, it is alleged that you attacked ships of the German Hanseatic fleet without due cause and brought the crown into disrepute. How do you plead?'

Richard looked into their impassive faces and wondered if whatever he said would make one bit of difference. 'Not guilty.' His confident voice echoed in the high ceilinged room.

They waited for him to continue and seemed surprised at his silence.

The Chairman cleared his throat and read aloud from his notes.

'We are commissioned by His Royal Majesty to examine the official complaint that the Hanseatic Bay Fleet, during its annual passage to transport salt from the Bay of Bourgneuf to the Hanseatic ports of Germany and the Baltic, was attacked by ships under your command and seized in an act of piracy.'

Richard stood and addressed the commission. 'My lords.' He tried to keep the anger from his voice. 'I have the king's warrant to keep the safety of the seas, which permits me to undertake such actions in the waters of the English Channel as I see fit.'

The commission regarded him in silence and he realised they could have no idea they were being used by the queen. 'May I also add that the court has unreasonably withheld the payments owed to me as Captain of Calais? I have to pay the men of the garrison by whatever means I can.'

The commission tried to continue questioning the legality of his claim. They seemed to have little else to say and Richard became increasingly irritated at their thinly veiled attempts to find a reason to remove him from his post. When they eventually adjourned for lunch Richard found Tully, who had been waiting all morning with the handful of men of his personal guard he had brought into Westminster Palace.

Tully looked at him enquiringly. 'Is it over now, my lord?'

Richard frowned. 'It seems they have been told to keep on until I admit I'm guilty!' He was tired and hungry. 'Where can we find something to eat?'

Tully pointed down the corridor. 'They said we have to go to the kitchens, down there.'

Richard felt annoyed. 'I've been visiting Westminster for many years. This is the first time I've been sent to the kitchens!'

Nevertheless he was hungry and followed his men. The place was poorly lit, with men and women baking and scrubbing, tending great ovens and steaming cauldrons. Curious faces turned in their direction as they entered and Richard was sure he heard his name as he was recognised by someone.

As they cut through the kitchen, one of Richard's guards bumped into one of the cooks preparing food. The man swung a punch and hit him in the face. In a moment the scene turned into a brawl. Luke Tully and the other men of Richard's escort tried to restrain him. A heavily built cook lunged angrily at Richard with a long steel roasting spit, yelling something about traitors. He dodged the blow by twisting sideways as he had been trained in years of fencing practice. Richard had left his sword behind when he went to the commission. He still carried his dagger and drew it, slashing one of his attackers on the arm.

The royal guards appeared and Richard spotted their commander. 'I am the Earl of Warwick and take full responsibility for my men. This was simply an accident. Can't you see?'

The guards ignored him and began to surround them.

'Stand back!' Richard held his dagger in the air. He looked round for Tully, who had picked up one of the carving knives and was using it to ward off the men behind them.

'We've been set up, Tully. The guards arrived too soon. They were expecting something to happen!'

'Let's get out of here, my lord!'

One of the king's men shouted. 'Cut off their escape!'

Tully looked where the guards were headed and spotted a door leading out to the courtyard. He dashed to it and held it open while his men helped Richard escape the brawl.

Tully glanced back into the steaming kitchens. 'One of my men is missing.'

Richard hesitated. 'I don't think we can help him. There are too many of them.' He made a decision. 'Quick, to the river. It's the last thing they will expect us to do. The river was busy with boats and they soon found a barge for hire. Richard tossed the owner a silver coin to take them away from Westminster as fast as he could.

Tully put his hand to a badly bruised eye as they floated down the river to safety. 'That was bloody close!'

Richard glanced down at his expensive black velvet tunic. It had been torn in the fighting. 'I think this charade was all a plot to discredit me, Tully.' He shook his head and remembered the thick set man who attacked him with a skewer. 'It could even have been an attempt on my life.'

✝

The bad news he had been anticipating finally arrived. Richard showed the letter to Anne. His uncle had been right. The queen was conscripting soldiers from every town and village in England. There could only be one reason and he had been called to bring as many men to the York cause as he could spare. His father was also making his way from the north to his uncle's stronghold at Ludlow Castle.

She read it carefully. 'Is this the war the Duke of York was talking about?'

'It might not come to that.' He looked into her troubled eyes and tried to reassure her. 'We need to make a show of strength. Win over the people.'

'You said that before St. Albans.'

'I believed it then and I do now.'

'Am I coming with you back to Warwick Castle?'

He thought for a moment. Six months had passed since he had been back to their home in England. The time had gone so fast, although he knew Anne was missing her home.

'You are safest here with the girls.' He smiled at her, trying to hide his concern. 'Calais is probably the safest place in England.'

Anne didn't laugh at his joke. 'Send word as soon as you can, Richard?'

He could still see concern in her eyes. 'Of course. I've no idea how long this will take.'

She held him close and whispered in his ear. 'I'll miss you.'

For a moment he found himself regretting that he had to go. There was a knock at their door and he opened it to find his flagship captain, one of Richard's most experienced men. The captain looked uncomfortable about the news he had to deliver.

'You need to come and talk to the captains, my lord. They're not happy about this.'

Richard was surprised. His men had loyally followed him in everything, even when they'd recently seized the salt ships of the Hanseatic fleet, a blatant act of piracy.

'What on earth do you mean?'

The captain was a blunt man. 'They won't sail against the king, my lord.'

'This isn't about the king.' He glanced back at Anne then turned to the captain. 'Who put them up to it?'

The captain looked uneasy. 'Andrew Trollope.'

'Trollope? The Sergeant Porter?'

'Yes, my lord.'

'He was Lord Rivers' man.' He shook his head. 'Thank you for telling me. I'll come and talk with them right away.'

Richard felt troubled as they made their way to the harbour. A lot of the men in the garrison had stayed after Lord Rivers left. Richard needed their experience and Andrew Trollope was an experienced soldier, popular and well respected by the men. He realised why his men were not prepared to side with York. His captains were glad to see he had come in person. Richard had always encouraged them to speak their minds.

'We are not sailing against the king.' He looked at them. Their faces were serious.

One of the older captains stepped forward. 'We hope you understand. We can't make our men traitors to the king, so would you swear to that, my lord?'

Richard could feel himself getting angry. He saw Andrew Trollope standing in the background, observing how he was going to handle the situation. Richard had come to expect absolute loyalty from his men. After all they had been through together it unsettled him to see they were on the brink of mutiny.

'On my honour, I intend to pledge my loyalty to the king, as does my father, the Earl of Salisbury, and the Duke of York.'

They sailed at noon. Every ship in Richard's fleet was needed and it had taken them three hours to load two hundred men-at-arms and four hundred archers, as well as all their horses, supplies and equipment. Richard had known this day would come, and preparations had started soon after his uncle's unexpected visit to Calais.

The town of Sandwich still showed traces of its ravaging by the French, with blackened trees and charred marks on the cobbled streets from the fires. Richard was glad to see that many of the houses had already been rebuilt and the people showed no sign of resentment towards him. His ships were soon unloaded and he made his grand procession through Canterbury to London.

Richard rode at the head of his red-coated men, flanked by his personal guard, drummers and fife players, with his standard bearer carrying his long banner of the bear and ragged staff. People came out of their houses, cheering. Richard noticed there were others in the crowd with worried faces as they watched him march past. Like his men in Calais, he realised they were unsure about his motives.

His plan had been to stay overnight in London then make his way on to Warwick castle where he would meet up with his father's army. Soon after he arrived one of his supporters, a wealthy merchant, asked to see him urgently. Richard was tired from the long ride and sent a message that he would see him in the morning. His servant returned saying the merchant was insistent that he must speak with Richard right away. Richard reluctantly agreed. He had done well through his alliances with the merchants of London and needed as many friends as he could in these troubled times.

The merchant was ushered in. He was a well-built man dressed in dark blue velvet with a heavy gold chain around his neck. Richard stood to welcome him and noticed the look of concern on the merchant's face.

'Good to see you again, my friend. What is it that can't wait until tomorrow?'

The merchant shook his head. 'Can we speak in private, my lord? This is for you alone to hear.'

Richard dismissed his servants, intrigued.

The merchant lowered his voice. 'The queen has an army lying in wait for you on the road to Warwick.'

Richard was shocked. 'How many men does she have?'

The merchant was unsure. 'I watched them march from here a week ago, my lord. I'd say at least two or three thousand men. I've heard there could be more now. They seemed a poor lot, conscripts mostly. There were also archers and plenty of knights with their retainers.'

'I have my best men here in London.' Richard frowned. 'There are not enough to take on a force that size though.' He looked earnestly at the merchant. 'I'm grateful for your warning. We could have marched straight into a trap.'

'Your father is still heading to Warwick?'

'As far as I know. My brothers ride with him and I expect he has been able to raise a few thousand men. He can look after himself.'

The merchant hesitated. 'I think it is well advised that you leave London as soon as you can, my lord. This place is full of spies and I've heard the queen has issued a warrant for your arrest. I fear it's too dangerous for you to stay.'

'I am in your debt. One day I hope to repay your service to me.'

The merchant forced a smile for the first time since he arrived. 'You have many friends here. We all wish you the best of luck in what you have to do, my lord.'

Richard thanked him and the merchant left by the side entrance, out of view of the queen's spies. As he watched the merchant go Richard called for a rider to take a message to his father. It might be too late, although there wasn't anything else he could do. It angered him to think the queen's forces had probably occupied his home at Warwick Castle and knew they would loot anything of value given half the chance. He consoled himself with the knowledge that at least his family were safe in Calais.

Richard was greeted by his father on his arrival at Ludlow and could immediately see something was badly wrong. His father's right hand was bandaged and his tunic had been torn at the shoulder.

His father spoke with his usual bluntness. 'Your brothers, Thomas and John, have been captured.' He shook his head. 'Thomas is wounded.' His father looked like a beaten man.

Richard realised he hadn't seen his brothers for over a year. 'Where are they being held? Can we get to them?'

His father's face was grim. He shook his head. 'I tried.'

'Let us hope they are being held for ransom.' He looked around. 'Where is the Duke of York?'

'Out on patrol with his sons.'

'I've been told the queen is bringing thirty thousand men?'

His father was concerned. 'They mustn't be allowed to surround us here.'

'The queen would hold a siege until we starved!'

'How many men do you have, Richard?'

'I have two hundred men-at-arms and four hundred archers and crossbowmen.'

'I still have at least four thousand and there were twenty thousand here already and more on the way.'

'Still outnumbered.' He forced a smile. 'Although we have the better men!'

His father smiled back for the first time. 'Get some rest, Richard. Tell your men to do the same. We've a long march ahead of us and a hard fight at the end of it.'

Richard couldn't rest and was waiting with his father when the Duke of York returned with the news that the queen's forces were on their way. He was flanked by two armoured knights and Richard realised these were his uncle's eldest sons, Edward and Edmund. He easily recognised Edward as he was a full head taller than the other two, his height made more noticeable by the York crest on the helmet he wore with the visor raised.

The duke dismounted and turned to them. 'We'll not wait for them to reach us here. We need to find a good position on the road and be ready.'

Richard's father agreed. 'Did you get sight of them?'

The duke shook his head. 'We couldn't risk being captured. Their conscripts are no match for our soldiers, though. What they have in numbers, we have in experience.'

Edward dismounted and removed his helmet. 'And determination!'

Richard studied his uncle's sons. Edward was tall and well-built with blond hair and an engaging sense of humour. His expensive armour had the dents and scars of a fighting man. Like his father, Edmund was sharp and observant, missing little of importance and already showing many of his father's qualities. Both were too old to be husbands for his daughters, although they had all the right qualities. He hoped the duke's other two sons would turn out as well.

When they were ready to ride he noticed Edmund was riding alongside the duke and Edward was sharing a joke with some of the young knights following behind.

He rode over to him. 'You're welcome to ride with me, Edward, if you wish?'

A broad grin flashed across Edward's face. 'Thank you. I'd be honoured, Earl Warwick.'

They rode side by side with the grandest York army ever assembled, to take on the Queen of England. Richard looked back and was pleased to see his red-coated men seemed in good spirits, with his banner flying proudly. It took most of the day to reach Worcester, only to see the king's standard flying over the enemy camp. It meant the king was with them.

He rode up to where the duke and his father had stopped in the road.

The duke turned to him. 'We'll have to change our plans. I suggest we withdraw to Worcester and see if the king will consider our demands. Agreed?'

Richard and his father both agreed.

'We can't blame them.' Richard looked back at the royal standard. 'There are men with us who will not fight against the king.'

'The queen knows it.' His uncle scowled. 'That's why she's made sure we all see it. Let's hope the king is mindful of the last time he was advised to ignore our oath of loyalty, at St. Albans.'

They found a priest in the town who agreed to take their message to the king. They had a long wait and when he returned he did not bring good news. With the priest was the stony faced Bishop of Salisbury carrying his bishop's crook and dressed in his gold-embroidered purple robes and mitre.

The bishop addressed the duke. 'The king will pardon you all, except for the Earl of Salisbury, if you will lay down your weapons and surrender now. I have to tell you he has over fifty thousand men and more are joining his army each day, my lord.'

Richard was concerned. They could not surrender to the queen. To do so would be madness. At best they could expect to be attainted, their lands taken from them. At worst, they could face charges of treason and incarceration in the Tower. The threat to his father meant the queen knew they would not surrender. It was a trap. They were being forced to fight against the king.

His uncle turned to the bishop. 'You can tell the king he'll have his answer soon enough.'

The bishop was unsurprised. 'God be with you all.' He crossed himself and returned to the king's encampment.

Richard's father said what they were all thinking. 'We've had a wasted journey. We should withdraw and dig in. Barricade the road and make them come to us.'

They took the Tewkesbury road and marched the men to Ludford Bridge, by the wide and fast flowing river Tern outside Ludlow. The men had lost much of their enthusiasm for the task so Richard personally led the work of digging defensive earthworks. Their few cannons were positioned to fire down the road and long sharpened stakes were cut and set into the earth banks. The work was hot and dirty and the sun was setting before he was satisfied.

The duke's son Edward rode up to them as Richard made his final inspection of their readiness, shouting words of encouragement to the men on guard duty who were watching for the first sign of the approaching army. Edward was popular with the men and seemed much older than his nineteen years and reminded Richard a little of himself at the same age.

'Do you think they have more than fifty thousand men, or was that a ruse?'

'I wish I knew, Edward.' Richard looked around at their defences. 'We must rely on our wits in the morning. They definitely have the advantage of numbers.'

Richard was woken at dawn by Tully. 'Bad news, my lord. Trollope has gone to the enemy with as many men who will follow him.'

Richard cursed and began strapping on his armour. 'How many? How long ago?' He wished he had dealt with Trollope at Calais, when he had the chance.

Tully helped him with the straps. 'At least an hour ago. A good few men have followed, my lord.'

The significance of the news hit Richard. 'He knows our strength, our positions, everything. He even knows most of our men won't fight against the king.'

Tully looked concerned. 'We can't fight them now, my lord.'

'Let's find my father and uncle. We don't have much time.'

Richard's father was already awake and waiting for him. 'The duke has left for Ireland, Richard. He had no choice.'

Richard was still coming to terms with the rapid turn of events. 'What about his family, his sons?'

'Edmund has ridden with him. Edward is going to stay and protect his mother and younger brothers.'

Richard looked at the sky. 'We'd best get away while we can. They'll be coming for us soon and we won't stand a chance in daylight.'

His father agreed. 'Who would have thought it would come to this? You must get away to your estates in the west, as soon as you can.'

'I'm not going to leave you here. You heard what the bishop said. They will pardon the men if they surrender.' He looked directly at his father. 'They won't pardon you.'

'You're right, Richard. We need to get going. We must take young Edward with us.'

'Edward?'

His father nodded. 'The king won't harm my sister or the boys. I imagine Edward will want to put up a fight. He'll take on fifty thousand men if we let him!'

Richard reluctantly agreed with his father and went in search of the young Edward, Earl of March.

✝

They were joined by Sir John Wenlock and Luke Tully. A tall, pragmatic, sometimes outspoken man, Sir John was a veteran of the wars in France. Formerly Queen Margaret's Chamberlain, like several of those who defended King Henry at the first battle of St. Albans, he turned his coat to the York cause and was appointed Speaker of the House by the Duke of York. Sir John now feared for his life if he was captured by the Lancastrians.

The five of them rode hard through the night with only what they could carry. Before they left they exchanged their plate armour for rough woollen tunics, although they all carried swords and Tully had his crossbow slung over his shoulder with a full quiver of bolts. Edward had reluctantly seen the wisdom of leaving his mother and younger brothers to the king's mercy. He also carried a heavy purse of gold coins rather than leave it to the looters.

Tully had told his men to give them a head start, then spread the word that Richard had ordered them to lay down their arms and accept the king's pardon. Those who were able to find their way back to Calais would be well rewarded for their loyalty when he could join them.

By the time the sun was turning the sky a dusty pink they had put enough distance behind them to slow down a little. They rode to the house of one of his father's loyal retainers, to recover their strength and agree a plan. The owner of the house served them a hot meal and produced an old mariner's map, which they spread on the table. Richard studied the map with interest. It showed the Bristol Channel and southern coast of England. Faded and crudely drawn, it had clearly been used for navigation at sea. Someone had plotted lines on the map and marked way points with crosses, to show the route they had sailed.

'They'll expect us to head east.' He looked at the others. 'I'll bet they've already realised we're not in Ludlow. They'll be sending men to cover the Kentish ports.'

Edward knew the area well and traced his finger down the Bristol Channel. 'We could take the long way round to Calais, by ship?'

Richard was impressed at his suggestion. 'If we can find a ship to take us and the weather holds.'

His father agreed. 'I'd rather take my chances at sea. Once we are at sea they won't be able to find us.'

They thanked their host and rode to the north Devon coast in search of a suitable ship. The long ride was made more difficult by the need to keep out of sight and constantly check they weren't being followed. An orange sun was setting on the western horizon by the time they reached the coast. Even though they were tired and hungry, they couldn't rest until they found a ship and put to sea.

The harbours were full of small boats that reeked of fish. They could only see one that looked fit to make the long journey, a three-masted carrack named *Kismet*, similar to several they sailed in Calais. Richard made a quick inspection with Sir John, who knew what to look for in a ship. The carrack was a merchant trader from Bristol, past its best and the bilges needed pumping. Otherwise she seemed watertight and the rigging was functional. Large enough to be stable in heavy seas, it had a high rounded stern and a cabin in the aftcastle, with a long bowsprit and bunks for the crew in a forecastle.

The owner was reluctant to sell it although his attitude soon changed when he saw gold coins. He was also rewarded with their horses in return for his silence. They were all tired and the hour was too late to start looking for a crew, so they spent a fairly comfortable night moored to the quayside, taking turns to keep a watch in case anyone came looking for them.

In the morning Richard and Edward went in search of provisions for their voyage and Tully accompanied Sir John in search of the crew, with silver coins to pay them. Richard and his father went to the cabin and began plotting their course on the old map. Although Richard had sailed the length of the English Channel many times, this was a new experience for him. He would have liked to sail to his own port of Cardiff. The problem was he was too well known there and word of his presence could soon reach the queen's informers. Their only option was to sail the long way, around the dangerous rocks of Land's End.

The tide was rising by the time they had tracked down a crew and the supplies were loaded. They cast off, unnoticed by anyone and headed out into the muddy grey waters of the Bristol Channel. Richard was pleased to see the old canvas sails fill with a strong north-easterly breeze, which soon had them speeding to safety.

Edward was enjoying their adventure, his first sea voyage. He got on well with Tully and was helping him to improve his sword hand in return for lessons with the crossbow.

'You know what Kismet means, Tully?'

'Good luck, my lord?'

'Good enough. It's one of the words brought back from the East by the crusaders. It means destiny, providence. God's will and what is written in the stars.'

Richard heard their conversation and joined them on the deck. 'A good omen. We could use some luck after being betrayed by our own men.'

Tully looked thoughtful. 'I'll bet a week's wages, my lord, that we haven't seen the last of Andrew Trollope.'

'He'll be an obvious choice to help whoever they send to winkle us out from Calais. We'll be ready for him.'

It took most of the day to reach the fishing village of Padstow on the Cornish coast, where they navigated the tricky sand bar and entered the busy harbour. Their ship blended perfectly with the others moored close alongside fishing boats. Although there were some soldiers in the town they seemed more interested in the taverns than the ships moored at the quayside. They decided to send Tully for fresh supplies, as no one would recognise him and they could stay out of sight.

They woke next morning to the tempting aroma of bacon frying and found Tully making breakfast from freshly baked bread, which they washed down with a mug of strong, dark Cornish ale. Richard checked the tide and plotted their course to Lands End. He knew many ships had been wrecked on the rocks rounding the tip of Cornwall and planned to give it a wide berth.

Heading out to sea they soon found the wind had veered and increased in force, making the ship heel over uncomfortably. The sky turned a brooding slate grey and the wind speed began to increase. Choppy waves started hitting them on the side, sluicing the deck with seawater. Edward joined Richard and his father in the cabin, steadying himself as the ship lurched heavily.

'Tully told me the crew want to put in at St. Ives.' Edward peered out of the open porthole. 'They say there's a storm coming.'

'We have to get around Lands End before any storm hits.' Richard braced himself as the ship lurched again in the swell. 'I'll have a word with the crew.'

It didn't take long for him to find out that none of the crew had ever sailed further than St. Ives. They admitted they were fishermen, not used to being out in heavy seas. Richard took charge.

'I'll take the helm.' He looked up at the towering mast, with its complicated system of ropes and pulleys. 'I'll need help with the sails. Do you know how to take in a reef?'

The men set to work and reduced the size of the mainsail, heaving on the ropes and tying the spare canvas to stop it flapping in the fresh breeze, slowing their speed a little and making the ship more manageable.

Richard could taste the salt in the air as he set a course to sail them clear of the rocky cliffs of Cornwall. The waves were higher now and Richard had to use all his strength as he braced against the wheel. He kept checking their course as they ploughed through the worsening seas.

His father looked worried as a huge wave crashed over the bows and flooded into the hatch.

'We can't take too many like that!'

'Have one of the men secure that hatch, Tully!' Richard had to shout now to make himself heard. 'They need to pump the bilges and get the water back out or the weight will slow us down!'

The bows of their ship lifted high into the air as they rode up a huge wave, then plunged down the other side into the deepest troughs Richard had ever seen. He looked up at the mast and guessed the waves must be twenty or thirty feet high. They were caught in a storm and there was no going back.

The next wave flooded over the deck, washing away anything not tied down and flooding into the open hatch. One of the crew struggled his way across the deck and began securing the hatch covering the access to the hold. The wind was howling now and the sea was strangely dark against the foaming white crests.

Another huge wave crashed over them. Richard was soaked through to the skin and he shivered in the cold wind. His concern was for the crewman who had been washed up against the side of the deck and nearly into the sea. Luke Tully had also seen him and emerged from the cabin with a coil of rope. He tied one end firmly around his middle and threw the other to the crewman, who was clinging on for his life. The man caught it before the next wave crashed across the deck. Somehow the crewman still held the rope and Richard watched as Tully pulled him to safety.

For several hours Richard worked to keep them clear of the dark shape of the high cliffs, until the muscles in his arms ached with the strain. The cold was making his hands feel numb. He found it difficult to see through the misty spray, which soaked his hair and clothes, chilling him to the bone.

He realised the storm was easing as they were rounding the tip of Land's End. Now they faced a new danger, as the old chart had shown rocks offshore and someone had written the name of the largest, the Runnel Stone. Richard heaved the wheel to starboard and looked up at the flapping sails. The wind was still in their favour so he kept on course, giving the rocky headland a wide berth.

Now the storm had passed Sir John took a turn at the helm and Richard was finally able to rest. Wet and exhausted, he plotted a course for the island of Guernsey, the furthermost part of his Warwick estates.

Richard woke to find they had sailed through the night and the island could be seen on the far horizon. He felt a huge sense of relief as they finally dropped anchor in the sheltered harbour. The disaster at Ludlow still weighed heavily on their minds. At least they were now safely out of the reach of Queen Margaret's army.

Richard's father and Sir John set off for the shore with Tully and one of the crewmen in the longboat to find fresh water and supplies for the final trip to Calais. Richard looked out at the island through the open cabin door. The sun was shining and flocks of hungry gulls pecked for crabs on the seashore. A few small fishing boats were tied up at the quay and some fishermen were busily loading their nets.

Edward sat down on the bunk. 'Well done, Richard. There was a moment when I thought we weren't going to make it.'

Richard rubbed his eyes. 'She's a seaworthy little ship. I think I'll have her refitted as part of my fleet when we get back to Calais.'

Edward was concerned. 'I wish I knew how my father is. He's either on his way to Ireland now or locked up in the Tower.' A look of regret showed in his eyes. 'I shouldn't have left my mother and brothers to take their chances.'

'We couldn't save them all.'

Edward stood up. 'Perhaps we can.'

Richard was confused. 'What do you mean?'

'I'll come back with you to Calais. We'll raise an army of loyal men and put my father on the throne.'

Chapter 14 - Summer 1460

Richard Earl of Warwick felt an overwhelming sense of pride as he rode into London at the head of his riding retinue of five hundred mounted knights and an army of more than ten thousand men-at-arms and archers. His father, the Earl of Salisbury, rode on one side and Edward, Earl of March the other, all three wearing armour with their banners held high behind them. His men were in good spirits and cheering crowds welcomed them, despite the steady summer rain.

An old woman shouted to them excitedly as they rode past. 'God bless you, my lord, God bless you all!'

Her shrill voice caught Richard's attention. He raised a gauntleted hand in acknowledgement of her support and felt a surge of pride as the crowd cheered even more loudly. He knew some of them were there simply for the spectacle and others out of curiosity. Most, though, were there to show their support for the new order. They were tired of the Lancastrians, with their mad king and French Queen. The time was now right to establish the House of York as the legal and military power in the land.

As he rode towards the towering cathedral of St. Paul's, Richard reflected on the unexpected events of the past few months. They had been expecting a fight when they sailed into the shallow harbour at Sandwich yet many of the king's men mutinied to join the York cause. The rest dropped their weapons and ran for their lives. Richard's growing army marched triumphantly to Canterbury, with fanfares of trumpets and the steady beat of his drummers, cheered on by the Kentish men who had followed Jack Cade and were tired of Lancastrian misrule.

He remembered his relief when they finally reached the safety of Calais and had news that the Duke of York was safe in Ireland. Richard was proud of how he'd been able to take the helm himself when the crew were too frightened to continue. In the spring he had taken to the sea again in his flagship and sailed all the way to Waterford harbour in Ireland to meet the Duke of York and discuss plans for their revenge.

His uncle was scathing about the Lancastrians and told him how he had been sent an envoy from the king to inform him he was charged with high treason. He'd ordered the unfortunate messenger to be hanged, drawn and quartered in the market square, a clear message to the Lancastrians that there was now no going back.

On his long return journey Richard collected a surprise for his father. His mother always refused to set foot on a ship, yet was finally persuaded to sail with him to Calais. She was terrified at first, despite Richard's reassurances, as she had suffered nightmares of drowning at sea and was unable to swim. Her desire to see her family helped her to overcome her fear and it had been good to see her finally reunited with her granddaughters.

Soon after they arrived the clanging of the alarm bell interrupted their lunch when a fleet of ships were spotted by the lookout. Richard was unsurprised. He knew the young Duke of Somerset had been given the Captaincy of Calais as a reward by the queen and was expecting him. The duke was welcomed by a salvo from Richard's cannons and was forced to turn back and land at Guines Castle in the marshes to the south. Unluckily for the duke, his captains were loyal to Richard and delivered his ships back to Calais. With them were some of the soldiers who had been disloyal to Richard at Ludford Bridge. He had them executed on the spot. Andrew Trollope had wisely stayed at Guines with the duke.

Richard had also sent Lord Wenlock on an audacious dawn raid on Sandwich. He captured Lord Rivers, who was caught sleeping in his bed. His son Anthony and beautiful wife Jacquetta of Luxembourg were also taken prisoner and paraded through Calais in triumph. Richard had been angry when Rivers was helped to escape to England by Lancastrian supporters in the town, although the raid had been a show of Yorkist strength and paved the way for their successful return.

Now they made their way through the crowded streets of London to St. Paul's Cathedral to give thanks for their good fortune. The cathedral was much more than a place of worship. Dominating the heart of the city with its towering spire, the great cathedral built by William the Conqueror was a gathering place and focal point, a landmark where important news was shared. Richard was well aware of this and had sent messengers ahead to make sure the people knew of his intention.

They were well aware of how religion united the people, even more than their loyalty to the crown. In front of a packed congregation, Richard knelt side by side with his father and Edward in front of the altar in prayer. God must be seen to be on the side of York.

They thanked him loudly and publicly for his good grace.

The peaceful tranquillity of the cathedral was interrupted by the thundering boom of a distant cannon, the dull sound echoing around the high stone arches of the nave. Richard's bodyguard immediately moved closer to protect him. They were all vulnerable to assassins and there were still plenty of Lancastrian sympathisers in London, as well as mercenaries in the pay of the king's supporters. Richard thought it unlikely that an attempt would be made in the sanctuary of St. Paul's and cannon fire was the last thing he expected.

Londoners were used to the sound of cannons to mark special events, yet when a second shot reverberated across the city people started muttering to each other as they speculated about the reason. A woman called out for her children in alarm and some of the congregation began moving towards the arched doorway, soon blocking the wide entrance in their eagerness to leave.

Richard turned to his father. 'It seems God has other work for us to do today.'

His father looked concerned. 'We have to see what's happening. It must be coming from the tower.'

Edward was watching the crowd at the entrance. 'This is no place to be caught if the king's forces have returned to London.'

Richard's father bowed his head and made the sign of the cross on his chest and the three of them walked backwards down the aisle, then turned. Their men had made a path through the jostling people and they passed through the great oak doors. The summer rain had finally stopped and the sun was unusually bright in the sky. The crowd was watching to see how they would respond to the unexpected Lancastrian attack.

Richard shielded his eyes and scanned the side roads for signs of trouble. People were running now, trying to reach a place of safety before the real fighting started. A fruit seller's barrow was overturned in the rush and apples rolled all over the cobbled street to be stolen or crushed underfoot. Their grooms brought the horses and Richard mounted, watching while his father and Edward did the same. He signalled to the waiting mounted knights to follow. Behind them came the men-at-arms and archers, no longer just a show of strength, they were now an army ready to fight.

They progressed as fast as they could through the crowded streets in the direction of the firing, arriving just in time to see another cannon fire directly into the crowd. A plume of smoke showed the firing position on top of the Tower walls and the stone cannon ball smashed heavily into the throng of people who had come out to see what was happening. Men and women screamed in pain and the crowd surged angrily towards the gates of the Tower. Richard could see there was nothing to be done.

He shouted to his father over the noise. 'It must be a Lancastrian rear-guard.'

'The only thing we can do is hold the Tower to siege and wait for them to come out.'

Edward joined them and looked at the carnage in the street. 'What are they thinking of, firing into the crowd?'

Richard took a firm grip on his reins in case the next shot startled his horse. 'They are playing right into our hands.' He watched the angry mob gathering around the Tower portcullis. Some had already armed

165

themselves with halberds and others brandished swords. Whoever was in command in the Tower had made a fatal mistake. The people of London would have his head on a spike as soon as he left the safety of the Tower, which he would have to do eventually.

Richard's father made a decision. 'I will stay here and keep them from leaving. You two should take the rest of the men and see if you can track down the king's army before they return to London.'

'I wish you luck, Father.'

Edward looked up at the high walls of the Tower of London. 'The guns have stayed silent for a while now. I trust you can keep them that way!'

As if to answer his words, an explosion sounded with deafening ferocity. They all flinched as the cannon ball thumped violently into the wall of a building, dangerously close to them. The shot was too close for comfort. Richard's father led them in a tactical retreat out of range of the high cannons.

'Don't worry about me.' He glanced back at the Tower. 'Make sure the king's army doesn't come back here until I've had a chance to sort this lot out.'

Richard raised a hand in farewell. 'We will be back soon with the king.'

The rain started again as they gathered their men to march north. They made slow progress as their heavy supply wagons dug deep ruts in the muddy roads. Fast afore riders were sent ahead on the main roads and by noon on the second day one returned with news of the Lancastrian army. The king's men had been sighted. They were camped in the grounds of an Abbey on the north bank of the River Nene, outside the town walls to the south-east of Northampton.

As soon as they arrived Richard climbed with Edward to the top of an ancient fort a mile to the west of Northampton known as Hunsbury Hill. They were both soaking wet and the ground was slippery underfoot. There was a clear view from the top across to the Lancastrian camp. Their enemy had been expecting them and was raising a massive earthwork.

Richard could make out the ominous dark shape of several heavy cannons. He scanned the sloping front of the embankment they would have to climb and saw men at work hammering sharply pointed wooden stakes into place.

'They've diverted the river to make a water filled ditch. That answers my question about where we choose to fight.'

Edward studied the defences. 'I can see archers. Hundreds of them.' He looked thoughtful as he spied on the enemy guards. 'They look even wetter than we are. You know what happens to a decent bow in the rain.'

'We needn't worry about them being accurate.'

'They look well prepared though. It's not going to be an easy fight.'

'I am well prepared as well, thanks to your suggestion. I've promised your friend Lord Grey of Ruthin an important post in our new council.'

'Grey's no friend. He's a turncoat!' Edward seemed surprised.

'Well, with luck he'll turn the battle for us. We both know how hard it is to be let down by your own side!'

'We can't rely on him.'

'We don't have to.' Richard looked back at their enemy. 'If he helps us reach the king I'll honour my promise.' As he stared out across the battlefield, he remembered the last time he had seen Lord Grey's wife, his cousin Lady Katherine. She would not forgive him for the death of her father, Sir Henry Percy at St. Albans; although he hoped she would be grateful if he made her husband Treasurer of England.

They slid back down the grassy bank of the hill fort and found Edward's tent in the hastily erected York camp. Their boots were covered in mud and the cold rain water ran in a constant stream from the thin canvas roof of their tent, adding to the puddles forming outside.

'Damn this rain!' Edward took off his armour. His doublet was soaked through and he pulled it off, revealing his broad muscular chest.

'They say it's the worst July for a hundred years.' Richard also stripped to the waist.

'I can believe it.' Edward grinned at him. 'I also believe we can turn this foul weather to our advantage.'

Richard was interested to hear Edward's plan. 'What do you have in mind?'

Edward looked at the sky. 'They won't have much stomach for fighting in this rain.'

'You think they will agree to our conditions?'

Richard's brother George, now Bishop of Exeter, had persuaded the Bishop of Salisbury to ride out with a message for the king, offering to exchange hostages and seeking a peaceful alternative to fighting. Edward's answer was interrupted by his groom, who brought dry clothes and gave them both a tankard of hot spiced ale.

Edward raised his tankard to Richard. 'If they won't agree terms, we'll seize the high ground in a frontal assault.'

The guards shouted outside and Richard looked to see their envoy had already returned. The Bishop of Salisbury was dripping wet with the rain and had a dour expression. 'I was only able to see the Duke of Buckingham, my lord. He asked me to tell you that the Earl of Warwick shall not come to the king's presence.'

Richard could tell there was more. 'What else?'

'He said if you come,' the bishop hesitated. 'You shall die.'

Richard shook his head. 'Buckingham's words not the kings! Did he agree to take our message to the king?'

'No. I don't think he had any intention of doing so, my lord.'

Richard appreciated his honesty. 'Thank you for your efforts, Bishop. I know you have done your best.'

The bishop took his leave. 'I must change before I catch a chill.'

They watched him go.

Edward was unsurprised. 'There's only one way you're going to get a message to the king, Richard. We'll have to take it to him personally.'

Richard had grown to like Edward's youthful exuberance. 'You're right. We have to at least try to prevent unnecessary bloodshed and anyway, it's still raining.'

✛

By one o'clock there was no sign of a break in the weather and Richard called his commanders together. He had to raise his voice to be heard over the steady drumming of the rain on the tent.

'This weather is hard for your men and horses. It also makes the king's cannon useless. Our scouts tell us their guns are mired in the mud and their crews gone.' He looked at their grim faces. 'We have to advance while we can. The road will soon be impassable. Make sure your men know we outnumber them two to one. No harm is to come to the king or to the men the queen has wrongfully conscripted to fight us. All who wear the badge of the black ragged staff are to be saved. It's the badge of Lord Grey, who will grant us entry into the king's camp. All other knights and their squires are to be killed on sight. No quarter. Understand?'

The king's longbow men added deadly arrows to the rain pouring on their enemies' heads as they advanced across the muddy field. Richard marched forward on foot, as the ground was too soft for a horse. He looked over to his flank and saw Edward plunging straight across the water filled ditch, up to his waist in the muddy brown water. He yelled at the top of his voice as he scrambled up the embankment at the head of his men, brandishing his sword and ignoring the arrows thudding into the ground all around him.

Richard's men followed, splashing through the deep ditch. The defensive earth embankment bristled with the sharply pointed wooden stakes. Designed to stop a cavalry charge, they made useful handholds for the foot soldiers, who grabbed them to stop from slipping back down the wet mud of the slope.

Richard cursed the heavy plate armour he had chosen to wear as he led his men, doing his best not to fall in the sticky brown mud. A trickle of cold rainwater had found its way into the padded lining. He lifted his visor to have a better view and saw the king's men-at-arms were waiting for them as his men crested the bank.

They clashed in brutal hand-to-hand fighting. Richard found he was being attacked by two men at once and was relieved to see Luke Tully appear at his side, using his sword with deadly efficiency as Edward had been teaching him. Despite their advantage of numbers Richard could see his men were hard pressed, yet they were steadily gaining ground. A rousing cheer made him look to see Lord Grey had been as good as his word, creating an opening in the defensive line and allowing his men to charge through to the king's camp in the Abbey fields. The battle was soon over and Richard met up with Edward, who was looking for the king.

They discovered the Duke of Buckingham lying dead inside his tent in a pool of blood. There were cuts to his hands where he had tried to fend off his attacker. His throat had been slashed so deeply his head was almost severed. More of the leading Lancastrian nobles, including Sir Thomas Percy and the Earl of Shrewsbury, were floating dead in the watery ditch. Many others had died on the muddy battlefield or drowned in the fast flowing waters of the River Nene, dragged down by the weight of their armour as they tried to escape.

King Henry was found sitting alone in his tent. He was unharmed and appeared dazed and confused, shocked by the violent scenes he had witnessed. Richard led him to nearby Delapre Abbey, where nuns took them to the cool chapel. A shrine marked the spot where the body of Queen Eleanor, wife of the first King Edward, had rested nearly two centuries

before. He knelt alongside the mumbling king and said
a prayer of thanks for the sparing of his life and their
victory that day.

Chapter 15 - Winter 1460

The joyous celebrations went on for days and Richard felt at last his luck had changed for the better. They had chosen to spend Christmas and New Year at their London mansion by the side of the Thames, which thankfully had survived the worst of the looting. Warwick Castle was stripped to the bare walls in his absence. Fortunately his merchant friends in London had kept at least one of his homes safe.

He had a successful past year to celebrate. His army returned from Northampton in triumph with the king and established a Yorkist Council with him in full control. The king allowed him to do much as he pleased now that the queen had fled with the young Prince to Harlech Castle in Wales with Sir Jasper Tudor, one of her few remaining supporters of any worth. The last he heard was she had sailed to Scotland, although from what he knew of the Scots he didn't imagine she'd find much sympathy there.

Anne and the girls had travelled with his mother from Calais for Christmas. Little Annie, his youngest daughter, was now a precocious four-year-old. She was his favourite and highly spirited, always asking questions and seeking approval, as he had done with his own father as a child. Her sister Isabel was now nine, a demure and attractive young girl, she was much more like her mother, observing and taking in every detail, yet giving little away. Margaret was now grown into a young lady. Although only thirteen, she looked older and he would soon have to think about who she could marry.

Richard thought of Megan and wondered how she was. Anne had allowed her to visit Margaret at Middleham when Richard was away, although as far as he knew Megan had never been to Warwick Castle or their home in London. He had honoured his promise to Anne that he would never see her and they had an unspoken agreement that Megan's name would never be mentioned.

Anne and his mother had been busy arranging lavish banquets and festive parties, inviting the best of London society, as well as important ambassadors from Burgundy, Italy and Germany. Now his wealth was restored he could once again afford the most expensive wine from every country in Europe and the finest minstrels played in their gallery.

The food they served was the talk of London. His kitchens worked tirelessly to produce endless courses of rare and exotic delicacies. That Christmas, in recognition of Richard's love of the sea, the banquet included fish of every kind. The giant head of a conger eel was filled with young lampreys. Live lobsters brought all the way from Cornwall were plunged into boiling water at the banqueting table and served piping hot. A whole baked porpoise needed several men to carry it to the table, to the delighted applause of his guests.

Richard felt truly relaxed for the first time in ages, finally enjoying the rewards of all his hard work. His one regret was that his uncle the Duke of York had not won over the council or the people when he returned from Ireland. The duke had left for his home at Sandal Castle to prevent his tenants from being harassed. Richard's brothers and father had travelled home to look into the rumours reaching London. It was said that Queen

Margaret was raising an army from the last remaining Lancastrian supporters in the north.

All his guests had left and Richard was enjoying having a quiet time with his family. A log fire blazed in the hearth and his daughters were playing happily with the new toys he had given them. Isabel had a perfect scale model of his flagship, complete with working rigging and little brass cannons on the deck. Annie had a beautifully carved set of wooden soldiers, led by a brightly painted knight on a white horse.

Margaret was reading a beautifully illustrated book of French poetry he'd bought her in Calais. Anne must have guessed the book was valuable yet didn't seem to mind him giving it to her. Richard looked across at Margaret as she read. She must have sensed his attention as she glanced up at him. She had the same enigmatic look in her eyes he'd found so hard to resist in her mother and he felt an unexpected sense of loss.

A noisy commotion outside the door disturbed their peace and Richard was standing up to investigate when the door burst open. His brother John stood there, his eyes red from riding hard into the wind. Richard knew at once the news was bad. He took him to his study, a large panelled room with bay windows overlooking the busy River Thames, and closed the door behind them.

His brother had never been one for words. 'I bring you the worst news, Richard. Our father is murdered. Our brother Thomas and the Duke of York are also dead.'

Richard stared out of the window, watching a small boat trying to sail up river against the current. He could feel tears welling in his eyes. The news was too much for him to take in. His father had always been so invincible. His brother Thomas had been in his study just before

Christmas, enjoying a drink with him and recalling their adventures as young boys. The Duke of York was supposed to be the next king and now he was dead.

He saw his brother was shaking with emotion. 'How did it happen?'

John wiped his eyes. 'That's the worst of it. Father was captured and held at Pontefract Castle. He somehow managed to escape and was set upon by his enemies. I don't know who they were.' He looked at Richard, a haunted expression on his face. He tried to compose himself. 'They cut off his head, Richard. Put it above the gates of York, next to the heads of our uncle and our brother.'

Richard had a whiskey decanter on his desk. Made from Venetian glass, it was engraved with his crest and had a pair of matching tumblers. He poured generous measures into the tumblers and handed one to his brother. They sat in silence for a moment, lost in memories of their father. The strong drink helped a little.

'What about Edward?' Richard spoke softly, hardly daring to know the answer.

'As far as I know he's safe. Never made it north.' John took a sip of his drink. 'His brother Edmund is also dead.' He shook his head. 'I liked him.'

'Do you know how the Duke of York died?'

'There are all sorts of stories going round. I spoke to one of the archers who escaped. He said Trollope's men wore your red livery and pretended to be reinforcements.'

Richard swore. 'That bastard Trollope. I should have had him executed!'

John crossed to the window to look out at the boats. 'Middleham Castle is yours now, Richard, and Sheriff Hutton, as well as all the lands as far as the border.' He drained his goblet and turned to Richard. 'I suppose that makes you the richest man in England?'

Richard was surprised at the note of bitterness he heard in his brother's voice and realised he was right. He would be even wealthier than the king.

'I'm sorry it had to be this way.' He looked across at John. 'I will raise an army and avenge our father. Our brother too. Queen Margaret will regret the day she ever set foot on English soil.'

Snow fell softly in St. Albans, the scene of Richard's first great victory and now the place he knew he may die. It had started so well, with his triumphant march from London to intercept the queen. His work to form an alliance with Philip of Burgundy had paid off. He detested the man yet five hundred battle hardened Burgundian soldiers now swelled the ranks of the men who came from as far as Kent to rally to his cause. The nervous Londoners raised funds to pay for equipment and supplies. The magistrates had even freed Luke Tully from his jail cell, where he had been locked up for brawling, to help rid England of the Lancastrian threat.

Richard was commanding the main army, with the Duke of Norfolk's men on his right flank and his brother John in command of the army on his left. Their spirits had been raised by recent news of Edward's victory over Jasper Tudor at Mortimer's Cross in the Welsh Marches. They could have used his army now. It was said that Edward had led the fighting himself, routing the Lancastrians with overwhelming savagery. Richard was unsurprised when he heard the news. It seemed his young friend was building quite a reputation.

Luke Tully raised his spade in greeting when he saw Richard riding up to inspect progress with defending the northern approaches to the town. His hair was longer and he'd started growing a beard to ward off the cold. Dirty and dressed in his work clothes, Tully was hard to distinguish from any of the men working on the trench.

'We've been digging for four days now, my lord.' Tully leaned on his spade and looked at his handiwork with pride. 'I hope they don't decide to turn around when they see what we've been up to!'

Richard dismounted from his warhorse to take a closer look. 'Glad to see you are providing a good example to the men, Tully.' He rubbed his hands together to warm them. 'How are your crossbowmen getting on?'

Tully picked up one of the new shields. 'It's large enough to protect a kneeling man. I've had them hammer these long nails so the points stick through.' He held it up to show Richard. 'Quite a weapon all on its own.'

'What about the caltraps?' Richard had ordered all the blacksmiths he could find in London to make him the deadly devices. If a horse or man stepped on one they would be out of the battle, possibly crippled for life or worse if the wound became infected.

Tully pointed to where sharp points could be seen poking through the dusting of snow. 'We've laid down hundreds of them.' He looked at Richard enquiringly. 'Who is going to collect them all up once we're done?'

'We'll have plenty of prisoners. It will be good to see them doing something useful before we let them go again.'

A cannon blast sounded and they both spun round to see where it had come from. The unmistakeable sounds of men yelling and fighting drifted across from the town. It seemed impossible. They had been taken by surprise.

Richard shouted. 'Trumpeters! Sound the alarm!'

Tully dropped the shield he was holding and called his men. 'Get your sallets on, men!' He pulled his own battered sallet onto his head and looked around for his sword, cast aside while he was working. 'To your weapons! We're under attack! '

Richard mounted his horse and galloped back towards the town, joining the other knights, who were responding to the sounds of fighting. As he rode he wondered how the queen's men could have possibly have got past without being seen by his lookouts. He charged into the town and headed towards the battle.

The narrow street ahead was filled with men fighting hand-to-hand. Powerful memories of his first battle in St. Albans came flooding back. Above the fighting Richard saw the archers he had stationed in the upper floors of houses were picking their targets with care, killing one of the enemy with every shot at such close range. His barricades were well built and doing their work. The problem was that too many of his men were still far away at the northern defences.

A man screamed in agony and fell backwards as an arrow struck him in the neck, another immediately taking his place. Then the barricade across the road gave way with the sound of splintering wood and yelling men surged through, brandishing halberds. Richard drew his sword and charged them, slashing viciously left and right.

He was losing control of the town. The queen's men must have marched through the night, arriving from the north-west much earlier than expected. She had caught him unprepared. The only thing to do was to ride back and rally his men. All their work on the northern defences was wasted. Worse still, the men were spread out over a wide front. He would struggle to organise them to defend the town.

He recognised the commander on his right flank, Sir John Mowbray, Duke of Norfolk, close by and rode up to him. 'What happened?'

The duke had been wounded in the face and was without his helmet. 'The men from Kent.' He wiped at the blood on his injured cheek and winced with pain. 'That bastard Lovelace has betrayed us and let the queen's cavalry through our line.' He shook his head. 'There were hundreds of them.'

Richard was astounded that the steward of his own household, Henry Lovelace, had been one of the queen's men all along. His disloyalty might have cost them the battle.

'My brother?' Richard had put Lovelace under John's command.

'I haven't seen him. I'm sorry, Richard.'

Richard saw his men were gathered ready to advance on the town.

'Wish me luck, Sir John.' He turned as he was about to go. 'Get yourself to the rear-guard. Take care!'

Richard led his mounted knights in a second charge at the enemy soldiers spilling from the town towards them. This time their fighting had the edge of desperation and men fell wounded and dying as they broke through. An arrow cracked off his breastplate with a violent metallic thud. The enemy kept on coming and Richard realised he was outnumbered. Reluctantly, he ordered the trumpeters to sound the retreat.

He waited in his furthest defences on the outskirts of the town. Scouts had been sent to see if the king was still in their keeping. After all the preparation and planning, he realised his life depended now on what he decided to do.

A familiar voice called out behind him. He turned to see Tully wearing his mail coat and carrying an expensive sword. Richard guessed he'd taken it from one of their attackers. Tully's red Warwick surcoat was ripped and he had lost his helmet in the fighting.

'You took a bit of tracking down, my lord.'

Richard was pleased to see a familiar face. He looked at the sky. 'The light is failing. We could be overrun once darkness falls.'

Tully was silent for a moment, scanning the dusk for any sign of movement. 'The men fought bravely today, my lord.'

Richard realised even Tully was starting to feel demoralised. 'They did.' He shook his head. 'We were betrayed again, Tully. And we are outnumbered. I don't know how the queen raised such an army.'

'It's getting colder.' Tully rubbed his hands. 'The men will be hungry.'

He knew what Tully was saying. The men were suffering in the relentless winter winds. Despite the harsh penalties for desertion they would soon start slipping away, knowing this battle was lost.

A movement caught his eye and his hand went instinctively to the hilt of his sword.

Tully pointed. 'It's only some of our scouts returning.'

They watched as the men came within hailing distance. 'What news?'

'They have taken the king, my lord. His guards are held prisoner and the town is lost.'

Richard cursed the queen and all she stood for. He should have left the king in the safety of the Tower. It had been an act of bravado to bring him with them and now he would pay the price. Few were loyal to the queen, yet he had seen how easily men would rally to the call of even such a weak king.

He called to Tully. 'Tell our trumpeters to sound the retreat. We must withdraw while we can.'

'We've lost, my lord?'

'We've lost this battle, Tully, not the war.'

As they rode in the darkness Richard looked back over his shoulder through the drifting snowflakes. There was no sign of anyone following them, although he could see flickering fires in the town of St. Albans. The aftermath of the battle would be looting and destruction. He had heard stories of how the Lancastrian army had pillaged and raped as they passed through towns and villages on the way to the city. He decided he must play on people's fears and make sure there was no welcome for the queen when she arrived in London.

They rode back through the night and found Edward's army. Edward was in celebratory mood after his victory at Mortimer's Cross. Richard listened to his account of the battle, where he'd had revenge for the death of his father by beheading Owen Tudor. Edward's mood changed once he heard what had happened at St. Albans.

Richard looked at Edward. He was no longer the boy he had first met. 'It's time, Edward. The people need a king who can sort this country out once and for all. Not one who is half mad and can't even rule over his wife!'

Edward looked at him for a moment and Richard wondered if he was remembering how they had planned this when they sailed around Lands' End in heavy weather. That seemed long ago now. Both of them had lost their fathers and a brother to Queen Margaret and he wanted vengeance.

'I'm ready, if you would have me as your king?'

Richard put his hand on Edward's shoulder. 'You are the king now. Wait here until I send for you.'

'Where are you going?'

'To London. To rally support for a new king!'

Richard began gathering supporters as soon as they reached London. The queen was still in St. Albans, her army preferring to pillage the town and in no hurry to enter the city. He couldn't believe his luck. She had let him get away. If he moved fast, there was time to put his plan into action.

He addressed the large gathering of worried Londoners. Nobles and merchants, soldiers and commoners had assembled to hear what he had to say.

'The queen and her army of thieves will be here soon, banging on your doors.' He paused, raising his voice so they could all hear. 'Are you going to stand by and let her take all you have worked for?'

Their reply was as he expected.

'Do you think this vengeful French Queen will look mercifully on those who sent her fleeing for her life?'

The mutter of dissent grew into a roar of disapproval.

One of the merchants shouted support. 'We must not let her into our city!'

Richard drew his sword and held it high for them to see. 'We are not defeated. Henry has recognised Edward of York as the rightful heir!'

The people cheered, calling out Edward's name.

Richard raised his sword again. 'With our new king we can keep our enemies from the gates of London!'

They knew the truth of what he said. Although many of them had sworn loyalty to Henry they were tired of living in the shadow of the Lancastrian threat. Many of Richard's men had been killed or wounded at St. Albans, with more than a thousand either deserted or taken prisoner. Now with Edward's army, he had more than enough to hold the capital. Word soon spread and more knights rallied to the cause, eager to be on the winning side.

He sent word to Edward, who rode into London with twenty thousand knights and forty thousand men in his silver and blue livery, the banners of York and his many supporters flying proudly. Richard had arranged for him to give thanks at St. Paul's and take the throne at Westminster Abbey. Richard watched proudly as his new king refused to be crowned until he had rid them of the Lancastrian threat.

The queen's men arrived too late. London was barred to her. Even when her envoys used King Henry's name the reply was the same. Now Richard knew he could pursue Queen Margaret of Anjou and deal with her. The time had come for a new king to show he could truly lead his people. Although he was only eighteen, Edward had proved he was ready to take the throne.

The men sang a bawdy marching song at the tops of their voices, in high spirits as they marched north, defying the bitterly cold wind. The Lancastrians were in retreat and were causing havoc and destruction as they went. The last reports were they had been camped near the River Aire in Yorkshire. Richard led the vanguard and reached the Ferrybridge, a small town on the great north road and an important crossing point to Pontefract Castle. The queen's men had destroyed the old stone bridge to slow them down. There was no other place to cross, so Richard's men had to close the gaps with wooden planks.

A yell from one of the men working on the bridge was followed by a splash as he fell into the freezing water.

Arrows filled the air. They had fallen into a deadly trap. Lancastrian archers were waiting for them and many more fell dead into the icy river before Richard rallied his men and managed to cross the makeshift bridge. They charged the enemy and were confronted by a determined rear-guard, left behind to slow their pursuit. The sheer weight of numbers meant the battle was short lived.

Richard set up camp on the north bank of the river. His men lit fires, tended to the wounded and settled down for the night. Richard and his commanders found lodgings at the inn in the town. Aware he was close to where his father had been killed by Lancastrian supporters, he took care to ensure his personal guard were alert and ready if needed.

He was woken early. 'My lord! We are under attack!'

Richard began strapping on his armour. 'Have my horse ready, be quick.'

He rushed back to the camp to find a full scale battle raging. Men in his red livery lay dead and dying. Once again, he had let the queen's men take him by surprise. Archers mounted on horseback were circling and firing a relentless hail of arrows from all directions, firing at close range at Richard's men with devastating effect.

Richard yelled as an agonising sharp stabbing pain told him he'd been hit. Glancing down, he saw the shaft of an arrow sticking from his leg. The bodkin arrowhead had pierced the closed greave on his leg, his armour slowing the force of the impact. He couldn't fight on with the wound and ordered the retreat, riding in search of someone to help remove the arrow.

✝

He recovered consciousness and realised Tully was carefully bandaging his leg.

'I caught an arrow.' His voice sounded hoarse and weak.

Tully continued winding the bandage. 'I was there when they took it out. You were lucky, it came out cleanly.'

Richard winced as Tully pulled the bandage tight. 'It hurt like hell!'

'They cauterised your wound.'

He remembered now. He had felt the numbing heat of the glowing red poker. Followed by the sickening smell of his flesh burning before he passed out.

He smiled weakly. 'Not the best start to our new campaign.'

Tully looked serious. 'We were ambushed by Sir Thomas Clifford's archers, my lord.'

'How many men have we lost?'

'A few hundred dead. Many more wounded, like you.'

Richard closed his eyes. He needed to recover his strength. His dreams were full of images of men with arrows sticking from their bodies. He tried to push away a horrific image of his father's severed head on a pike at the gates of York. The eyes were wide open and looking at him, accusingly. He woke in a feverish sweat, wondering where he was.

When Edward arrived with his main army Richard was well enough to ride out to meet him. Although still freezing cold, the sky was bright and clear. All traces of the battle were gone, except for the ruined bridge and the newly dug soil of mass graves.

Edward looked fresh, despite his long ride. He frowned at the bandage Richard still wore on his leg in place of his protective greave. 'You look like hell, Richard, how are you?'

Richard was glad to see Edward again. 'At least I have some good news. My uncle, Lord Fauconberg took his cavalry upstream. They crossed at Castleford and pursued Lord Clifford. He's dead. Killed by an arrow in the throat.'

'Now we must find the rest of them.' Edward sounded like his father.

'Scouts came back this morning. They are close by, Edward. At Towton.'

Chapter 16 ~ Spring 1461

They spent a cold and miserable night with little shelter from the flurries of snow that showed winter was refusing to give way to spring. Richard wished for the warm bed and roaring log fire he'd left behind in London. He missed the comfortable fur-lined cloak he liked to wear. His armour did little to keep out the cold, although he was grateful for the thick wool padding underneath. His breath turned to white clouds in the frosted air and tiny flakes of snow glistened in the thick dark mane of his horse.

He shifted in his saddle to ease the throbbing pain of the slowly healing wound in his leg. This battle would decide the rest of his life and which of the two kings would rule. To win would mean a glorious return to his family in London, to King Edward's triumphant coronation. To lose would mean a quick death, if he was fortunate, or a slow one if he was not. Worst of all, the whole country would suffer the misrule of their French Queen and her self-serving council.

Richard knew the area they were in well. He was so close to home he could almost have enjoyed the comforts at Sheriff Hutton, instead of sleeping rough in a freezing cold field with his men. It still seemed strange to him that he now owned Sheriff Hutton and Middleham Castle. He felt a sudden wave of sadness as he thought of how his father had died for the cause.

The sleepy village of Towton lay north of the battlefield, along the old London Road. His enemies now stood between him and the city of York, where King Henry cowered with his queen and their son Edward, the Lancastrian heir to the throne. Richard shivered as he remembered that York was also where his poor father's head had been impaled on a pike at Mickelgate Bar, next to the heads of his brother and the Duke of York.

The thought should have made him even more ready for the fight. It didn't, as instead Richard found himself wondering if this was to be his last battle. He looked out at the Lancastrian army facing them now across the snow-covered dale. Three times as many banners flew there as were flying for Edward. There could hardly be a noble family in the land not represented on one side or the other.

He breathed deeply of the cold northern air and reminded himself there was still much to do. He had yet to make good his promise to his father. He had no son and heir. There was also the need to find suitable husbands for his daughters. He looked across to where Edward was rallying his men and made a mental note to discuss Isabel with him. She was only ten, half his age, although that wouldn't matter if he could persuade Edward to wait a few years. Not for the first time he wished Edward could marry his daughter Margaret. She had just turned thirteen and was every bit as pretty as her mother, with her father's sense of adventure. Perfect for Edward in almost every way.

He cursed under his breath and looked out again across the snow-blanketed fields. The young Lancastrian commander Henry Beaufort, Duke of Somerset, had chosen their high ground well. His men were arranged in deep ranks on the north side of the valley, their flanks protected by waterlogged marshes. The steep, wooded banks of the river known as Cock Beck meandered between them, a natural barrier.

Richard rode along the ranks of his waiting men, nodding to those he recognised and raising a gauntleted hand in thanks for the loyalty of those he didn't. A few paces behind him followed his faithful squire Luke Tully, hardly recognisable in his new armour, and a soldier carrying his banner of the bear and ragged staff. He stopped in the centre and turned to address his men.

'This day history will be made. You are to give no quarter. We have marched a long way to let them escape us and fight another day.' He pointed to where Edward sat proudly under the royal banner. 'You fight for your new king. The rightful heir to the throne, King Edward of E/ngland.' He looked at their frozen faces. 'God is on our side!'

A rousing cheer went up from the men, turning heads all over the battlefield.

'A Warwick!' More men joined in to the call until it rang out across the valley.

'A Warwick!' They hammered noisily on their armour to show they were in good spirits despite the relentless cold wind that chilled them to the bone.

Richard ordered the trumpet call to ready for action and his army formed up in ranks opposite their enemies as heavy flakes of snow began to fall. Rows of his best archers marched to the front, then battle-hardened men-at-arms with heavy bills and poleaxes. His mounted cavalry waited in the rear, the heat from the flanks of their warhorses rising as steam in the freezing air.

Richard was proud of the men who followed him yet still had a nagging concern at the back of his mind. He wondered how many of them shared his secret fear that they would not see another day. The strength of their enemy bothered him. In the cut and thrust of close hand-to-hand fighting, numbers mattered more than skill with a sword.

He turned to Tully, keeping his voice low. 'We look outnumbered yet again, Tully. Is there no sign of Sir John De Mowbray?'

Tully frowned. 'Not yet, my lord.'

'Have you seen whose banner is on their right wing?'

'Henry Percy, Earl of Northumberland!'

'Yes, and somewhere out there is that bastard Trollope.'

'It seems Somerset is waiting for us to make the first move.'

'Then let's not disappoint him, Tully.' He drew his sword and raised the shining blade high so Edward could see his men were ready.

His father's younger brother William, Lord Fauconberg, commanded the archers. A tough soldier, he was well respected by the men. William fought with King Henry V and helped bring the king's body back to England when he died at the siege of Meaux. Now he was dressed in his old-fashioned, heavy armour and mounted on a fully armoured war horse, flanked by his squires and a man carrying his colourful banner. He reminded Richard of one of the knights in the illustrated books of chivalry he had read as a child.

Lord Fauconberg acknowledged Richard's sign and looked across to see Edward also draw his sword and hold it high in the air, the signal he'd been waiting for.

'Archers! Step forward!' A thousand men brought their powerful longbows up to position, pointing arrows up into the grey-blue sky. Richard noted that the icy wind was freshening and to their advantage.

Lord Fauconberg shouted to the archers, his deep voice echoing across the field. 'Nock!' He made sure they were all ready. 'Draw!' A forest of powerful longbows were drawn as one. 'Loose!'

The sharp whoosh of a thousand arrows being unleashed was followed by a moment of silence as they flew in a high arc, carried by the wind to strike deep into the rows of men on the opposite slope. Sharpened bodkin arrow heads pierced Lancastrian armour like daggers through paper. Anguished cries of pain from wounded and dying men drifted across the shallow valley to Richard and he knew they had passed the point of no return.

The archers watched closely to judge the range of their first shot, then began to empty their quivers of arrows in a fluid motion, the best of them managing to loose a dozen arrows in a minute. Richard watched as the Lancastrian forces suffered heavy casualties before they had even moved. Great swathes of the enemy ranks collapsing in shouts of pain and panic as the men at the front lost their nerve against the relentless onslaught.

The freezing wind blew harder now and returning Lancastrian arrows fell short, slowed by the wind against them and blown off course. Richard watched with grim satisfaction as the white expanse of virgin snow ahead of his men was soon bristling with arrows sticking harmlessly into the ground.

Lord Fauconberg was ready and shouted again in his loud baritone voice.

'Archers! Advance!' The line of bowmen stepped forward into the snow, firing their six-foot longbows as they went. Richard watched as many casually bent to pull the Lancastrian arrows sticking from the ground and fired them back where they had come from.

Their plan had worked. The Duke of Somerset showed his inexperience of command by ordering his army to advance down from their high position to the plateau of the open field. This was what Richard had been waiting for.

'Trumpeters, sound the advance!'

The shrill sound carried well and the archers moved aside as they heard the signal to let the men-at-arms pass. The heavily armoured men carried long bill hooks and poleaxes that could wound and maim without even coming in range of a sword. Used with both hands the savage poleaxes could slice even a helmeted skull in two with one blow. A hammer on one side could deliver a crushing blow and many had a sharp spike on the top which made them potent thrusting weapons.

As the men-at-arms were marching to engage the enemy Richard saw a sudden flurry of movement to his side. The Lancastrians had been saving a deadly surprise for his men.

'Cavalry! To the left flank!' Richard shouted a warning as hundreds of mounted knights swept from their hiding place in the trees with a thunder of hooves on the frozen ground. Swinging heavy broadswords and deadly maces they cut into the men on the ground, hammering forward, killing as they went. Others carried long lances that speared through men before they even had a chance to fight.

Richard saw Edward in the thick of the fighting, surrounded on all sides. He could hear Edward's voice shouting for his men to stand and fight. Archers loosed their arrows into the enemy horses at close range, causing them to wildly rear in panic, throwing their riders to the ground and trampling over men with their iron-shod hooves. Even as those at the front fell, more appeared from behind and Richard felt a familiar sense of foreboding as he realised how badly they were outnumbered. His men were being steadily pushed back. Some had already turned and run off.

He called to Tully and they charged into the fray, hacking at the heads of the men trying to pull them from their horses, ever wary of the ground that was now slippery with blood spilling into the melting snow and ice. Richard felt a sharp thump as a crossbow bolt glanced off his armour. He saw Tully's horse go down, mortally wounded by a savage blow to its chest from a bill hook. Tully rolled as he fell and sprang to his feet, ready with his sword as two men attacked him at once.

Richard raced to his rescue, slashing at one of them and deliberately riding over him as Tully speared the other in the neck with the point of his sword. The fighting was relentless and desperate, with more men pressing forward as the York army was driven back up the slope. A shrill trumpet blast sounded close by and for a second Richard thought it marked the retreat. He looked to the high southern ridge behind them as the Duke of Norfolk's men charged in to join them. Now the Lancastrians desperately tried to hold their ground. Although the duke's men had been on a long march they were fresh to the battle and routed the tiring soldiers, who had been fighting for hours.

The Lancastrian line broke as men began to run for their lives. Richard's men started shouting his old battle cry as they realised the day was won.

'A Warwick!' The call became a roar across the battlefield. 'A Warwick!'

They ran in pursuit of the fleeing enemy. Some tried to surrender, throwing down their weapons. They were cut down without mercy. Richard looked across the snowy field and knew the tide had turned. Edward was still high on his horse, rallying his men, his royal standard flying proudly next to that of his father.

Richard knew Edward's father would have been proud to see his son. He made his way through the dead and dying men towards his new king. The ground was littered with abandoned weapons and armour cast away by the Lancastrians as they ran. In the distance he saw the battle was not yet over for some.

Shouts rang out in the frozen air as commanders encouraged their men.

'No quarter!'

They chased the fleeing army towards the fast-flowing river, where many were swept away in the icy water. Archers fired at the running men, choosing their targets with deadly efficiency. One by one the last of the Lancastrians fell, bodies twisting with the impact of each blow. Richard looked around him. There was no sign of Tully and he felt a pang of sadness. He was going to miss Luke Tully, his loyal companion for so many years, one man he could always trust.

Groups of soldiers were already busy stripping the dead of their armour, the reward for risking their lives for the new king. They showed little respect for those who had no further use for their armour or weapons. Richard recognised one of the half-naked corpses lying in a dark red circle of his own blood in the snow. Andrew Trollope stared up at him with sightless eyes. He had finally paid for his treachery at Ludlow field and his part in the murder of Richard's father and the Duke of York, although he felt little satisfaction. Whoever removed his armour must have also recognised Trollope and had cut off his nose as a final punishment.

Richard could see their new king enjoying his moment of victory in the distance, surrounded by cheering men as he gave a victory speech. Richard knew he should have been elated at their triumph against such odds, to see the Lancastrians well and truly defeated. Instead he felt cold and tired. He couldn't remember when he last had a hot meal and the dull ache from his wounded leg troubled him.

Before he left for York Richard called to visit the windswept tents where the wounded were being tended by nuns from the convent. It saddened him to see some of his men who were plainly never going to recover from their wounds. He did his best to thank them for their service and was about to leave when a familiar voice called out.

'My lord, the battle is won, the war is not!'

He turned to see Luke Tully, his head bandaged, his grin a sign that he would soon recover.

Richard laughed with relief. 'Tully, you bastard, I thought you were dead!'

Richard rode at Edward's side, followed by their battle weary army through the gates of York, stopping to reverently oversee the removal of the heads from the Micklegate Bar. They already knew that Henry and his Queen had fled the city with the young Edward, Prince of Wales. It seemed impossible that the Duke of Somerset could have escaped the carnage at Towton, yet despite a careful search his body had not been found. They also knew that Queen Margaret would already be planning her next move.

Edward had to be crowned before the people would truly recognise him as king. Richard's brother John was left to deal with the Scots as best he could while he returned to London to organise the coronation. He had a hero's welcome, as rumours had somehow reached Anne that he was badly wounded. She was so relieved to see him safe and well she broke down in tears. He had little time to spend with his family, as the parliament was in disarray and many people needed to be won over to King Edward.

In late June, Edward's grand coronation procession made its way through the streets of London, to the adoration of cheering crowds. In full armour of burnished silver and gold, with victories at Mortimers Cross and Towton behind him, Edward was everything King Henry had failed to be. Richard rode proudly behind the king with his personal guard in fine red tunics and the long flowing banners of Warwick and York flying high.

At Westminster Abbey Thomas Bourchier, Archbishop of Canterbury, placed the crown of state on Edward's head and made him King of England. Richard watched from the side with Anne, just as he had at the coronation of Queen Margaret. So much had happened in those intervening years yet so much was still the same. Even as he watched Edward being crowned, he realised Margaret was still Queen, still a real threat to them all.

The wine flowed freely at the grand coronation banquet in the great hall and there was much merrymaking. The king's champion, Sir Thomas Dymoke, rode noisily into the hall in full armour on his warhorse. Throwing down his gauntlet, as required by the old tradition, he challenged all who disputed Edward's right to the throne to do battle with him.

Edward now rewarded those who had been loyal to him, knighting and giving new titles to his followers. His mother and two brothers had returned from exile and he made twelve year old George the Duke of Clarence, and nine year old Richard, Duke of Gloucester. Richard's brother John was rewarded for his courage with the title of Lord Montague. His brother George became Lord Chancellor of England, a position formerly held by his father.

Richard looked at the new king at the head of the table and recalled his own moment of self-doubt on the snowy battlefield at Towton. He still had much to do. The old King must be recaptured and held somewhere safe where he could do no harm. Queen Margaret could be allowed to return to Anjou with her son, if she would promise to never return. Most importantly of all, Edward must be found a wife, a Queen fit for such a king. He stroked his beard and wondered where he should start.

Chapter 17 - Autumn 1462

Richard rode to Middleham Castle as soon as he heard of his mother's illness. As always he travelled with his personal guard, a mounted force of his most loyal men. He had learned the value of what some called showmanship and the need to give people something to cheer about. He was now one of the richest men in the country and considered it a good investment to provide his men with fine black horses and red livery trimmed with gold braid. Scouts and heralds were sent ahead and fanfares played, so that each town they passed through became another opportunity to build his popularity.

Richard now liked to dress well and had black plate armour specially made by the best craftsmen in Germany. The black breastplate was cleverly designed to accentuate his muscular physique and he wore it now as much for show as for protection. He only used his heavy gold chain of office on state occasions although he always wore his sword and dagger. They were a reminder that although his time was mostly spent dealing with matters of diplomacy and the politics of state, he was still a warrior knight.

It had been a busy year for Richard, as Edward had asked him to take full control of the new reforms. He steadily replaced the council of selfish nobles and dithering clerics with respected men of learning and ability, including some of the most powerful merchants in London. They had rewarded him by bringing the finances of the country back from the brink of disaster and restoring confidence in parliament.

Now he could focus on his other great responsibility, the defence of the country. The threat from the north still hung over them like an ominous black cloud. King Edward decreed that Richard was to have whatever resources he needed to ensure the safety of England. As well as maintaining the largest standing army ever seen in peacetime, he continued to build his fleet at Sandwich and kept them in readiness as a precaution against an invasion from France.

He was welcomed by his brother John, who had become his right hand man and guardian of his estates in the north. John had always been the one who looked most like their father and now he had the same heavy build and assertive confidence. His voice had even taken on the same gruff tone that commanded unquestioning obedience. Richard was glad he could rely on his brother, who never showed resentment or complained at the huge disparity of their wealth.

Richard dismounted and handed the reins of his horse to a waiting groom. He pulled off his black leather gauntlets and shook his brother warmly by the hand.

'It's good to see you again, John.'

'You too, Richard.' He watched the army of men riding through the gates and filling the courtyard. 'Have you brought Anne and the girls?'

'Yes, and we have a special guest.' He turned to watch the fine coaches following his men.

'Edward has entrusted me with the wardship of his young brother Richard.' He looked with mock seriousness at John. 'I think he wants us to make a man of him.'

'That's not a problem, if he has an ounce of his father's spirit!'

They watched as the black and gold coaches drew near, each pulled by a fine team of black horses and driven by liveried coachmen. First Anne, then Isabel and little Annie and finally Margaret were helped down by a footman. Richard felt a momentary pang of recognition as he saw Margaret, now fourteen and the image of her mother. They all wore fashionable silk dresses, with tall veiled hats that made them look older than they were. Anne wore a necklace of diamonds with a heavy solitaire pendant that flashed as it caught the late autumn sunlight.

Their young guest hesitantly climbed down and joined them. He was dressed in black and carried a sword that looked too long for him, its tip nearly touching the ground. He regarded them with the same questioning expression that reminded Richard this was the son of his uncle, the Duke of York. At his brother's coronation the ten-year-old Richard had been named Duke of Gloucester as well as being made a knight.

John welcomed them. 'Welcome back. Mother will be so glad to see you all.'

He took the trouble to shake hands with Richard. 'Welcome to Middleham, Sir Richard. You've grown into a fine young man.'

The young Duke shook his hand. 'I am honoured, Lord Montague.'

'Are you good in the saddle, Richard?'

'Yes, my lord.' His voice was clear and confident.

John looked appraisingly at the young Duke. 'We must ride together.'

Anne put her hand on his arm. 'How is your mother, John?'

'Some days she is better than others.' John frowned and turned to Richard. 'The physicians don't seem to know what to do. They bleed her every day yet still she worsens.'

Richard brushed the road dirt from his sleeves. 'Take me to her, John.'

✠

The room was lit by the glow of beeswax candles which burned with a clear, bright flame and flickered gently in the cool air coming through the partly open window. A vase of freshly cut long-stemmed white roses stood on a table by her bed. Richard picked up their delicate scent and remembered they were his mother's favourite. Someone had gone to a lot of trouble to find them so late in the season. Next to the roses on the table was a miniature portrait of his father. He was surprised at the powerful mix of emotions he felt as he glanced at the picture.

His mother reached out and took Richard's hand in her weak grasp. She smiled up at him from her bed. She looked pale and thin. John told him she had hardly left her room for weeks now, relying on her servants for everything. He knew as soon as he looked at her that she didn't have long.

'Thank you for coming, Richard.' Her voice was a whisper.

'How are you feeling?' He put his hand to her brow to see if she felt feverish. Her forehead was cool to his touch, as if life had already passed from her.

'There are some things I want to tell you, Richard.'

He could see speaking was an effort for her now. 'You need to rest for now, Mother.'

'I wanted to thank you for making me sail with you to Calais on that ship.' Her eyes shone with the memory. 'That voyage was a great adventure. It helped me understand how much you have achieved.'

Richard looked at his mother and wished he had not always been so busy. He should have spent more time with her. 'I didn't think you would come.' He forced a smile, remembering how stubborn she had been.

'I want you to know something, Richard, about your father. He was proud of all our children.' Her eyes twinkled in the candle light. 'He was especially proud of you.'

Richard struggled to control his emotions. 'I miss him. We all do.'

His mother was silent for a moment, seemingly lost in her memories. She looked into his eyes. 'You should know. Megan has been so kind to me.'

'Megan?' He was confused. He hadn't seen Megan for years.

'Yes. She came here when she heard about your father. Megan has been looking after me since your father died.'

'Megan is here now?'

'Yes. Take care of her, Richard.' She looked at him as she had when he was a boy. 'I'm glad you listened to me.'

For a second he saw the strong woman she had been.

Richard was out riding with John when they saw someone on a fast horse charging towards Middleham. It could be important news so they headed back to the castle to investigate. The messenger proved to be one of Richard's informers from France, come in person rather than entrusting his news to a messenger. Richard met him alone in his study.

'Queen Margaret sailed from Harfleur with a fleet of over forty ships, my lord.'

Richard did a quick calculation. Forty ships were enough to carry an army. Not enough to threaten London although if they took one of the Channel ports by surprise they could be a serious threat.

'How long ago?'

'A week, my lord.'

'My God!' He was thinking fast. She clearly hadn't crossed the Channel.

'Do you know where she was headed?'

'North, my lord. We think for Scotland.'

'They got past our patrols at Calais?' He was thinking aloud now.

'They sailed under the command of Marshal Pierre de Breze.'

'Marshal de Breze knows to avoid Calais. I saw him off from there once.'

'What are they planning?'

'That's all I can tell you. I don't think even the crew knew where they were sailing,'

'Thank you anyway. I appreciate the warning.'

He paid the messenger in gold coins for his trouble and watched him go. It seemed Queen Margaret managed to surprise him every time he thought his life had settled down. He had to admire her determination. Even now Edward had been crowned she was still clinging on to the idea of her son one day taking the throne. He called for his brother and told him the news.

'We have to go north, John.' He stared out of the window into the courtyard below where his girls were playing a game with young Duke Richard.

'How long do we have?'

Richard turned from the window and frowned. 'I wish I knew, John. The worst of it is that she seems to finally have the backing of the French. I'll send word to the king in London for him to bring as many men as he can. My guess is that she's planning to land somewhere up the coast and will try to win back her army.'

John knew what he was saying. 'We still don't have control of the far north, or Wales, come to that.'

'It's going to be up to us to hold them off for as long as we can. Whatever the cost.'

'There is a way we can do it. If we take one of the northern castles we can use it as a base to rally our supporters.'

Richard agreed. 'The worst thing we can do is sit here and wait while they consolidate their position.'

The impressive outline of Warkworth Castle loomed like a stone cliff over the town in the early dawn mist. Richard had never been so close to the home of his old rivals in the north before. In the heartland of the Percy family, this was their home and would have been a dangerous place for a Neville to be caught off guard. Richard immediately saw why Sir Henry 'Hotspur' Percy had originally chosen Warkworth as his base. The high, rocky site had the benefit of natural defences, with the river Coquet on three sides, less than a mile from Warkworth harbour on the Northumberland coast.

Encouraged by the news that King Edward was on his way north with an army of more than forty thousand men, they had chosen Warkworth as the ideal location from which to halt the Lancastrian invasion. Marching ninety miles directly north of Middleham Castle, Richard's men had silently moved into position by the dim light of a quarter moon, sealing off the lanes into the town and effectively surrounding the castle.

Richard studied the three-story stronghold for signs of life. Only the tall central tower with its Percy standard flying on top showed any lights. He guessed these were where lookouts were posted. Whoever the men were, they had failed. His brother John returned and gave him a grin and thumbs up sign to show his men were also ready.

Richard had sent Tully and some men from his personal guard to the Anglo-Saxon church of St. Lawrence in the village. They had roused the grumbling old priest from his bed and he now stood terrified between two burly soldiers, apparently fearing for his life. Richard signalled for them to let him go.

'I'm sorry to have disturbed you. I had good reason.' He pointed up at the castle. 'You might be able to help me save a lot of lives.'

The priest still looked dazed. 'What do you mean, my lord?'

'Can you see how many men we have?'

The priest glanced around. Richard's men were behind every tree, heavily armed and ready to fight. As he was led to their position he would have also passed Richard's cavalry, waiting in fields, as well as the hundreds of archers his brother John had brought from Middleham.

'I want you to go to the castle. Tell them they are completely surrounded.' He looked at the sky. The sun was starting to show in the east. 'I'm not a vengeful man, so I'm giving them the chance to surrender. You can give them my word. On my honour they will not be harmed if they do. Understand?'

'Yes, my lord.'

The priest looked unhappy at his task and was about to go and turned to Richard. 'Who are you, sir? They will want to know who it is that has them surrounded.'

'You can tell them I am the Earl of Warwick. They may like to know that King Edward will also be here soon, with his entire army of fifty thousand men.'

Richard watched him go and muttered a prayer under his breath. Warkworth Castle was probably the most easily defended fortress in the whole of the north. He had no information about how many men were in the castle. There was still no news of how far away Queen Margaret's army was or if she had even raised an army. If he had to take the castle by force, they could have supplies to withstand a siege all through the winter. The thought of that didn't appeal to him at all and he found himself remembering the icy conditions at Towton.

Tully pointed as lights began flickering at several of the castle windows. It could mean the priest was now there with his offer of amnesty. Richard looked across to where his brother John was waiting, a tense expression on his face. An audacious plan, it could work. If it didn't, all they would have lost was the element of surprise.

As Richard was starting to wonder if the priest was ever going to return, they had their answer. The Percy standard flying from the high tower was lowered. He ordered his men to form up in ranks, men-at-arms to the front, archers providing cover and the cavalry of mounted knights to the rear. They cautiously approached the massive stone gatehouse in the centre of the south curtain wall. The drawbridge was down and the huge iron portcullis had been raised. It could be a trap. Ahead, in the centre of the castle courtyard, stood the commander of the garrison, unarmed and ready to surrender.

Richard rode across the drawbridge with a clatter of hooves, following his men-at-arms, who had secured the entrance. The men looked tense as he approached the grim-faced garrison commander. Many of the men seemed as if they had rushed from their beds. Some still carried weapons and appeared unsure of what would happen next.

'In the name of King Edward, rightful King of England, I accept the surrender of the garrison.'

The garrison commander stepped forward and Richard saw the priest from the village waiting behind him. 'You will allow my men to leave for the coast?'

Richard nodded. 'I gave my word. Tell your men to lay down their arms. If any of them wish to remain, in the service of King Edward, they will be well rewarded.'

The garrison commander ordered his men to surrender and handed the massive iron keys of the castle to Richard. Those of his men who were still armed laid them to the ground. A few mercenaries who must have had no particular loyalty to the Percy family formed a group by the keep, ready to join Richard's men.

The soldiers of the former garrison marched out of the castle and down the road towards the sea. One of Richard's men let out a spontaneous cheer, that was soon picked up by the others and soon the high curtain walls rang to the sound.

'A Warwick! A Warwick!'

✝

Their plan had been an even greater success than Richard had dared to hope. Without a single arrow being shot they had secured the grandest of the northern castles and gained a base from which to besiege Alnwick. His brother

John was appointed garrison commander and ordered a full accounting of the arms and provisions they had secured. As well as the castle, Richard found he had secured valuable bronze cannons, ammunition and gunpowder, as well as enough arrows to last them well into the following year.

He established his own quarters in one of the upper storey rooms in the tall central tower, with panoramic views across the town of Warkworth all the way to the sea. The old stone walls of his room had heavy tallow candles set in iron brackets and he watched as one of his servants lit them from a taper. An old tapestry of a wild boar hunt hung on one wall. It had seen better days although he realised it must have once been expensive. He ran his fingers over the surface of the ancient oak table, feeling the scars of the centuries and wondered if this was the same room Henry 'Hotspur' Percy had planned his rebellion against King Henry IV sixty years before.

Richard stood looking into the night from his window and wondered if he had been too generous letting the garrison go free. He unbuckled his sword belt, removed the breastplate he was still wearing and loosened his tunic. The sun was setting after a long day and he felt tired. He had chosen the room because it had a comfortable looking bunk behind an old velvet curtain where he hoped to have a peaceful night's sleep. He checked the feather-filled mattress for bed bugs and not finding any was settling down when there was a firm knock at his door.

A letter had arrived from Anne. It had been sent soon after they had left for the north. Anne was in the habit of writing to him if he was away for more than two or three weeks. He'd only been gone a couple of days, so Richard guessed the contents before he even read her neatly written words. His mother was dead.

He read Anne's letter a second time. His mother had passed away peacefully in her sleep soon after Richard and John left for the north. Richard knew even if he had been at Middleham there was nothing he could have done. All the same he was angry at Queen Margaret for robbing him of the precious last few hours with his mother and swore to have his revenge.

Chapter 18 - Winter 1463

Warkworth Castle proved to be the ideal base from which Richard and his brother John could lay siege to the other northern castles. Easily supplied by sea, Richard could ride out and check on progress with the sieges, returning to Warkworth before nightfall. He found the well-appointed apartments to his liking and kept a roaring log fire burning in the huge stone fireplace in his room.

The massive stone fortress of Bamburgh Castle was on the Northumberland coast twenty-five miles directly north of Warkworth. Richard had spent weeks laying it to siege the previous year, only to see it lost as soon as he returned to London. His brother John took up the challenge to win it back for York and had now successfully taken Bamburgh from its commander, no less than Henry Beaufort, Duke of Somerset.

The Lancastrians seemed to have lost heart following news that their Queen was shipwrecked and her army lost. Reports had reached Richard that the North Sea storms had overwhelmed Margaret's fleet of ships on passage from France to her new allies in Scotland. Some had sunk with all hands and others washed ashore and wrecked on nearby Holy Island. Richard learned that Queen Margaret had landed at Berwick in a small boat and almost drowned, saved by her loyal French follower Pierre de Breze.

As soon as the weather allowed, he sent part of his army in search of them. He also sent a ship full of men-at-arms to Holy Island to make sure none of her men escaped. There was no sign of Queen Margaret and Richard guessed she had somehow made her way back across the Scottish border. Her men on Holy Island had nowhere to escape. They put up a brave fight but many were killed and the few survivors of the short battle surrendered and were taken prisoner.

One of John's men arrived one evening at Warkworth Castle with a message for Richard from his brother. He brought the news that the Duke of Somerset wanted to meet to discuss terms. After he had left Richard called for Luke Tully to prepare for the short trip to Banburgh.

Tully was surprised. 'You are going to negotiate with the Duke of Somerset, my lord?'

Richard frowned. 'I have mixed feelings about even meeting with the man who commanded the Lancastrians at Towton.' He shook his head. 'We both had a hand in the death of each other's fathers.'

Tully knew better than to comment and instead poured Richard a goblet of whiskey from a bottle he had brought with him. He watched as Richard tasted it appreciatively.

'Good stuff, Tully. Where did it come from?'

Tully handed him the bottle. 'We found several barrels in the cellars, along with some good wine.'

'See to it that the drink is shared out between the men. It's the least I can do after keeping them here all winter.' He handed the bottle back. 'Just make sure they don't turn up drunk on duty.'

Tully looked pleased. 'They will appreciate it, my lord.'

'This winter has been hard on us all, Tully. The king has ordered us to take all the northern castles for York, yet I don't know if we can cope with any more long sieges.' He took another sip of the whiskey and could feel its warmth flowing through his body. 'An extended siege in winter is as hard on the besiegers as the besieged.'

Tully agreed. 'I have heard the men complain of the cold. They would be glad to see an early end to this siege work.'

'I try to do my best for them, although there have been too many times when they had to live off salt fish or go hungry. I know Edward well enough to be sure if I can do a deal with Somerset he will grant him a pardon.'

John greeted him when he arrived at Banburgh. 'Come and look, Richard, I have something to show you.'

Richard followed his brother down the long corridors to the oak panelled state rooms, the best in the old castle. They had spectacular views of Lindisfarne Island out to sea. Richard stood at the window watching the dark grey rolling waves. He watched a sailing ship braving the white crests of rough seas further from the shore. The castle was the perfect place to guard against an invasion from across the water.

'You've made me curious now, John.'

His brother opened the silver catches on a finely crafted wooden casket, decorated with gold fleurs-de-lis, and gestured for him to look inside. He could see valuable jewellery, necklaces and diamond broaches that sparkled in the light, as well as some parchment letters and other documents. Richard picked up one of the letters. It had a broken wax seal he couldn't recognise. He unfolded the letter and started to read. The flamboyant writing was in French, addressed to Queen Margaret from her father.

'Good God.' He recalled the proud figure of the Count of Anjou at Margaret's coronation. He hadn't liked him much then and liked him even less now. 'Have you read all of these?' Richard carefully re-folded the letter and replaced it in the casket, feeling strangely intrusive.

'My French isn't too good.' John looked at the casket. 'I know they belong to Queen Margaret. She left here in such a hurry I think she could only take what she could carry. We probably have all her personal effects!'

He opened a nearby wooden chest and showed Richard velvet and silk dresses. They were creased, as if hurriedly packed. Richard picked up a white linen chemise and held it to his face. The delicate scent of lavender immediately reminded him of Megan's cottage and triggered a rush of images in his mind. The powerful connection when the young Queen Margaret looked directly into his eyes, all those years ago. He remembered how the humiliation of his defeat by her army at St. Albans was tinged with a grudging admiration for her leadership and courage.

Richard realised he had a special bond with his enemy Queen. He completely understood her obsessive determination to see her son crowned King, despite all that had happened. He recalled the stories he had heard of how she bravely survived shipwrecks, attacks from robbers and numerous defeats, yet still persevered. There was an undeniable connection between them. He sensed that connection now, more powerfully than ever.

John picked up one of the diamond necklaces. Obviously worth a great deal of money, the polished facets of the precious jewels sparkled in the light as he ran it through his fingers. 'What do you think we should do with it all?'

Richard spotted an unusual crucifix on a chain at the bottom of the casket and picked it up for a closer look. Made from solid silver and beautifully crafted, the fine detail was worn smooth from many years of handling. He guessed it had some sentimental value to Margaret and slipped it into the pocket of his tunic.

He turned to his brother, who was securing the bronze clasp on the chest of clothes. 'Let's send the whole lot to Edward. It will amuse him.'

'Good idea, I'll do just that.' John turned to Richard. 'I almost forgot why you are here. Henry Beaufort is waiting in the great hall. He says he's had enough of the north and is ready to discuss a deal.' John looked concerned. 'Do you think we can trust him?'

Richard was uncertain. 'Do we have any choice?'

'Yes. I could have him locked away somewhere they'll never find him.' Anger flashed across John's face. 'I know what our father would say.'

Richard put his hand on his brother's shoulder. 'We can't be sure what part he had in our father's death, John. If his men will follow him it would send an important message to all the people round here who think it's a good idea to support the queen. Take me to him.'

The duke was about eight years younger than Richard, although they looked about the same age. He was wearing an expensive black velvet brigandine with silver rivets fixing the protective steel plates in place. There was an empty scabbard on his hip belt. Richard could see from his bearing that the duke was rarely without his sword and felt deprived of the weight of it. He had an engaging smile and was well built and handsome despite his unshaven appearance and the old wound on his face. He saw Richard looking.

'I got this at St. Albans.' He smirked, touching the jagged scar and rubbed the stubble on his chin. 'First battle, not the second.'

Richard was in no mood to be reminded. 'You told my brother you want to discuss terms?'

'Yes.' He looked directly at Richard. His eyes were a deep blue and had a confidence that seemed at odds with his situation. 'I can't follow the French Queen any more, none of us can.'

'And?' Richard forced himself to forget who the man in front of him was for a moment. There would be plenty of time for that later.

'I'll help you take Alnwick.'

'What do you want in return?'

The duke looked amused. 'A full pardon. A place at court. My lands restored. An end to sleeping rough. The usual things.'

Richard wondered what to make of him. Beaufort was a survivor. He had his share of bad luck, yet always seemed to recover. 'We could use your help with Alnwick. As for the rest, that will be up to King Edward.'

Henry Beaufort held out his hand and Richard shook it, still wondering if he was doing the right thing.

'Agreed.'

Richard led the siege of the garrison at Alnwick Castle, barely two hours' ride north of Warkworth. As he approached the well-positioned Percy stronghold on the coast he recalled his last visit there so many years ago, when he agreed a truce with Sir Henry Percy, who had died at the first battle of St. Albans. Against Richard's better judgement Henry Beaufort had disappeared inside the castle to talk to the commander of the garrison, Baron Hungerford, his fellow survivor of Towton.

The weather had turned colder. A chill wind was increasing in strength and the persistent rain soaked them all to the skin. The light was also failing, making Richard regret his decision to trust the Lancastrian Duke. He could be plotting with the Baron right now. His suspicion seemed proved when one of his border lookouts returned with alarming news. An army of Scots and mercenaries had been sighted crossing the border. One of their banners was thought to be that of Richard's adversary Marshal Pierre de Breze.

Richard called to his men. 'Fall back to the line of the trees. Take cover where you can!'

The men looked at him in surprise then followed his order. They waited in the freezing rain. Richard decided he would have the duke and the Baron both publicly executed when he could. He looked across at the grim faces of his men. They would be hoping he would soon order the attack and end the siege. He was reluctant to leave their good defensive position now he knew the Scots were coming.

His wounded leg ached in the cold and reminded him of the danger they faced. He wasn't prepared to risk his life for a northern castle. They changed hands so often it simply wasn't worth it. Richard put his hands inside his tunic to warm them and his fingers touched the polished edges of the queen's silver crucifix. He held it tightly in his hand, taking some comfort from it.

He thought again of the queen and how she must have feared for her life to run without taking any of her possessions with her. He wondered if she was riding towards him, having secured an alliance with the Scots. He had spent so many years with his father keeping the Scots from the border, yet now they rode freely into

England without a challenge. Richard considered ordering a retreat rather than risking capture by the Scots.

Richard's thoughts were interrupted by the sound of boots and horses' hooves on cobble-stones. Muffled voices carried a long distance in the still night and he strained to hear. Men were moving on the road leading to the castle entrance yet they seemed to be in no hurry. He peered into the darkness and could make out the shape of a cart drawn by a team of heavy oxen.

'They're leaving the castle, my lord.' One of his commanders pointed into the distance where lines of men could be seen disappearing into the fading light.

Richard told no one that his eyesight was not as sharp as it used to be, particularly once darkness fell. The clank and rattle of weapons against armour suggested the men were armed, yet they carried no banners and the way they marched without looking back suggested they were not planning to fight. He couldn't understand why they would leave if the Scots were on the way.

They waited in the rain, watching the Lancastrian garrison depart. The wintry night sky was almost dark now, with only a thin sliver of new moon. The Scots had a reputation for not fighting fairly. Richard realised they could be surrounding his position in the near darkness.

'A light, there on the battlements!' Tully spotted it first. A swinging lantern, the secret sign from Henry Beaufort that he'd been successful.

Richard still didn't trust him. They were all freezing cold and hungry now. 'Forward, men, and keep your wits about you.'

The castle was completely unguarded. Richard didn't know how the duke had done it and didn't care. Another Lancastrian castle had fallen to their cause without a fight. He was wet and cold. He realised he was also hungry and couldn't even remember when he had last eaten a hot meal. Now at last he could change into some dry clothes and celebrate the new Yorkist garrison in Alnwick Castle.

Richard had decided he needed respite from the constant skirmishes in the north. The time had come to honour the memory of his father, who stated in his will that he wished to be buried at Bisham Priory. Close by the Thames near Marlow and once a mystical place of worship for the Knights Templar, the priory had become the mausoleum for the Earls of Salisbury through the ages.

A team of masons were commissioned to carve two heavy stone coffins and the bodies of Richard's father and brother were exhumed from their graves in the grounds of Pontefract Castle and brought to York Minster, where their heads were reverently restored. Richard and John had decided this was to be a military funeral, so Richard's wife Anne and John's wife Isabel travelled separately to the service.

The funeral procession was the grandest the people of York had ever seen. Richard and his brother John rode behind the coffins of their father and brother Thomas, which were carried on a specially constructed, black-draped chariot, pulled by six fine black warhorses. Both were dressed in expensive armour with flowing black capes to guard against the chill wind. On each side of them rode eight knights, carrying their banners, followed by a dozen drummers, beating out a sombre rhythm on heavy bass drums as they marched.

Behind that came his mother's coffin, brought from the crypt at Middleham Castle in a gilded carriage draped in pure white silk. A bouquet of her favourite white roses lay on top of her casket. One hundred men-at-arms marched behind, all in the Warwick livery of red with the badge of the bear and ragged staff.

The Earl had been a prominent figure in the area and almost the entire population of the city crowded onto the streets to pay their last respects, despite the cold. The procession made its way through the Micklegate Bar and began the long journey due south, through Nottingham, Leicester and Northampton, the heart of England. Richard looked back down the road. The long lines of marching men and horses seemed more like an invading army than a funeral cortege. He knew that was how his father would have wanted it.

They were cold and tired by the time they finally reached Bisham Priory. John saw to the arrangements for the funeral the next morning. Richard had something else he had to do. He went to the crypt of the priory to inspect the newly made alabaster effigies he had commissioned. He stood in silence before them, overcome with emotion. The effigy of his father was dressed in his best mail and armour, wearing the surcoat bearing the brightly painted quartered arms of Neville and Montacute. The finely modelled face regarded Richard impassively, as his father often had. A good likeness. Richard ran his fingers over the carved mail coat and marvelled at the craftsmanship.

Next to his father's effigy was his mother, wearing her favourite dress and with a perfectly serene expression on her face. His mother's head rested on a pillow supported by two perfectly carved angels and she looked at peace next to his father. Like his father's, her hands had been carved in prayer. Richard reached out and clasped them in his own. At that moment he would have given all his wealth, every inch of land and every castle he had ever owned to have his parents back. He sank to his knees and wept.

Chapter 19 - Autumn 1464

Richard was on the most important mission of his life, to find a wife for the king. Edward had been a single man too long. The last straw was when he more than pardoned Henry Beaufort. The king also restored all his lands and titles and even invited him to his bed. Richard's strongly worded warnings about Beaufort's untrustworthy character had been ignored, causing a minor rift between Richard and Edward.

Edward's mood did not improve when Richard was proved right and Henry Beaufort returned to the side of Queen Margaret. After the unsurprising treachery of the Duke of Somerset, the Lancastrians soon retook the northern castles which were so hard won and so easily lost. This time Richard had no patience for long sieges and blasted the walls of Bamburgh Castle with great cannons until the garrison ran. His brother John captured the duke in a battle at Hexham and had him publicly executed for his treason. He was rewarded by being made the Earl of Northumberland and given the lands that once belonged to the Percy families.

Delicate negotiations with King Louis of France had been going on for almost three years now, with emissaries and ambassadors crossing the Channel in both directions with gifts and letters. Not for nothing had they nicknamed King Louis l'araignee, 'the spider'. His webs of intrigue were testing Richard's powers of diplomacy, challenging work which could hold the key to lasting peace in England.

If Richard could secure a marriage which tied Louis to Edward he could be sure France would never support Queen Margaret. There was at least one promising candidate for Edward to marry. The young Queen Charlotte of France had a sister, Princess Bona of Savoy, who was unmarried and, at fifteen, about the right age. The problem for Richard was that Louis was unpredictable. He was used to doing what he pleased, when he pleased and didn't act like a king.

Richard decided the time had come for him to meet the King of France in person. The meeting would be held in secret, a chance for the two of them to speak frankly, and the journey was not without danger. Although Richard carried a letter of safe conduct from the king, he was not allowed to bring his personal guard. The Loire Valley was known to harbour men who had fought the English and still had scores to settle. He travelled light, with Luke Tully and a few servants to avoid drawing attention to his presence.

He arrived at the castle at Amboise not sure what to expect. More of a family home than a castle, the favourite residence of King Louis was positioned high over the River Loire, with views across the open countryside. It had taken much longer than Richard expected to ride from Calais, stopping for a day in Paris, then deep into the heart of rural France to Amboise.

After waiting for half the morning, he was unhappy to be informed that the king was indisposed. Richard asked for an audience with the queen and after more waiting was finally shown to her state rooms. He had expected the French court to be richly decorated. As he was led through long, narrow corridors, Richard noticed that even the royal apartments were simply furnished, with little sign of the extravagance he had seen on visits to Duke Philip of Burgundy.

Surrounded by her ladies in waiting, Queen Charlotte, the king's second wife, was almost half the age of her husband and heavily pregnant. Richard knew she had a reputation for easily losing her temper and studied her for a moment, conscious of the need to somehow win her support. The queen's white dress contrasted with her jet-black hair, most of which was covered by a tall pointed hat in the latest French fashion. She fed morsels of food to a small lap-dog as he watched. Charlotte spoke only in French, so softly that Richard had to strain to hear.

'Earl Warwick, we are honoured to have you in our court.'

Richard bowed. 'Thank you, your Highness. I have important matters to discuss with the king, on behalf of King Edward of England.' Although his French had greatly improved during the time he had been living in Calais, he still felt at a disadvantage.

The queen regarded him with her piercing blue eyes. 'The king is going hunting.' She looked out of the high, arched window to the castle grounds, as if expecting to see him. 'Sometimes he goes hunting for days, forgetting me and his duties.'

Richard wasn't sure how to respond. He had travelled too far to return without something to show for his time, so he tried again. 'Your sister, the Princess Bona of Savoy. I would like to meet her, if it is possible for that to be arranged?'

'My sister is in Milan.' The queen stroked her dog absent-mindedly. 'I can send a message to her for you?'

'Please will you tell her that the King of England is minded to ask for her hand in marriage, to bring together the great houses of York and Valois?'

'My sister would be honoured, I am sure.' She whispered something to one of her ladies in waiting, who looked at Richard with new interest. 'We will look forward to the wedding.'

The doors burst open and King Louis appeared with his entourage. A plain looking well-built man wearing ordinary hunting clothes, Richard recognised him immediately from his bearing. He also noted that the king's nose was as large as it had been described, although tales of his legs being so thin they could hardly support him were obviously an exaggeration.

'At last we meet, Captain of Calais!' His voice boomed in the high ceilinged room in heavily accented French.

Richard bowed. 'Your Grace, I am here to discuss arrangements for the marriage of King Edward.'

'Good. Princess Bona will make him a fine wife.' King Louis seemed to consider the matter closed. 'You will come hunting with me now.' His words were a statement rather than a question.

Richard was happy to agree. 'Of course, Your Grace.' He turned to Queen Charlotte. 'It has been a pleasure to meet you, your Highness.'

He followed the king to the stables and was glad to see Tully, grooming their horses.

'I'm going hunting, Tully, for wild boar with the king.'

Richard felt a great sense of relief as they rode through the wooded French countryside behind the pack of hunting dogs. He hadn't known what to expect of King Louis yet it had been less difficult than he thought. Now he could return to England secure in the knowledge that he had personally brokered the first meaningful alliance between England and France for over a hundred years.

King Louis rode up to him. 'You hunt boar in England, Earl of Warwick?'

'Not for a long time, Your Grace.' He smiled. 'We've been too busy hunting Queen Margaret of Anjou.'

The king laughed, understanding the joke. 'And what will you do when you catch her?'

Richard grinned. He was glad to have found common ground with the king. 'I think we'll send her back to France!'

The excited barking of the dogs in the woods ahead interrupted his reply.

The king shouted urgently in French. 'The dogs have the scent!' he pointed to his hounds that were barking more loudly now. 'To the boar!'

They rode deeper into the woods, ducking to avoid low branches and not slowing even as the forest became more overgrown. The king was a skilled rider and charged ahead without a care for the danger. Richard had not been on a boar hunt for years, as the wars and politics of England had kept him completely preoccupied. The thrill of the chase was exhilarating and he felt young again for the first time in ages.

The baying of the dogs told them the boar must have been cornered. They rode to where the barking was loudest to see a heavy black boar with large tusks, surrounded by the hounds. It bellowed angrily, pawing the ground and threatening the dogs with its tusks. Now the king turned to Richard.

'It is traditional in France for the guest to finish the boar.' He gestured with exaggerated generosity. 'The honour is yours, Earl of Warwick.'

Richard understood the challenge in the king's voice. A test, to see if they had anything in common or if Richard was playing a role to secure the alliance. He slid from his saddle and drew his dagger, taking a firm grip on the handle.

The wild boar charged the hunting dogs, deeply goring one in the flank with its long tusks. Another dog grabbed the boar by the snout, locking its teeth deep into the flesh. With a high pitched squeal of anger and pain the boar made a sudden sweep of its muscular neck and swung the dog high into the air, smashing it hard into the trunk of a tree. Somehow the dog managed to keep its hold and the boar tried again, tiring now. The other dogs joined in the fray, biting and snapping. One tore at the boar's ears, making it even angrier.

Richard approached the boar warily, knife at the ready. It seemed enormous as he came closer, at least four feet long, with mud caking its coarse black bristles. He knew of men who had been killed by wounded boars. There would not be a second chance if he missed his mark. The boar was roaring now, its eyes glittering with black fury. He lunged forward and struck deep between its front legs, below the base of the neck. A gush of blood showed his blow had been fatal. The boar died instantly as Richard's sharply pointed blade pierced its heart. He stood back and wiped the blade of his knife, hoping no one would notice how much his hands were shaking.

One of the hunters called off the dogs. The king slapped him on the back.

'Good kill, Earl of Warwick, good kill.'

One of the men produced a flask of strong brandy and they passed it round. Richard raised the flask in a salute to his new alliance with the King of France.

The news hit him like the blow from a war hammer. Edward had secretly married a commoner, Elizabeth Grey, widow of Sir John Grey and the daughter of Lord Rivers. It seemed impossible that such a thing could happen. There had been no discussion, no consultation. Worst of all, he appeared to be one of the last people in the country to have heard about it. Richard could barely control his temper when he was finally granted a private audience with Edward.

'Are you out of your mind, Edward? You are the King of England.' He struggled to keep his temper. 'You cannot marry a commoner!'

Edward looked at him with a stern expression. 'Mind your manners, Richard. Elizabeth is not a commoner. She is the daughter of Countess Jacquetta of Luxembourg.'

Richard didn't answer. He was still reeling from the turn of events. He had always known that Edward had a weakness for the common women who managed to catch his eye. He just couldn't accept that he had secretly married one of them behind his back, while he had been going to so much trouble to find a suitable match for him in France.

Edward squared up to Richard. 'My wife.' He paused, to give the words emphasis. 'My wife is the daughter of the widow of the Duke of Bedford, brother of King Henry the fifth.'

Richard was exasperated. 'Your wife,' he stared directly at Edward, 'was a lady in waiting to Queen Margaret of Anjou.'

'That was a long time ago.'

'Her father, her husband and her brother have fought against us! What would your father have said?'

Edward looked at his shoes and said nothing.

Richard continued. 'You have put the future peace of the country at risk!'

Edward raised his hand to silence him. 'How, exactly?'

Richard raised his voice in exasperation. 'We need to secure a treaty with the French, to stop them ever supporting Queen Margaret against you.'

'I might not need the French. You have seen to it that there are few Lancastrians left to be concerned about. Anyway, I'm in talks with Burgundy.'

'Burgundy!' Richard felt a second hammer blow. 'We agreed that Philip of Burgundy is not to be trusted?'

Edward seemed surprised. 'You don't know?'

'Don't know what?' Richard hardly dared imagine what further surprises Edward had for him. He could see all his hard work unravelling, quicker than he would be able to restore the damage done.

'Philip of Burgundy is handing over to his son Charles. I've had people talking to him about marriage to my sister Margaret.'

Richard was incredulous. 'He's already married.'

Edward frowned. 'His wife is dying, Richard. My father was planning for him to marry Margaret. He had to marry a Frenchwoman because of some treaty. Once she is dead he's free to do what he wants.'

'What about all the work I've been doing in France? What about our alliance with King Louis?'

Edward looked disdainful. 'The man is a peasant, Richard. Surely you've seen that?'

Richard refused to agree. 'He's our best hope of peace.'

'The price was too high.' Edward sounded irritated. 'You would have had me marry his wife's ugly sister.'

Richard knew the meeting was over. There was no point in arguing. Even if he could somehow prove the marriage to Elizabeth invalid, the damage was done. There was not even a hope that Edward would now marry his daughter Isabel. Although she was only thirteen she was almost a woman and attractive enough. He was turning to go when Edward stood and looked at him, an earnest expression on his face that reminded Richard of the younger Edward who had sailed around Lands End with him.

'You need to understand, Richard. I don't have to put up with a dreadful arranged marriage.' He put his hand on Richard's shoulder. 'I love her. I married Elizabeth because I am in love with her. Nothing else matters.'

Richard had one more marriage to arrange, the betrothal of his own daughter Margaret. Margaret had gained a good education and fulfilled her mother's ambition for her to become a lady. Now she was sixteen and ready to be married. His choice was Sir Richard Huddleston, a promising young knight from a respectable Cumbrian family and heir to the Lordship of Millom.

The morning of Margaret's wedding was a perfect autumnal day, so he decided to ride alone to the old Norman church of St Michael in Spennithorne, across the meandering River Ure from Middleham Castle. A single bell rang musically, echoing across the Yorkshire dales. Anne and the girls were travelling to the service in a carriage so he waited for them in the peaceful churchyard.

The tall, square church tower could be seen from Middleham and was one of his favourite places when he needed somewhere quiet to think. His argument with the king troubled him deeply. He would not find it easy to accept the Woodville family and there was a real danger now that France would support Queen Margaret, after all he had done to prevent it.

Not for the first time, Richard began to wonder what he wanted out of life. He had more money than most men could ever dream of. His lands and properties were so vast he could never hope to visit them all in a single year. He had been Chief Minister, Admiral of the Seas, and Captain of Calais, yet despite it all he still felt unfulfilled.

A woman's voice spoke his name and he turned to see Megan, looking almost as he remembered her all those years ago. A jolt from his past. He'd had no contact with her for most of Margaret's life yet it seemed he had only seen her yesterday. He took her hand in his. She looked beautiful in a flowing cotton dress. Her hair was under a simple hat made from white lace and her eyes still sparkled with the energy he had always found so attractive.

'You look well, Richard.'

He stood in silence for a moment, lost in recollections of their life together. 'So do you, Megan.'

'Your daughter has turned out well, don't you think?'

Richard looked into her eyes. 'She is her mother's daughter.'

'Can you believe it's been sixteen years?'

Richard still held her hand. Their close contact felt natural, without a trace of awkwardness. 'I've missed you, Megan.'

Sadness filled her eyes then she brightened. 'Margaret seems happy with your choice of husband for her.'

'He's an honest man. With prospects.' He looked at her again, amazed at how little she had changed. He noticed she no longer wore the sapphire around her neck. The ring he had given her was now on her finger. Richard struggled to keep his emotions in check.

'I have decided to give them a manor house at Blennerhasset as a wedding present, as well as lands at Penrith with the income from the rents in Coverdale.'

'Thank you. She is to be a lady now, thanks to your mother.'

Richard remembered. 'I must thank you for what you did for my mother.'

Megan looked sad again. 'She was kind to me.'

He hesitated to ask the question that formed in his mind as soon as he saw her. 'And have you also now become a lady?'

Megan laughed. 'I don't usually dress like this, you know.' She glanced at Middleham Castle in the distance and squeezed his hand absent-mindedly. 'I moved to York to be closer to Margaret when she came here. I found work as a seamstress.'

Richard was surprised. 'I didn't know.'

'No. I've seen you coming and going and stayed out of the way for Anne's sake. I never married, if that's what you're asking.'

Richard gave her hand a gentle squeeze back and reluctantly let it slip from his grasp. 'I would have married you, Megan, if I had been free to do so.'

She looked across at the church. People were starting to gather outside in the late autumn sunshine. She smiled at him, a twinkle in her eyes. 'You know, I believe you would have. We must go now, Richard, Earl of Warwick. Your guests are arriving, my lord.'

He walked with her to the church, not caring what the people would say.

Chapter 20 - Summer 1465

Richard was out of the country at trade discussions during the extravagant coronation at Westminster Abbey of Elizabeth Woodville. He knew Edward was simply keeping him out of the way. Almost all the nobility of England were present, with the exception of himself, and his absence had been seen as a sign of his diminishing influence. He was also certain that changes would be made at Westminster while he was away and, to make matters worse, he had been sent to negotiate with the Burgundian merchants who knew he was close to their enemy King Louis of France.

His wife and his daughters Isabel and Anne made sure he was represented at the coronation ceremony and gave him their detailed impressions of the day. Richard was unsurprised to hear that Elizabeth had succeeded in outshining even the extravagance of the coronation of Margaret of Anjou. Despite his disappointment at the way her marriage had been contrived, he had to admire the new Queen Elizabeth for the skill with which she managed her rapid rise of fortunes.

The coronation was overshadowed by news on his return that King Henry had been captured at last. His brother John had nearly apprehended the king twelve months before at the battle of Hexham. Henry escaped, leaving behind his personal belongings, including his ceremonial helmet with a gold crown that now graced John's hallway.

Despite an extensive search the trail grew cold. They knew the king was being kept in safe houses by supporters in Cumbria. He was finally spotted at Waddington Hall, the home of the Sheriff of Yorkshire, Sir Richard Tempest. Even then he fled down a secret staircase and almost escaped across the River Ribble until he was captured in the nearby woods.

Richard immediately saw an opportunity to regain some of his popularity with the people of London. He decided to escort the king from Islington to the Tower. The same people who had once cheered just at the sight of Richard's standard had short memories. His long absences in Calais and France meant they readily believed untrue stories put about by his enemies. Being seen to bring King Henry back to London would help restore his popular image.

He arrived at the manor house in Islington where the king was being held and found him with two doctors, who seemed concerned about the king's health. Richard was shocked at the physical change in King Henry, who had grown an unkempt beard which was turning grey. Worse still was the king's mental state. He regarded Richard with a curious expression, apparently unaware of who he was or the reason for his visit.

The king was seated on a small horse, his feet tied to the stirrups with leather thongs and a rope tied around his middle to prevent him falling from the saddle. A straw hat was placed on his head and the procession made its way through the city. People jeered as he rode through the dirty streets to his prison. Richard had a hundred guards as escort to ensure that it didn't get out of hand. As well as the risk of some Lancastrian sympathisers attempting to rescue the king, there was almost as great a danger of someone attempting to assassinate him, the feelings ran so high.

One man ran into the street and shouted into the king's face.

'Usurper!'

King Henry sat upright on his small horse and shouted back at the man in an unexpectedly confident voice. 'My father was King of England!' He looked around as if aware of his surroundings for the first time. 'He was peacefully possessed of the crown for the whole of his life.'

Richard brought his horse alongside King Henry and tried to calm him. He was concerned that despite Henry's obviously poor mental condition, there were still plenty of Londoners who would be loyal to the old King, many believing that he had been ordained by God. They were no longer jeering at King Henry and Richard knew how easily they could be incited to rescue him. He was fairly confident his guards would be able to ensure the king's safety, but it would be a disaster if he was seen to have mishandled the simple task of returning the king safely to London.

A man at the back of the crowd shouted. 'God save the king!'

Henry continued, louder this time, seeming to find new energy from the way he was drawing more attention from the crowd. 'His father, my grandfather, was king before him. I was crowned almost in my cradle!' His voice faltered and he spoke more quietly now, a note of sadness in his voice. 'I was accepted as king by the whole realm. I wore the crown for nearly forty years. Every lord swearing homage and fealty to me, as they had done to my forefathers.'

The king's sudden new-found spirit vanished as soon as it had come and Richard signalled to the guards, who rode up and surrounded the king, almost cutting him off from public view with their black warhorses. They were not far from the Tower. He looked into the crowd and realised they were now less certain. He suspected that the king's outburst would now be the talk of London, repeated in all the taverns and bawdy houses. Word of this was bound to reach the royal circle and there was nothing he could do to stop it.

Richard forced himself to smile at the crowd as they continued on their way, appearing more confident than he felt. He laughed when a woman started shouting about Queen Margaret being a harlot as the procession passed. King Henry just rode in silence, apparently oblivious of what was happening around him. Richard felt some relief when the familiar sight of the Tower of London came into view and he could hand over his prisoner to the Captain of the Guard.

He looked at the king and felt a sudden pang of compassion for the man as he was untied from his mount and led off by two burly yeomen of the Tower to his place of imprisonment. He noticed Luke Tully was also watching with a look of concern.

'You are wondering why he has to be locked up in the Tower?'

'It does seem harsh, my lord.'

'It's partly for his safety,' He looked around to make sure he couldn't be overheard, 'and as surety against Queen Margaret having ideas about raising another army.'

'Do you think that likely, my lord?'

'She has a son, Prince Edward. What mother would not do everything in her power to ensure her son has his rightful inheritance?'

Tully looked back to where King Henry had been led away. 'I can't help wondering how things would be if he had a little of his father's spirit.'

'I'll see to it that he is well treated. I suspect he hardly knows what is going on. It will be interesting to know who visits him and why.'

They watched until the king disappeared from view then Richard went in search of Edward. He found him alone in his private rooms in the Palace of Westminster. The guard on the door tried to refuse him entry, then relented under Richard's stern order to stand aside. Another sign of how things were already changing under the influence of the new Queen Elizabeth.

This was Richard's first opportunity for a long time to speak to the king without Elizabeth being present. The room was in semi darkness, lit only by large candles which flickered in the still air as Richard walked past. Edward sat alone at the head of a heavy oak table. Richard immediately realised why the guard had not welcomed him. Edward had been drinking.

Edward raised his goblet. 'Richard, you've come to celebrate with me.' He looked around for a second goblet.

Richard glanced at the almost empty bottle of red wine on the table. 'I'll not join you in a drink, thank you, Edward.' He pulled up a chair and regarded the king he had worked so hard for. 'You will be pleased to know that there was little support for Henry as we rode through London.'

'And now he's safely in the Tower?'

'Yes. It will give Queen Margaret something to think about, now you have him in your keeping.'

'You think she is still plotting against us, after everything that has happened?'

'I do, Edward. While her son lives, she will want to see him on the throne. She is a determined woman, despite all the setbacks she has suffered.'

Edward poured himself more of the dark red wine while Richard watched. He could smell the faint aroma of it, reminding him of happier times. He wondered if this was the time to mention his plans for a peace treaty with France.

'I have resolved to return to Calais, with your consent, to nurture your interests in France.'

Edward took a sip from his wine and looked at him questioningly. 'To see your friend King Louis?'

'Of course.' Richard guessed from his tone that Edward was up to something.

'I've heard that Louis wishes you to rebel against me.'

Richard caught his breath. The king was in a dangerous mood.

He decided not to over react. 'You have been misinformed.'

'Maybe I have.' Edward looked at him, as if making a judgement. 'I don't need you to prove your loyalty to me, Richard. I know you have always put my best interests before anything else.'

Richard relaxed a little. 'I believe I can secure a peace treaty with King Louis. As well as stopping him from supporting the Lancastrians, we could improve our trade with France.'

Edward shook his head. 'The thing is, Richard.' He took another generous drink from his goblet, seeming to enjoy having the advantage over Richard. 'The thing is I don't trust the man. I don't like him. Never did.'

Richard had heard it all before, several times. He knew better than to try to persuade Edward. It wasn't necessary to like the French King to secure a treaty with him. The problem was the Burgundians. He still had reliable sources at court who informed him of Edward's meetings with ambassadors from Burgundy. If news of this reached King Louis it could put an end to the treaty.

Edward continued. 'There is also the question of my sister Margaret. She is nineteen and needs a husband worthy of the house of York. It would suit me if she was to wed Charles, Count of Charolais.'

Richard was shocked. All the work he had done to win over King Louis would be undone, yet he had to admit he could see how Edward's plan could work. Charles would soon inherit Burgundy from his ailing father. He had almost married Margaret of York previously, only being prevented from doing so by the Treaty of Troyes.

'You are too late, Edward. Charles of Burgundy has married Countess Isabella.'

Edward looked scornful. 'You know as well as I do that she is on her deathbed. I've been reliably informed that she is not expected to last another month.'

Richard saw a possibility. 'Louis would use such a marriage as reason to side with Lancaster. Queen Margaret has been to see him several times to ask for money to fund her campaign. I understand why you would have your sister marry Charles of Burgundy. We have to keep Louis on our side.'

'I think he'll support the Lancastrians anyway. You'll be wasting your time trying to persuade him otherwise.'

'All I ask is your consent to try.' Richard looked imploringly at Edward. 'You have nothing to lose if I fail and everything to gain if I succeed.'

Edward sat back heavily in his chair, causing it to scrape on the tiled floor. 'You always had a way with words, Richard. If anyone can match King Louis it is you.'

Richard wasn't sure if Edward meant it as a compliment or an insult and decided to change the subject. 'There is one other thing I would ask of you, Edward.'

The king sat in his chair. 'What is that?'

'My daughter Isabel is fourteen years old now.' He looked at Edward, trying to judge his mood. 'I thought that George would be an ideal suitor for her.'

Edward looked surprised. 'My brother?' Edward was condescending. 'And young Richard for your daughter Anne, I suppose?'

Richard held his ground. 'They are cousins, as you know. It would need a special dispensation from the Pope.'

Edward turned on him angrily. 'I forbid it. Do you hear, Richard? I absolutely forbid it!'

Chapter 21 - Spring 1466

Richard returned to Calais after a difficult year doing his best to reconcile his differences with the king in London. He had tried to set aside his distrust of the Woodville family, knowing he had to make the best of Edward's choice, and made a point of being seen to publicly support the new queen. She was an attractive woman and genuinely attentive to him, listening carefully to his views and opinions. As with her father and brother, Richard respected her abilities, so it had not been too difficult to forget how she had spoiled his plans.

He could also see Elizabeth had done nothing in protecting and promoting the interests of her family he would not have done himself. The new queen was a steadying influence on Edward, turning a blind eye to his amorous liaisons when necessary and playing her part as his queen, bringing more modern thinking to the royal court. Edward had been appreciative and asked Richard to act as godfather to his new daughter, who he had named Elizabeth, after her mother. He even stood in for Edward at Elizabeth's side at the churching banquet, which tradition dictated the king could not attend.

Richard's brother George had finally been made Archbishop of York and Chancellor of England. They ensured the event was used to remind people of the undiminished importance of the Neville family. No less than twenty-eight peers, fifty-nine knights, ten abbots and seven bishops attended the ceremony. There was a great banquet with thousands of roasted pigeons, served with exotic cranes and peacocks, as well as four hundred swans and six bulls roasted whole. The feasting was the talk of the country, as was the fact that the king and his new queen were noticeable by their absence.

The early spring sunshine and chill sea air of the English Channel were refreshing after the often tense atmosphere of the Woodville court, as Richard now thought of it. He'd been looking forward to returning to Calais after a longer than expected absence and hoped to finally prepare the way for a peace treaty with France. His family sailed with him, as well as his servants and Luke Tully, with men of his personal guard.

He complained to Anne on the evening of their arrival. 'I am in charge of foreign policy, yet right in the middle of my negotiations with King Louis, Edward tells me I have to entertain Charles of Burgundy.' He felt the now familiar sense of irritation. 'Edward does test my loyalty to him at times.'

Anne was conciliatory. 'I know you have high regard for King Louis.' She frowned. 'Is it impossible for you to establish some compromise with Charles of Burgundy?'

Richard was pacing the room to help himself think. He stopped and turned to her.

'If I do, it could compromise my understanding with King Louis.'

'What are you going to do, Richard?'

'I plan to see what I can make of negotiations with the French.'

Anne looked concerned. 'Is it a good idea to confront Edward? You could be playing right into the hands of our enemies at court.'

'He has no idea how much work it has been to secure peace with France.'

'I think he does.' Anne frowned. 'Queen Elizabeth's mother, Countess Rivers, openly supports the Burgundians. They turned up in force to her coronation.'

Richard sat heavily in his chair. 'My information is that Philip of Burgundy is not expected to live much longer.' He rubbed his eyes, feeling tired from the journey.' I also know that Charles is still aggrieved because I tried to put a French Princess on the English throne.'

'Charles will see it differently now, if he is married to Edward's sister?'

Richard could feel his anger rising. 'The man is a Lancastrian supporter. He is friends with Henry Beaufort and openly assists Margaret of Anjou!' He stormed out of the room, slamming the door behind him. The noise echoed down the corridor of the old castle. As he passed the guards they were careful not to make eye contact.

He made his way to the castle balcony, a favourite spot he went to when he needed to think. It had been built above the state rooms to allow splendid views of the estuary and on a clear day, the white cliffs of Dover. The late summer sunset now turned the entire landscape a shimmering golden pink. A single sailing ship made its way up the Channel, the sails full despite the light breeze. Richard identified the ship as a merchantman and watched as it sailed past Calais. Sometimes he wished he could have had a simpler life, like the captain of the merchantman, plying his trade without any concern for the frustrating politics of the English court.

He heard soft footsteps behind him and turned to see Anne. She put her arm around his waist and stood at his side in silence, watching the sun descend towards the western horizon. Richard put his arm around her, pulling her closer. They had almost been living separate lives in London, as he went early to Westminster, often returning late and tired. The warmth of her body felt good. Anne's waist was a little broader from fine living in London, yet he still found her attractive, even though she was now turning forty.

He turned to her. 'I've been thinking about our daughters. Isabel is fifteen now.'

Anne looked up at him. 'We need to decide soon. Our new queen has been busy marrying her family to the most eligible bachelors in the country.'

Richard's new plan formed in his mind. He had a different perspective on England from this side of the Channel and needed to start putting his own interests first. His influence had been so rapidly eroded by Edward's marriage into the Woodville family there was almost a danger he would become an irrelevance, the many sacrifices he had made for the house of York soon forgotten. Decisive action was needed. He was still one of the wealthiest men in the country and had two beautiful and marriageable daughters.

'Edward himself argued he should be allowed to marry who he pleased.' He watched Anne's reaction as he spoke.

Anne looked thoughtful. 'We would have to be careful. It would mean going directly against Edward's wishes.'

Richard looked out across the familiar estuary. The sun finally set below the distant horizon, replaced by the light of a luminous new moon shimmering on the tranquil sea. As he watched, stars began to shine brightly in the dark sky. There were just a few at first, then the whole sky seemed full of their twinkling light. He wasn't superstitious, yet it seemed a good omen of the need to change.

'I would have to sound George out in secret.'

'What do you think he'll say?'

Richard was certain. 'George will agree to marry Isabel. Her inheritance would completely change his standing at court. He is the male heir to the throne after Edward.'

'Only while Elizabeth fails to provide Edward with a son and heir.'

Richard didn't answer. It saddened him to think they would probably never have the son he'd always longed for. When he promised his father an heir he imagined he would have plenty of healthy sons, yet since his daughter Anne there had been no sign of another child. It had unquestionably put a strain on their relationship, although he was starting to accept it now he had other things to worry about.

Anne broke the silence. 'From what I've seen of George he seems a likeable young man, although he does have something of a reputation.'

'George, Duke of Clarence is ambitious, opinionated, yet discontented despite all his wealth and the lands in the West Country the king has given him. He reminds me a little of myself at seventeen.'

Anne smiled at the memory. 'God help us all.'

Richard studied the tersely worded summons from Edward and feared the worst. The king had signed it personally and it bore the royal seal. No reason was given, only that a most urgent matter required him to attend the king's presence with utmost haste. The problem was that Richard could think of many ways in which he could have earned the king's displeasure. He knew that despite the efforts he had made to publicly and privately accept

Elizabeth as his queen, the Rivers family bore a grudge against him that went back many years.

He recalled the coolness with which Lord Rivers had handed over Calais to him and the outrage when he had been captured at Sandwich in his bed, to be paraded before the townspeople. Now he had been made Earl Rivers, as well as being appointed Treasurer of England and was in a position, through his daughter Elizabeth, to exact his revenge. As he rode towards Westminster Richard guessed it would be Elizabeth's way to take it slowly, seeing it as her duty to her family, a matter of defending her father's honour.

Richard felt a chill shiver at the back of his neck as he realised the summons could be about his letter to King Louis of France. He had taken an unnecessary risk, sending a letter to Louis without Edward's knowledge. As well as promising that England would not invade France, the letter expressed support for the quashing of an uprising in Normandy by Louis. Richard now regretted ever writing the letter, penned in a moment of anger at Edward's interference with his negotiations.

Although he could always deny what had been said in discussions, to deliberately misrepresent the king in writing was quite a different matter. He worried the letter would surface in the future. In the wrong hands it could be used to do him great harm. Even the usually tolerant Edward could be persuaded that such a letter was firm evidence of treason.

Word could have already reached Edward about his unsatisfactory meeting with Charles, Duke of Charolais. At Edward's insistence, Richard had ridden from Calais to Burgundy to meet the young duke and discuss the prospect of marriage to Edward's sister Margaret. Charles was dismissive and confrontational and the meeting had ended in heated arguments about Richard's promises to King Louis.

Another worrying possibility was that young George, Duke of Clarence, had already betrayed his trust and failed to keep their discussion confidential. George had a problem showing proper discretion, particularly when he had been drinking. He could well have been bragging about how the Earl of Warwick had offered his eldest daughter's hand in marriage. Richard appealed to George's jealousy of his elder brother. He pointed out that Edward forbade their marriage because he didn't want George to have the power that came with the Neville fortune.

Richard knew Edward's real concern would be that if the marriage took place, he might start trying to make Isabel queen by whatever means he could. There was still the question of Edward's legitimacy, although he found it hard to see George ever taking Edward's place, although the idea of his daughter one day becoming queen certainly appealed.

Richard could already see further changes at court in the short time he had been away. New people he had never met before replaced the familiar faces. Forty new Knights of the Order of the Bath had been created at Elizabeth's coronation. He guessed they were Woodville supporters and self-serving opportunists, appointed through favours rather than through merit. To his annoyance, he was kept waiting outside the king's chamber. Richard recognised the king's voice and heard him laughing at some joke through the heavy wooden door, which was guarded by two armed men in royal livery.

When at last he was ushered in, Richard was surprised to see Edward was seated with the dour Sir William

Herbert, Earl of Pembroke. He nodded to Sir William, a loyal supporter of the York cause, rewarded for his service with the lands and title of the Lancastrian Jasper Tudor. He was also now the guardian of young Henry, Earl of Richmond, son of Edmund Tudor and Margaret Beaufort.

Richard was also aware that Sir William's son and heir had recently been betrothed to Elizabeth's ten year old sister, Mary Woodville. There was every possibility he would agree to take part in Richard's downfall in return for his son to marry into the royal line. Richard doubted that Sir William had been enjoying a joke with Edward and realised whoever he'd heard could have left by another door. Worse still, they might be listening out of sight behind one of the decorative screens. He guessed it could have been the queen or her father Earl Rivers. The thought of either made him feel at a disadvantage.

Edward greeted Richard without a smile. 'We have a most serious matter to discuss. A messenger was captured when we took Harlech Castle.' He looked across at Sir William and gestured for him to continue.

William Herbert spoke with a deep Welsh accent. 'He carried a letter from Margaret of Anjou.' He glanced at Edward, who gestured for him to go on. 'The letter was intended to be delivered to you, Earl Warwick, in secret.' He produced a folded parchment with a broken red wax seal and handed it to Richard.

They both watched Richard's reaction as he opened the letter and read it. Written in French and not in the neatly written hand of a scribe, the style was difficult for him to read. Although in different circumstances he wouldn't be certain the signature was Queen Margaret's, he knew it to be genuine. Incredibly, his sworn enemy was asking him to support her in a Lancastrian uprising against the house of York.

Richard's mind raced as he wondered where all this was leading. There was no need to deny any knowledge of the letter and he decided to simply dismiss it. He refolded it and handed the letter back to Sir William. Aware that he was in a dangerously vulnerable position, he looked across at the two men, trying to judge Edward's mood.

Edward finally broke the silence. 'The letter indicates that Margaret of Anjou is hopeful of support from your friend King Louis of France.'

Richard spoke as confidently as he could. 'The King of France has agreed to sign a treaty promising not to support the Lancastrians. You need have no concerns on that account.'

'I hope you are right, Warwick.' Edward's voice was firm. 'I mean to deal harshly with those who would plot against my family. The messenger has provided Sir William with the names of conspirators here in London.' He looked directly at Richard. 'He has named a servant of your deputy in Calais, Lord Wenlock.' He waited for Richard to respond.

It was the first time Edward had called him Warwick. 'You have my word, Edward. The last I heard of Margaret of Anjou, she was living in poverty, abandoned by even her most loyal supporters.' He looked at Sir William dismissively. 'I hope you agree Lord Wenlock has more than proved his loyalty to you?'

Edward thanked Sir William, who collected his papers together and left. Richard knew Edward well enough to know that there was more to come.

Edward looked at him sternly. 'I am concerned, Warwick. It seems I have not made myself clearly understood.' He held the silence, waiting for Richard to respond.

Richard tried to sound confident. 'What are you referring to, Edward?'

'I forbade you to discuss marriage of your daughters with my brothers, yet I learn this is precisely what you have done.'

He was being lured into a trap. If he denied his secret meetings with George he could be proved a liar. If he admitted them, it would be seen as a direct affront to the authority of the king. His only course of action was to admit his transgression.

'You will understand, Edward, I only wish to do the best for my daughters.'

Edward eyed him impassively.

Richard continued. 'It is my duty to make a good marriage for them both.'

'It is your duty to obey your king and liege lord!'

Richard remained silent. The last time Edward shouted at him, he had been certain the drink had affected his judgement. This was different.

Edward seemed to calm himself a little. 'At least you don't try to deny your actions. I have spoken to my brothers and told them they are not permitted to marry their cousins.' He gestured for Richard, who had been standing, to sit in one of the empty chairs.

Edward lowered his voice, so as not to be overheard. 'You know, Richard, that I do not question your loyalty or forget our friendship?'

'Of course, Edward.'

'I want you to make sure King Louis of France does nothing to support Margaret of Anjou. I will give you a letter of goodwill to take to him.'

Richard was grateful. 'I'll leave for France as soon as I can. I believe the prospect of a peace treaty is closer now than it has ever been.'

Edward stood, a sign the meeting was now over. 'Take care, Richard.'

Richard thought over those words, replaying the meeting in his head as he rode back to Warwick to make the arrangements for his journey to France. He was glad to be at last able to finalise the treaty with France, yet now his plan to marry Isabel to George was compromised. He knew only Edward's good nature had saved him from the Tower. Richard cursed Margaret of Anjou for placing him in such danger. His enemies would make mischief from her letter once word of its contents got out, which it surely would.

Chapter 22 - Spring 1467

The entire population of La Bouille, a normally peaceful Normandy village on the wooded banks of the Seine, turned out to see the King of France. Although the king had wished to be there to meet them, Richard took advantage of a favourable combination of wind and tide, sailing up the river from the port of Honfleur, where he had been welcomed as royalty and presented with the keys to the city.

The main road through the village was decorated with colourful flags and banners, which fluttered in the light spring breeze, creating a celebratory atmosphere. Richard's fleet of ships carried two hundred men from Sandwich, including trumpeters, a dozen mounted knights and their squires. Together with his personal guard, dressed in new red livery with banners of the bear and ragged staff, they lined both sides of the road.

The sound of trumpets and cheering people echoed through the village, heralding the arrival of the king's party as it made its way to where Richard waited. King Louis seemed keen to impress, as for once he wore his royal robes and was escorted by chevaliers. The elite knights of the king's guard were mounted on white chargers and each carried the flowing blue banner of the king, with golden fleurs-de-lis.

Richard approached them as the king dismounted from his horse. 'Welcome, my lord, you do me a great honour.'

The king bent double coughing at the effort of his ride, then greeted Richard in French. 'Earl of Warwick, it is good to see you after such a long time.' He hugged Richard warmly.

Richard was concerned to see that despite his effusive manner the king looked unwell and his cough sounded like the symptom of a deeper problem. He also looked much older than at their secret meeting three years before at the grand castle of Amboise.

'It is good to be meeting officially at last, Your Grace.'

The king acknowledged his reference to their secret meeting and lowered his voice. 'I regret there will not be any hunting this time, although there is much for us to discuss.'

'This time I also have authority from King Edward to finalise a truce between our countries.'

The king seemed pleased. 'Good. I will escort you to Rouen, Earl Warwick.'

Richard pointed back to his ships, moored at the quayside. 'Will you sail with us to the city, Your Grace?'

King Louis seemed to consider it for a moment then made a decision. 'I am not much of a sailor. I will ride ahead and arrange a grand reception for you.'

Richard watched the king's party leave. He studied the river and turned to his captain. 'Am I right in thinking the tide is no longer in our favour?'

'You are, my lord. We will have to wait. The Seine is noted for strong currents and shallow water.'

Richard stared at the fast-flowing river, watching as an uprooted tree flowed past. Its branches stuck out of the water like skeletal hands and he tried not to think of it as a bad omen. 'I've heard the spring tides bring a flood?'

'Yes, my lord. They call it the mascaret. It has claimed many ships on their way upriver to Rouen.'

'In that case the main fleet will return to the deep water at Honfleur. We need only three ships to carry the rest of the men to the city.'

While he waited for the tide Richard pondered on his mission and what he could hope to achieve. The treaty was not a forgone conclusion, as the prospect of a Burgundian marriage with Edward's sister would displease King Louis. There was also the question of how Edward would react on his return. Their last meeting had been amicable although he wondered how he would ever regain Edward's trust, whatever the outcome of his negotiations in Normandy.

By mid-afternoon their ships were ready to sail. Although the tide had turned, the water was still low. Richard was keen to arrive in Rouen in daylight and gave the order to sail. There was a real danger of running aground on the raised banks so they made slow progress, the sailors swinging lines weighted with lead and shouting out the depth. Richard felt the keel of his ship grinding on the gravel of the river bed at one point, and was relieved when the rising water floated them clear.

At last the tall spires of the city of Rouen came into view. Richard had never visited the historic city where King Edward was born and Anne's father had died. He frowned as he remembered how his old rival Henry Beaufort lost the city to the French eighteen years before.

They were welcomed by a band of musicians as they moored at the quayside. The crowd of curious onlookers cheered as Richard shook hands with the king, who greeted them on the quayside with his entourage. Once the men and horses were safely ashore, the king led them in a grand procession through the town to the old cathedral of Notre Dame, where they gave thanks and prayed for peace in front of a packed congregation.

Richard was shown to his rooms at the lodge of the Dominican friars and was invited to a royal reception at the king's palace, the Château Bouvreuil. A grand banquet was prepared, with Richard as guest of honour. He was surprised to be introduced to the queen, who had travelled to Rouen for the banquet. Surrounded by a chattering group of ladies in waiting, Queen Charlotte was now slim and attractively dressed in a flowing silk dress decorated with silver and gold. As they were introduced she gave no sign they had met before, although Richard saw a flash of recognition in her eyes.

Many important nobles from all over France arrived and were all keen to be introduced, curious to see the man they had heard so much about. Richard sensed that some were still reserved about a peace treaty with England, although they were all duly respectful to him and his officers. Afterwards the king invited Richard to join him in his private rooms. Unlike the finely decorated reception rooms at the chateau, the king's apartments had low ceilings and rustic furniture.

King Louis had changed into his more comfortable, plain hunting clothes and could see Richard was surprised at the simple furnishing of his rooms. 'We can talk privately here.' He poured them both a generous goblet of brandy. 'And there is also a connecting passage to your lodgings.' He lowered his voice almost to a whisper. 'Out of sight of Burgundian spies.'

Richard thanked the king. 'I am most grateful for your hospitality, Your Grace.'

Louis looked pleased. 'And I am grateful that you travel all the way to Normandy in person, Earl Warwick. It is so unsatisfactory to discuss such important matters through intermediaries.' He took a sip of his brandy, savouring it for a moment. 'Now we must discuss your terms for an agreement.'

Richard tasted the brandy before answering. He felt its warmth flowing through his body. 'All we ask, my lord, is that you do not support Margaret of Anjou or her Lancastrian supporters against the house of York.'

'And what do you offer me in return?'

'We commit not to support Burgundy in any action against France.'

Louis looked at Richard quizzically. 'Yet your king is planning to take Charles of Burgundy as a brother-in-law?'

Richard could see his plans unravelling. 'That has been discussed, although nothing has been agreed, Your Grace.'

Louis looked pleased. 'In that case I would like to find a French suitor for Margaret of York.' He noticed Richard's hesitation. 'And I will provide a dowry of gold fit for the sister of the King of England.' He warmed to the idea. 'I will also pay the king in gold for each year our treaty of peace endures, and remove the restrictions on English merchants, as a gesture of our continued goodwill.'

'I am sure, Your Grace, that King Edward would be most interested to hear your proposals.'

Louis leaned forward in his chair. 'What if he persists with his plans for a treaty with Burgundy?'

Richard was prepared for the question. 'I am confident that I am able to persuade him.'

'It would be useful to have a plan.' The king paused significantly. 'Just in case?'

Richard recalled how one of the French ambassadors mentioned the possibility of the Lordship of Normandy. He took another sip of the fine brandy. He had been drinking wine at the reception and was aware he needed to keep a clear head. 'What do you have in mind, Your Grace?'

'You could restore King Henry to the throne.'

Richard realised from the way Louis was watching his reaction this was not an idea that had only just occurred to him. He wondered if the hand of Margaret of Anjou was behind the suggestion. 'King Henry is a good, pious man, although not fit to rule England.'

'Henry would be a good King if he had you, Earl Warwick, to oversee the rule of the country in his stead?'

Richard looked at Louis and saw a twinkle in his eye. He was enjoying the intrigue. 'I don't need to remind Your Grace that King Henry has a wife waiting for the chance to put her son on the throne?'

Louis lowered his voice. 'The suggestion was made to me by her brother the Duke of Calabria. If King Edward rejects our offer of peace, I could ensure my cousin Margaret of Anjou sets aside past differences between you.' He sat back, looking pleased with himself.

Richard had to think fast. 'You are full of surprises, Your Grace. You can be assured I'll do everything in my power to see a lasting peace with France.'

Louis leaned forward again. 'All I ask is that you think on this, and also another offer I have for you.'

'And what would that be, Your Grace?' Richard was interested.

'If it comes to war with Burgundy, I could make you a prince. All of Holland and Zeeland could also be yours, your own kingdom.'

Richard was surprised. This was something he had never considered. He suddenly saw how his base at Calais could be extended to become an empire. Tired from the long day and feeling slightly dazed by the strong brandy and the unexpected turn their discussions had taken, he thanked the king for his hospitality and returned to his rooms to think on all he had heard.

His meetings with the king continued for eight days, with grand banquets and tours of the city, including a visit to the market square where Joan of Arc had been burned at the stake. News of the death of Philip of Burgundy surprised no one, although it meant Charles was now to become the new duke and even more of a threat to their plans.

On the final day of his visit Richard watched with Louis while a scribe prepared two copies of the agreement, which they both signed. It would have to be ratified by Edward in person, although that should be easier now the document had been signed by the King of France. As Richard bid farewell to King Louis he had mixed feelings about the deal they had agreed. In his heart Richard knew Edward would not hesitate to break the hard won truce at the first opportunity. If that were to happen, he would need to be ready to act.

Richard's brother George was waiting with Anne and his daughters for Richard's return to Warwick Castle. Richard hugged his wife and shook hands with his younger brother, pleased and surprised to see him, although he immediately knew from his brother's demeanour that the news he brought was not good. The death of the Duke of Burgundy would change Edward's position regarding Charles and he was keen to catch up with events in his absence.

'What is it, George?'

'Edward rode out to my residence with his men and demanded my seal of office.' George looked directly at Richard. 'He has replaced me as Chancellor.'

Richard was tired from his long ride and sat in his favourite chair, trying to make sense of the shocking news. Their father had been Lord Chancellor, one of the highest ranking of the Great Officers of State, second only to the Lord High Steward. This was not merely a slight against his brother George. Edward's action was a slap in the face for the reputation of the entire Neville family.

'Who has he appointed in your place?'

'The Bishop of Bath and Wells.'

Richard frowned. 'He was somehow involved in the secrecy surrounding Edward's marriage to Elizabeth, although I've yet to discover in what way.' He looked at his brother. 'The important question is why?'

George seemed uncomfortable. 'I think I was a little outspoken about the Burgundians and have been working to secure a dispensation from the Pope to allow your daughter to marry the Duke of Clarence. I try to be discreet but Edward has spies everywhere now, even in my own household.'

'Is Earl Rivers behind all this?'

George shook his head. 'I understand why you could think that. Rivers has reason enough to bear a grudge against us all, yet he seems to be an honourable man, despite our differences in the past. I suspect William Herbert is plotting to bring us down, Richard.'

'Lord Herbert? What have we done to wrong him?'

'Herbert accompanied Edward when he came to demand my seal of office. He looked rather pleased with himself.'

Anne had been watching their exchange in silence. 'I am afraid there is worse news, concerning you, Richard.'

'What now?'

George answered. 'Our enemies have been spreading a damaging rumour. They are saying you went to France to meet with Margaret of Anjou.'

Anne looked worried. 'They also say you have made a secret pact with her. It's being repeated everywhere.'

Richard felt a wave of anger. He looked at them both and saw they were waiting for his reaction. Even his wife and his brother were prepared to believe the rumours were true. His reputation would be ruined unless he could convince everyone of his innocence.

'I can show them who I've been meeting with!' He realised he was raising his voice and took a deep breath in an effort to calm himself. 'I returned with the senior ambassadors of the King of France.'

Anne still looked concerned. 'What are we going to do about it, Richard?'

He put his arm around her. 'I will take the French ambassadors to meet the king. Then we will just have to see.'

✛

The rhythmic stroke of the oarsmen pulled the gilded barge through the murky water of the River Thames with deceptive ease. There was a light breeze coming down the river. Although almost summer, Richard was glad of the fur coat he wore. He leaned across and pointed out Greenwich Palace to his guests, led by the Count Louis de Bourbon, Admiral of France and chief ambassador of King Louis. Fluent in English, the count was an amiable young man who had risen to his important post despite his nickname of the bastard of Bourbon.

Richard was doing his best to conceal his concern at the reception they would receive from Edward. He had only grudgingly agreed to meet them at all, yet he had also made no mention of the rumours about Margaret of Anjou, for which Richard was grateful. Now as they neared the stone jetty of the Palace of Westminster, he saw there was only Luke Tully, with Richard's personal guard, waiting to welcome them.

He had foreseen this possibility and asked George, Duke of Clarence to assist. He had also ordered Tully to have drummers and trumpeters standing by. As their barge drew alongside the old jetty the drums and trumpets struck up on an unseen signal, causing interested passers-by to gather in a small crowd. There was no royal banner or any sign of the king, which in itself was a breach of protocol and contrasted starkly with his own reception at Rouen. George played his part well, however, making a short speech of thanks and explaining that the king was waiting to greet them in Westminster Palace.

After an embarrassingly long wait in the king's antechamber they were finally ushered in. The king was dressed informally in riding clothes and instead of the advisors Richard expected to see attending such a meeting, Lord Herbert was at his right side, regarding them suspiciously, with Earl Rivers on his left. Richard wondered if Edward planned to embarrass him further in front of the two men he most suspected of trying to harm his reputation.

He stepped forward and formally introduced Count Louis and the other French ambassadors. Edward regarded them with poorly disguised disinterest. His welcome was cold, as if he would rather not have met with them at all. He did not invite them to be seated, although there were empty chairs at his table.

'Good day to you, ambassadors. You will understand that this meeting is a short one.' He looked at Lord Herbert, who nodded in confirmation. 'There are rumours of plague in the city. My court is moving to Windsor right away.'

Richard was disappointed. 'There are significant matters regarding the details of this treaty that cannot be rushed, Your Grace.'

Edward looked up at him, unsmiling. 'In that case, Earl Warwick, I shall appoint representatives to study these matters in detail.'

Richard knew he was about to dismiss them, before any of the ambassadors had even spoken. 'King Louis of France has signed the treaty, which now needs to be ratified by Your Grace.' He looked directly at Edward. 'I recommend you to invite the French ambassadors to attend your court in Windsor.' Richard knew he was making a bold suggestion and risking a stern rebuttal. He hoped he knew Edward well enough to be confident he would avoid confrontation where he could.

Edward agreed. 'If we must.' He turned to the Count of Bourbon. 'We will continue this discussion at a later date, Count Louis.'

Richard thought he saw a gleam of triumph in William Herbert's eyes as they thanked the king and returned to the waiting barge. As they made their way back down river the count spoke to him quietly, so the others would not overhear.

'It seems, Earl Warwick, that Charles of Burgundy has been here ahead of us?'

Richard disagreed. 'The people don't trust Burgundy. They never have and I doubt they ever will.' He lowered his voice, concerned that even on his private river barge his words could be overheard and repeated. 'The problem

I have to address is that the king is surrounded by those who put their own interests before those of their king.' He looked at the young count, one of the few people he now felt he could trust to keep his words confidential. 'They are traitors to our cause, Count Louis, and I will deal with them.'

Chapter 23 - Autumn 1468

The grand banqueting hall of Middleham Castle was turned into Richard's headquarters in the north, with messengers at all hours, lords and knights rallying to confirm their support. Although the leaves had barely begun to fall from the trees, the chill of winter was already making itself felt. Richard had a log fire blazing in the grate, filling the air with the familiar warmth of wood smoke. He sat in his father's heavy wooden chair at the head of the table, reflecting on the change in his fortunes.

King Edward and his Woodville court at Windsor had paid scant attention to the French ambassadors, despite his best efforts. In the end the ambassadors had to leave with only the gift of a pair of mastiffs and a hunting horn for their troubles. It contrasted starkly with the gold chalice and other gifts he had been given in France. Richard knew this was a poor outcome and one which could permanently damage his standing with the King of France.

There had been extravagant banquets to celebrate the formal announcement of Charles of Burgundy's engagement to Edward's sister Margaret of York. After that the affronts to the Neville family name had come thick and fast. At the urging of his brother George, Richard made one last effort to put his own feelings to one side and agreed to escort young Margaret to Dover for the start of her new life.

Duke Charles was waiting to greet them in all his Burgundian finery. Swaggering and overbearing, he had clearly not forgotten how their last meeting had ended and treated Richard with thinly veiled contempt. Aware his every word could be reported back to the king, Richard ignored the duke's posturing and wished him every happiness with his new bride.

In truth, Richard's heart was heavy with pity for Margaret of York, a beautiful princess and a Plantagenet daughter of York. Trained to expect her fate from childhood, she was now forced to spend the rest of her life with a man they both detested. There was sadness in her eyes when she bid him goodbye, but as her ship sailed he realised that as the Duchess of Burgundy, young Margaret could be a useful friend to him in the future.

On his return to Westminster he learned disturbing news. Edward was planning a truce with Brittany and successfully petitioned parliament for money to make war on France. He was planning an invasion by sea with an armada of warships. They were to be commanded by the queen's brother, Lord Scales. There was no role for Richard, despite the fact he was still Captain of Calais and the most experienced admiral in the country.

While he was still trying to come to terms with this, Edward ordered him to send four hundred of his best archers to support Brittany in the new war against France. The final insult. There had been a great argument which only served to remind him how little power he now had. Richard left for the north on bad terms to consider his future.

Now he sent for his brother George to help decide how to proceed. He was approaching forty and his black beard was starting to turn grey. There was now no prospect of a son and heir, yet for the first time in ages he felt a sense of excitement at being back in control of his own destiny. He had tried his best to retain some influence at court, yet Edward crossed him every time.

At great personal risk he exchanged secret messages with King Louis in France. His messages were frank about the people's unease with the relentless rise of the queen's family. He also confirmed what he knew Louis wanted to hear about the unpopular relationship with Burgundy, yet he had so far stopped short of warning of the planned invasion. Richard knew the king could read between the lines.

George arrived in the early evening and Richard greeted him warmly. 'You look more like a soldier than a man of the cloth.' He looked at his brother. Without his bishop's robes he looked a true Neville, although he had his mother's insightful temperance and none of his father's bluff manner. He also lacked Richard's bitterness at the way they had been so badly treated by Edward, yet they shared the same determination to defend their family name.

'Such are the times we live in now, Richard. Even the Archbishop of York cannot visit his own brother without tongues wagging.' George pulled off the heavy black cloak he was wearing and threw it on a chair. 'These riding clothes allow me to travel as I please without drawing attention.'

They sat in the comfortable chairs on each side of the massive stone hearth, booted feet on the wrought iron firedogs, enjoying the heat from the blazing logs. A servant brought a bottle of wine, with a supper of thick slices of roast beef and freshly baked bread for George. He poured them each a goblet of the good French wine, then Richard gestured for the man to leave and closed the door behind him.

'I am troubled by the knowledge that Edward's spies are almost certainly watching our movements.' He scowled. 'We must take care not to be overheard, even in our own castle!'

George shook his head. 'When the papal legate came to visit he told me he was followed as soon as he reached our shores.'

Richard looked across at his brother. 'I need your help, George. Will you secure the dispensation for Isabel to marry the Duke of Clarence?'

George was enjoying his roast beef. Richard waited patiently for his brother to answer, knowing that more than just his daughter's future depended on his reply. Papal dispensations were difficult to obtain at the best of times and almost impossible now, unless George felt able to convince the Pope.

'I must advise you it will not be easy while King Edward opposes the match. He has even threatened the Pope that to grant a dispensation will incur the displeasure of England.' He shook his head. 'I've never heard the like.'

'Every man has his price, George, even the Pope of Rome. You can negotiate on my behalf as you see fit.'

George took a sip of wine and nodded in approval. 'It might not even be necessary to travel to Rome. I am still Archbishop of York. It will give me great satisfaction to personally preside over Isabel's wedding.'

'Thank you.'

Richard watched as his brother ate hungrily, tearing at the bread and wiping his plate with the crust just the way he had in this same room when they were boys. He remembered his surprise when their father first announced his wish for his youngest son to study for the priesthood. Only now did he see what a clever move his father had made to secure the power of the church, although he never envied his brother's apparent life of chastity.

George finished eating and set the now empty plate on the table, refilling his goblet with wine. 'And I would ask something of you in return, Richard, if I can.'

'Of course. All you need do is ask.' Richard was curious.

'I am probably right in thinking you had a hand in the ransacking of Earl Rivers' mansion by the men of Kent?'

Richard didn't reply, although he knew his silence would tell his brother all he needed to know.

George continued. 'At least you had the decency to make sure neither he or his family were at home this time.'

Richard knew he was referring to the way his men had dragged Richard Woodville and his wife Jacquetta from their bed in the raid on Sandwich and paraded them through the streets of Calais. It had seemed a good idea at the time. He wasn't to know that Rivers would one day be the king's right hand man, or that Edward would marry his daughter.

'What are you asking me to do?' He sat up in his chair, trying not to become annoyed at his brother. 'Is it my fault the Woodvilles are making themselves unpopular?'

George looked exasperated. 'Richard. I am asking you to try harder to make your peace with the father of the queen. He is a decent man. Edward and Elizabeth both listen to him, so you could have no greater ally to protect your interests at court.'

'You are right. If we have the dispensation, he might be able to moderate Edward's feelings about Isabel marrying his brother.'

'Then it is your plan to look at how Edward can be deposed?' There was a casual note to George's voice, as if he wasn't talking of treason against the king.

Richard hesitated before answering. It had saddened him when he realised he could no longer be entirely sure of his brother John, who was still fiercely loyal to Edward. Richard had never been close to George, who had followed such a different path, so still wondered how open he could be.

'George, Duke of Clarence, has reached his majority. My daughter Isabel is now seventeen.' He took a large log and threw it on the fire, which crackled and spat then burst into new orange flames. 'All I want is for them to be married while it's still possible.'

If George sensed Richard's unwillingness to share his plans, he gave no sign of it. 'What will we do if I cannot convince the Pope?'

Richard looked at his brother and decided to be more open with him. He had few enough allies now. 'You know our brother John recently quelled an insurrection aimed at restoring the Percy family to power?'

'Yes. York is full of it.' George reached for the wine bottle and refilled his goblet. 'This man who called himself Robin of Holderness was an agent of the Percy family.' He stared into the flames. 'He was inciting people to protest at the new taxes, when they were really campaigning for Henry Percy to be restored to the Earldom of Northumberland.'

'John hanged the ring-leaders, so I think we'll hear no more of it, although it has given me an idea.'

George looked interested. 'What's that?'

'Sir John Conyers visited me to express his support. He has a sizeable band of retainers.' Richard looked at his brother, watching his reaction. 'I've suggested he could help me by reminding our neighbours in the north of how little Edward has done for them. He is calling himself Robin of Redesdale.'

'And in the meantime you continue to act as a loyal Yorkist?'

'We are loyal Yorkists, George. I don't forget how our father and brother both died for the cause.' He took a sip of his wine and stared into the fire. 'In the meantime I don't see any harm in building support from those who are disaffected with the Woodvilles. If it ever comes to a fight, I need to be sure that people will rally to our banner.'

✝

The silver bells on the hooded falcon's leather traces tinkled musically as Richard and his hunting party rode towards the woods in the early autumn sunshine. George, Duke of Clarence, had arrived at Warwick Castle in style the previous day, wearing a shining silver breastplate adorned with a heavy gold medallion. Richard had invited him to come hunting with falcons, a good opportunity to get to know his future son-in-law better. He also needed to hear the latest news from London from someone inside the royal circle.

As well as the falconers, his squire Luke Tully and half a dozen men of his personal guard rode behind them, armed and ready if needed. Warwick Castle was a true fortress now. Lookouts stood guard on the battlements and patrols marched around the perimeter night and day, with guard commanders ready to sound the alarm at the first sign of trouble.

The threat of an attack was even felt inside the castle, where only the most trusted servants now remained in the household. A generous supply of provisions had been stored so they could withstand a siege if necessary, although Richard hoped it would never come to that. He had seen too many sieges in the north where those defending castles were simply trapped inside, their castles becoming their prisons.

He glanced at the young duke riding alongside him. If he didn't know he would never have guessed this was Edward's brother or Duke Richard's, for that matter, the three of them were so different in every respect. For all his faults, Edward looked and acted like a king, while Richard was serious and controlled. George was lighthearted and easily bored by politics or government. Fortunately he was excited about the prospect of hunting with the hawks.

Richard turned in the saddle to speak to George. 'How is the mood in London?'

'London is awash with rumours. Nobody knows what to believe.'

'So how is the king responding to these rumours?'

George shrugged. 'Edward is the same as ever. Nothing seems to worry him, even rumours of assassins on their way from France. Although he is angry with you about the fall of Brittany.'

Richard already knew. There was no way he could possibly send archers to support the Duke of Brittany in a fight against King Louis. Fortunately the opportunity had passed, as the duke had reached an amicable agreement with France, much to Edward's displeasure.

'Has Edward heard that Margaret of Anjou is gathering a fleet at Harfleur?'

'Yes. He ordered Lord Scales to patrol the Channel and keep our shores safe.'

'That should keep at least one Woodville busy for a while, before he learns the truth.'

George was quick to understand. 'There is no French fleet?'

'No. It is an unfortunate mistake. I understand the weather in the Channel is most unfavourable this time of year.' Richard smiled at George. 'I don't envy Lord Scales his task.'

'There is concern at how it's taking money meant to fund the invasion.'

Richard was unsurprised. 'That money will be needed at home soon.'

They reached the beaters with the dogs in a field at the edge of the woods and stopped to put on thick leather gauntlets. The trained peregrine falcons were handed to them and looked around with bright intelligence in their curious eyes as their hoods were removed. Richard felt the powerful grip of the bird's talons as it clung to his gauntlet. He held it high, careful not to startle his horse, the leather jesses securely held in his hand.

On Richard's signal, the beaters entered the woods to flush out game birds. He could hear the muffled sound of their dogs yapping excitedly, searching through the dense trees. He continued riding around the edge of the field at a slower pace, George at his side. Richard could tell George was an experienced falconer, his keen eyes already scanning the sky in anticipation.

A fat wood pigeon came flying out of the trees. Richard held tight to his falcon's tether, allowing George the satisfaction of the first kill. He watched as George's peregrine soared into the air after the flapping pigeon, swooping over the field to catch up with its prey. The pigeon saw the danger, putting on an impressive burst of speed in its bid to escape the grasping claws and savage beak.

George shouted to his bird as it set off in pursuit, then looked disappointed as the wood pigeon disappeared back into the trees. Two more wood pigeons flew out as the beaters progressed through the woods. Richard loosed his falcon, spurring his horse into a canter to keep the birds in view. There was a clash of feathers as the falcon grabbed its prey and dropped to the ground to make the kill. They watched the head of the peregrine stab down and rise again with a morsel of red flesh in its sharp beak.

Luke Tully emerged from the cover of the trees and shouted from behind them. 'Well done, my lord.'

Richard smiled. It felt good to forget the intrigue of London for a while. 'I was lucky.'

They all continued to watch the progress of George's falcon, which was determined not to give in. They rode closer, in time to see it turn in flight and head for one of the other birds. Folding back its wings the peregrine dived. This time the arrow-like hawk was faster than the pigeon, with deadly results. There was a squawk from the wood pigeon, the last sound it would make.

George was pleased. 'A good falcon, Richard. I knew it could do it!'

Richard grinned. 'All it needed was a little encouragement.'

George appreciated the joke. 'The thing is, Earl Warwick, are you the falcon or the pigeon?'

Richard was surprised at George's clever reply. 'Always the hawk, Duke Clarence. The pigeons fly for their lives, yet the hawk will always live to fight another day!'

As they rode back to the castle George recalled their earlier discussion. 'The merchants of London are unhappy that there are no concessions with Burgundy, despite my sister's marriage.' He looked across at Richard quizzically. 'It's as if someone is stirring up their discontent.'

Richard had good connections with the merchants. It was easy enough to remind them of Edward's promises. It had got a little out of hand, with talk of a riot, although no one could put the blame for that on him.

George continued, not seeming to need an answer. 'Is it true the French have equipped Jasper Tudor with ships to attack from the West?'

Richard was not ready to admit how well informed he was about the actions of the French. 'If it's true, that will give Lord Herbert something to think about, instead of spending all his time worrying about spies.'

George turned to him. 'You know they are going to set up a Royal Commission to look into the allegations Lord Herbert has uncovered?'

Richard felt a chill premonition. He had taken great risks sending letters to King Louis, more than enough to raise the suspicion of any commission. The last time he had been summoned to Westminster to face questions from a Royal Commission he barely escaped with his life.

George seemed to sense a change in Richard's mood and laughed. 'Don't you know? My brother has decided that the best person to oversee this commission is me, with you at my side.'

Richard could hardly believe his luck. 'I am grateful to you, George. Am I right in thinking you suggested this?'

George looked pleased with himself. 'Edward was glad to have the matter taken out of his hands. I thought we could use it to build support. Some of those accused by Lord Herbert would be grateful for a pardon.'

Richard smiled. 'I'm sure they will, George.'

Chapter 24 - Summer 1469

The masts of Richard's flagship, *Trinity*, dominated the bustling shipyard on the banks of the River Stour near the town of Sandwich. Richard was inspecting her with Lord Wenlock, who had been helping oversee the work. Luke Tully followed them at a respectful distance. Tully had fought on board *Trinity* as much as any man and had a keen interest in the improvements. He knew Richard had been personally involved in every detail of her building. She was the symbol of his successful domination of the seas.

Trinity was also a working ship, providing protection to merchant ships making the crossing between Calais and the Cinque Ports. Over the years she had become battle-scarred, her weapons and rigging outdated. She had also been captured by French pirates, then fortunately returned by King Louis as a gesture of goodwill.

The re-fit was needed to restore her former glory. The work had taken over a year and cost a small fortune, as he had engaged only the best craftsmen and spared no expense of the materials. Lord Wenlock ran his hand down the smoothly sanded wooden handrail and looked pleased with the quality of the finish.

'Better than she was, even when new, Earl Warwick.'

'Yes. It's good to see her finished at last, Sir John.' He looked up to where his banner flew proudly at the top of the mainmast. 'I've been so preoccupied with business in the north I'd almost forgotten her refitting was due to be completed.'

Lord Wenlock showed them the powerful new cannons, specially cast in bronze and fitted in special gun ports along each side. 'These are the latest design, more powerful than much heavier cannon, with an effective range of over three hundred yards. The carriages are English elm, good for resistance to splitting.'

Richard saw Tully looking at how the carriages were held down by thick ropes, shackled to the deck. 'We used to haul the old guns around the deck to give a wider field of fire. Aren't these ropes going to be a problem?'

'You should have seen the recoil when we tested the new guns.' Lord Wenlock bent down alongside Tully. 'That's why we have these breeching ropes, to keep them in position.' He led them to the stern, where *Trinity* now had smaller swivel guns, as they had seen used by Spanish warships to devastating effect.

Tully tested the range of movement and nodded in approval. 'These are going to be useful when we close in on Burgundians.'

Lord Wenlock looked pleased. 'We've had them mounted fore and aft. They fire buckshot, as well as the smaller cannon balls.' He looked serious. 'You just have to make sure they don't swing round and fire across the deck!'

Richard was keen to see what had been done with the accommodation and they went below. As well as Richard's luxurious cabin at the stern, which had views out to sea, there was a generous cabin for guests and another for the captain. All the cabins were fitted out with new wood panelling. The spacious wardroom and adjoining galley had low headroom for the tall Lord Wenlock. The even taller King Edward had hit his head more than once aboard *Trinity*.

276

They were completing their tour of the ship when one of the crew advised of the arrival of their guests. The relaunch of *Trinity* provided the perfect excuse for Richard to gather his family in Sandwich. Anne had travelled from Warwick Castle with their daughters and household the previous day and were in lodgings in the town. His brother George had ridden from London and George, Duke of Clarence had brought a small army of servants and retainers from the west. Only his brother John remained in the north, still dealing with sporadic Lancastrian uprisings.

Richard welcomed them both and they all assembled on the deck for the formal blessing of the ship. Richard's brother looked once again like the Archbishop of York in his full regalia as he conducted the ceremony. After the blessing Richard met privately with his brother and the duke in his cabin. They had both brought important documents for him.

First his brother handed Richard a large letter bearing an impressive lead seal. 'The Papal dispensation.'

Richard examined the seal on the document. 'Thank you. There was a time when I wondered if I'd ever see the day this was granted. It has been almost three years.'

His brother looked pleased. 'I am glad to be able to help you, Richard, although I fear there will be consequences of this marriage. I have to leave now, Richard, as I must return to London.' He looked at the young duke. 'You have my blessing, as well as that of Rome.'

George, Duke of Clarence, studied the seal. 'Thank you, archbishop. Your brother told me you succeeded, although it's good to see this with my own eyes.'

After Richard's brother had left, George handed Richard an official warrant from the king, this time bearing the royal seal.

Richard unfolded the warrant and studied it carefully. 'Good.' He looked at the young duke and his brother, aware that they were about to pass the point of no return. 'Edward has agreed my request to return to Calais to again defend the shipping of the English Channel against Scottish and Breton Channel pirates. I shall look forward to that in due course. First, we have a wedding to attend to.'

George frowned. 'Edward is going to be furious with us both when he finds out.'

'That's why the wedding needs to be in Calais. Once we are safely across the Channel there's not a lot even he can do about it.'

George still seemed concerned. Richard knew the young duke was still capable of running back to London, given the opportunity. As well as making any prospect of his marriage to Isabel impossible, George knew enough now to have them all condemned as traitors.

Richard tried to look more confident than he felt. 'Your brother seems to have overlooked the fact I've been Captain of Calais for a long time. Calais has England's only standing army, loyal to me and mine to turn to whatever course I choose.'

'What about the Duke of Burgundy? He has more than enough men to attack Calais if Edward gives him leave to do so.'

Richard was surprised at the young duke's grasp of the situation. 'I can deal with the Duke of Burgundy. I have been in correspondence with your sister. Margaret will help us win over her new husband.'

There was a surprise waiting for them both when they returned to Richard's lodgings in the town. George's mother Duchess Cecily of York was waiting for them. It had been a few years since Richard had last seen her. In that time her hair had turned a soft shade of grey and even on the warm day the duchess wore black gloves and a heavy dark cloak with a fur trim. She had a reputation for her short temper and glowered at them as she dismissed their attempted warm welcome.

'Word has reached me that you are once again saying that Edward is low born.'

Richard could not deny it. Once again he felt the prospect of Isabel's marriage slipping from his grasp right at the last moment.

The duchess took his silence as an admission. 'Tell me it's not because you plan to replace him with George.' She scowled at her son, as if noticing him for the first time.'

George could not restrain himself. 'You have as good as admitted it yourself!'

Cecily gave him a withering look. 'You should know better than to raise your voice to your mother. Such talk is treason, George, and well you know it.'

Richard was becoming increasingly concerned. 'Do you deny it, here and now, Duchess Cecily?'

'Of course I deny it. Shame on you, Richard, for such betrayal of Edward. Is it true that you accuse the queen's mother of using sorcery to bring about Edward's marriage to her daughter?'

Once again, Richard chose not to answer.

His aunt turned on him accusingly. 'You are planning to make George king, regardless of the consequences, so your daughter can become queen!'

'I simply ask your blessing for my daughter to marry your son, that is all.'

The duchess had heard enough. 'Rest assured, Earl Warwick, the king will hear of this and he will not think well of it.'

Richard hoped he could appeal to her better nature. 'I ask you as my father's sister, as a Neville, to consider what is best for your family. There is no better suitor in England, and she is heiress to half my fortune.' He took comfort from the flicker of compassion he thought he saw in her eyes.

The duchess looked at them both. 'I cannot give you my blessing, knowing it would be against Edward's wishes, although in memory of both your fathers, I will pray for you all.'

✢

The *Trinity* sailed with the tide, followed by a fleet of ships carrying archers and men-at-arms to reinforce the garrison, as well as wedding guests, servants and cooks to assist with the wedding banquet. Richard breathed a sigh of relief as they tied up at the familiar quay, overlooked by the dark shape of the old Rysbank Tower.

After a busy few days of preparation for the wedding everything was finally ready. The cathedral-like church of Notre Dame, which had been damaged and repaired so many times in battles for control of Calais, was filled with the delicate scent of hundreds of fresh flowers. Isabel and Richard made the short journey from the castle in a coach drawn by two white horses. She looked happy and beautiful in her wedding dress of brilliant white silk. Her long dark hair was combed down over her shoulders and she wore a diamond tiara, which sparkled in the bright Calais sunshine.

Richard took his daughter's hand in his and led her along the aisle to where George, Duke of Clarence waited in his colourful knight's regalia. Richard was pleased and relieved to see so many knights and nobles had made the crossing to Calais to show their support. All were aware this was not without the risk of their attendance being reported to the king, although for now all that mattered was the wedding.

Richard's brother, the Archbishop of York, conducted the service and young George's voice was clear and confident as he said his vows. Richard stared up to the high arched ceiling of the old church. His eyes rested on the brightly painted effigy of Christ on the cross. He said thanks to God his daughter had found a good marriage at last and prayed that he had led his family on the right path.

The wedding celebrations were barely over when a ship arrived with urgent news from England. Followers of Robin of Redesdale had begun rallying in the north and King Edward had left for Fotheringay Castle with an army to deal with the uprising. Events were moving faster than Richard had planned. He met with his new son-in-law and they agreed to return to Sandwich and call for the good men of England to be ready to defend their rights.

Trinity sailed back to a rousing welcome from his supporters in Kent which reminded Richard of the old days. Hundreds of well-wishers were waiting on the quayside and the word was that an army of thousands were now marching from the north. He wondered what his brother John would do, knowing he would be torn between his loyalty to the king and his family.

Richard also learned that there was no time to lose, as his old adversary Sir William Herbert, now Earl of

Pembroke in place of Jasper Tudor, was bringing an army of Welshmen in support of the king. This could be his only chance to take control of the capital. The time had come to march on London. As they approached the city Richard looked back over his shoulder and could see the black bull of Clare on the banner of the Duke of Clarence, his men following behind. Behind them a straggling line of riders and foot soldiers dressed in Warwick colours stretched far back into the distance. It looked as if the numbers of their followers had now grown to several thousand.

Luke Tully rode at Richard's side and saw him looking back at their growing army. 'We have a lot of hungry mouths to feed when we arrive in London. What kind of reception do you think we'll have, my lord?'

Richard wasn't sure of the answer. 'I've heard that people have had enough of the Woodvilles.' He looked across at Tully. 'Earl Rivers will have already found there is nothing so unpopular as new taxes.'

Tully frowned. 'Why are they needed, now the king no longer plans a war on France?'

'Good question, Tully. King Edward has promised much and delivered little. The Woodville's have been living beyond their means.'

'Now they want the people to pay for it?'

Richard scowled. 'Rivers should never have been made Treasurer.'

A rider was approaching them. Richard recognised him as one of his agents from the north. The man slowed and rode up to Richard. He wore Richard's ragged staff badge and his clothes were dusty from riding hard. His expression was serious. 'I have important news, Earl Warwick.'

'What is it?' Richard silently prayed that Edward hadn't routed the northerners and returned to the safety of London. It could be serious for them all.

'We have engaged the army of the Earl of Pembroke, at Edgecote, near Banbury.' He removed his hat and wiped his brow. 'The Welsh have good numbers with poleaxes. We can see no artillery and few archers. If you can send reinforcements it will help us win the day.'

Richard was relieved at the news. 'I can send half my men right away. Can you lead them to the place?'

The man nodded. 'We must be quick, before the king's army can reach them from Nottingham.'

Richard watched as his best men rode off. 'I wish we were going with them, Tully.' He looked up the road to where the gates of London waited.

There hadn't been time to send scouts ahead, so he was relying on his judgement. He was fairly confident that the people would welcome them, although he knew they could be riding into a trap. Their arrival in the city was uneventful. There were no cheering crowds, although people did stop and stare as hundreds of men in the colours of George of Clarence and Warwick rode through the streets. If Edward was angry at news of George's wedding there was no sign of it.

Richard arranged supplies and purchased new equipment for his men. He originally planned to spend some time in London, regaining the confidence of the merchants and winning more support at the council in Westminster. Instead he knew he had to march north. His life could depend on the outcome of the battle ahead.

George rode at Richard's side. He wore his new armour which gleamed in the bright summer sunshine and had never been used in battle. George seemed completely unconcerned at having to leave his bride of less than a week behind in Calais. Instead he wanted to understand Richard's plans for when they arrived in Northampton.

'What will we do with my brothers if they are defeated?'

Richard had been reflecting the problem since they left London. 'I think it rather depends on Edward.'

George rode in silence for a short distance, apparently reflecting on Richard's words. He turned in his saddle, his polished breastplate flashing in the sun. 'Edward has a forgiving nature. If he is defeated he will take it with good grace. My brother Richard will not. He is vengeful, with everything to gain and little to lose.'

'I intend to persuade Richard of Gloucester to take the hand of my daughter Anne.'

George was surprised. 'He is loyal to Edward and would never agree!'

'Quite the contrary. She is heir to half my fortune.' Richard smiled as he remembered how Annie had pretended to be disinterested in the young duke, yet spent every spare moment with him. 'They were close when Richard lived in my household.'

'She's just a girl. They were like brother and sister, from what I recall.'

'Be that as it may, my daughter is thirteen now and will soon be a woman. I would much prefer to have your brother Richard tied to our interests rather than working against them.'

George looked unhappy at the prospect and continued riding in silence. Richard had chosen not to share his fears with his new brother-in-law. He was far from certain that Edward's forces would be easily defeated, although as far as they knew he had still not joined forces with the advancing Welsh army. Richard was more concerned with the quality of his own supporters marching south under Robin of Redesdale. Many were untrained retainers, armed with whatever they could lay their hands on. Not for the first time, he wished his brother John was commanding them.

As they finally approached Northampton Richard recalled the battle there nine years before. The road had been mired with mud and he didn't have dry clothes for a week, yet it had been one of their greatest victories. Now the road was dry and dusty from lack of rain. They slowed as one of the scouts reported dust rising into the air. There were riders ahead.

Tully squinted as he tried to identify the approaching men. Richard's hand fell to the handle of his sword.

Tully shouted. 'Warwick colours. They carry your banner, my lord!'

'They must be men from the advance party we sent.' Richard felt a sense of relief which was quickly replaced by concern. 'It could mean another victory or they could be coming to warn us of danger ahead.' He held up his hand to stop his men and they waited as the riders approached.

The leading rider was one of his commanders. 'Good news, my lord Warwick.' He reined in his horse and rode closer to Richard. 'The Welsh are routed.'

'What of the king?'

The man shrugged his shoulders. 'The word is he is still in Fotheringay Castle, my lord.'

Richard was pleased, it was exactly what he had been praying for. 'And Sir William Herbert, the Earl of Pembroke?'

'Captured, my lord. Together with his brother, Sir Richard Herbert and other nobles.'

Richard turned to George. 'It looks as if your men have been spared a fight. We will make camp in Northampton and decide what to do next.'

The details of the battle began to emerge as more men found their way back to the town of Northampton. The Earl of Pembroke's forces had been driven back by the archers of Robin of Redsdale. The earl and his brother fought back with men wielding poleaxes and nearly won the day, until Richard's reinforcements arrived. When they saw the banner of the bear and ragged staff the Welshmen broke and ran.

Richard billeted his men in the old castle of Northampton and found himself more comfortable quarters in a merchant's mansion overlooking the market square. He slept badly and lay awake in the darkness wondering what the future held. His scouts had returned with news that King Edward remained at Fotheringay Castle, with many of his men deserted. Richard had no wish to confront his former friend until he could be sure it wouldn't end in a battle.

Another problem that troubled him was what to do with his prisoners. He could have them locked up, although the earl was well connected and could rally support, even from within the Tower of London. Richard decided to send a message to those who would oppose him. The next day the people of Northampton gathered in the market square to witness the execution of Sir William Herbert and his nobles. Richard watched from a high window and turned away when he heard the crowd cheer. He had beaten the man who played a part in turning Edward against him. It gave him little pleasure. For all his faults, Sir William had been a loyal supporter of the house of York and was merely guilty of underestimating his enemy.

Richard arrived at Fotheringay Castle with George, Duke of Clarence, only to discover that the king was no longer there. They decided to make it their base for organising a search and sent men to all the seaports to prevent Edward escaping by sea to Burgundy. Although there was no sign of the king, his soldiers captured Earl Rivers and his son John and took them to Kenilworth for trial.

His brother George arrived from York to plead for the Woodville earl. 'Remember your promise to me, Richard. You agreed to do your best to reconcile your differences with Earl Rivers.' He looked exasperated. 'You can't just round up all Edward's nobles and have them murdered without even a trial by their peers.'

Richard had to tell his brother the truth. 'I am afraid you are too late. Earl Rivers has already been executed.'

George was shocked. 'Dear God. His son as well?'

'They were dangerous, George. If I let them live they would soon have found a way to turn against us.'

'The Earl of Pembroke was following the orders of the king.' George looked concerned. 'What crime was Earl Rivers charged with?'

'He ill advised the king through his own greed. He had always worked against us, George. You know it.'

'And his son John, was he guilty of the same?'

'Calm yourself, George. The public response to these executions has not done us any harm. A clear message has been sent to those who would march against us.' He looked at his brother. 'I gave orders that their heads were not to be displayed, as they did our father and brother. They were given a Christian burial.'

George shook his head in disbelief. 'You have clearly lost touch with what the people think, Richard. I can tell you they are horrified at your action.' He glared sternly at Richard. 'And what of Edward? When you find him, will you execute the king?'

Richard knew his answer was going to surprise his brother. 'I was going to ask you to escort him to Warwick Castle. He can be safe in your care.'

Edward relaxed in Richard's study at Middleham Castle and seemed worryingly unconcerned at his situation. He had been found in the house of one of his supporters and had agreed to be escorted by the Archbishop of York to Warwick Castle, for his own safety. As soon as the Lancastrians realised the king was captive they renewed their revolt in the north. The king's army would only act on his authority so Richard had no choice other than to move him to Middleham, then to Pontefract Castle, where he could sign the necessary orders. The revolt was soon crushed and the ringleaders executed, although the mood in the country remained on the edge of anarchy as Richard struggled to assert his authority.

Now Edward had called for Richard to come to Pontefract, as he had something important to say. Edward had been surprisingly amiable about being held under effective house arrest, although there had been an incident the previous week. Edward had been hunting in the castle grounds and almost rode away from his escort. Fortunately the men had been able to stop him escaping. Their captain told Richard that the king's intentions were clear. He had been testing their resolve.

Edward didn't stand when Richard entered the room and sat looking at him for a moment, before speaking. 'It is my intention to leave for London.'

Richard tried to hide his surprise. 'When the time is right, Edward, I will personally escort you back to London.'

'As you did with poor King Henry?' There was a note of ridicule in Edward's voice this time.

Richard felt his anger rising and did his best to control it. 'London has become a dangerous place these last few months. Every day I've had to deal with people taking the law into their own hands.' He looked at Edward. 'I'm keeping you here for your own safety and it's for me to decide when it's safe for you to return.'

Edward stood and stared out of the window. 'Since when was it the place of an earl,' he turned to give Richard another of his disarming smiles, 'to decide the king's pleasure to travel as he wishes?'

Richard heard hooves clattering on the cobble-stones outside and joined Edward at the window. The castle yard was filling with men not in Warwick livery. They were the king's personal guard. He could also see men wearing the badge of the white boar. Somehow Edward had sent message to his brother, Richard of Gloucester.

Edward gripped Richard's upper arm. The pressure of his hand was firmer than necessary and the threat in his voice was obvious. 'For old time's sake, Richard, I'll not have you clapped in irons.' He released his grip and turned for the door. 'Take care, Earl Warwick.'

He left without waiting for an answer. Richard watched through the window as King Edward joined his men in the courtyard below. He couldn't hear what they were saying although he could see Edward asking questions and looking satisfied with the answers as he put on a thick fur cape and hat. A groom appeared, leading the king's horse, already saddled and fitted with a bridle, making Richard wonder what had become of his own guards. Without looking back, King Edward led his men out through the castle entrance with a clatter of hooves.

Richard watched them go then stormed to the guardhouse to confront the guard commander. It seemed inconceivable that the king could simply ride out of one of the best defended castles in the country without even a challenge.

'What the hell is going on?' He looked at their surprised faces and realised that he had somehow been outmanoeuvred by Edward. 'Why did no one stop the king from leaving?'

The guard commander explained. 'Lord Montague, my lord. He ordered us to make way for the king.'

Richard was thrown. His brother John had finally decided which side he would support and had joined Edward. It shouldn't have been too much of a surprise, as his brother's son had been promised the hand of Lady Elizabeth, Edward's eldest daughter, although she was barely four years old. Nevertheless, he was still bitterly disappointed.

Chapter 25 - Spring 1470

Richard hammered on the door of George, Duke of Clarence's lodgings. It took time for the duke's servants to answer. On Richard's insistence they roused George from his bed and he reluctantly agreed to see Richard in his rooms.

'What's going on?' The duke looked as if he had been drinking.

'Edward is summoning people to York and asking them about a plot.' Richard lowered his voice, conscious of the danger they could be overheard. 'To put you on the throne. In his place.'

George looked worried. 'Who told you this?'

'My brother, the Archbishop. He sent a rider to warn me. It is only a matter of time before we too are summoned.'

'What are we going to do?'

Richard looked at George's crumpled nightshirt. 'Get dressed. We have to get back to the safety of Calais until all this dies down.' He saw George was trying to take in the implications of what he was saying.

'What about Isabel?'

Richard frowned. His daughter was close to having her first child. 'She will have to come with us, as will my wife and daughter.'

'She can't. Isabel will have to stay at Warwick Castle.'

'I can't risk having her used as a hostage to force us to return. I'm sorry, George. This timing is not of my choosing.'

A thought occurred to George. 'They'll be watching the ports. Surely Edward will guess we're headed to Calais?'

'Which is why we'll take the long way round. I've sent messages for ships to be waiting at Exmouth. If we are quick we can be safely out to sea before they even realise we are gone.'

✦

It proved easier than Richard expected to move his family in secret, travelling at night and staying at the houses of loyal supporters. He was able to muster a dozen ships at Exmouth and as many again were to join them from Weymouth. Although feeling immense relief once their fleet headed out to sea, Richard paced the deck, worried about Isabel's condition. She had been horrified at the prospect of travelling to Calais and Anne nearly persuaded him to leave them to take their chances at Warwick. Part of him wished he had now, as the sea conditions were far from ideal, with a squall on the way.

The problem was of his own making. Although he had been careful to stay clear of the queen, she would never forgive the execution of her father and brother. Worse still, in an act of bravado, he had ordered the arrest of her mother on charges of sorcery, only to see her released soon afterwards. Now he had no choice other than to keep his family close.

George joined him on the deck. He wore a thick cape and a fur hat to keep out the Atlantic chill. His usual good humour was replaced by a heavy frown as he regarded the choppy seas ahead of them.

Richard greeted him with an attempted smile. 'How is Isabel?'

'Dammed if I know.' George pulled his cloak more tightly round him as the spray from a wave spattered them with salty water. 'Your wife is with her, there's nothing I can do.'

'I'm hoping the weather improves before we reach Southampton.'

'Southampton? We need to give any of the English ports a wide berth!'

Richard disagreed. 'My flagship, *Trinity*, is berthed in Southampton. We'll be needing her in Calais.'

George looked amazed. 'It would be madness. For all you know your crew has been replaced with Edward's men. You can't just go sailing in and take her?'

'It's the last thing they'll expect us to do. *Trinity* has the best guns of any ship I know. She's worth it, George.'

'Worth risking all our lives?'

Richard stared out at the grey waves, now with white crests, a sign of worsening weather. He knew the young duke was right. 'I'll have the captain ready to take us out to sea at the first sign of trouble. We have the advantage of surprise, so let's surprise them!'

✦

He would have liked to be in the leading ship as they approached the more sheltered waters of the Solent. For once he had to let others take command and keep his family out of harm's way. Luke Tully had agreed to go in his place, with the best men from Richard's personal guard. The mission was reckless and carried a high risk, as there was no way of knowing how many of the king's men could be on board the *Trinity*.

They sailed a course close to the wooded shores of the Isle of Wight, hoping to stay out of sight from the mainland before making the turn that would take the fleet into the shelter of Southampton Water. Everything now depended on the element of surprise. Richard knew there was a danger of so many ships raising the alarm, so had sent two-thirds of them the long way around the island. He followed the rest of his fleet into Southampton Water and studied the outlines of the ships moored at the quayside. He could see distinctive high masts in the distance. His banner no longer flew from the topmast, although there was no mistaking the *Trinity*.

Like the bait in a trap, his flagship lured them right into the mouth of the old harbour before they realised the danger they were in. The roar of cannons sounded as a heavy iron ball crashed deep into the hull of the leading ship in Richard's fleet. Soldiers on the deck fell dying and wounded as hidden archers carefully selected their targets. There was a boom as another cannon ball smashed into the rigging of a second ship, shattering the mast and sending the mainsail to the deck in a tangle of rigging.

'Ready to go about, Captain!' Richard shouted at the top of his voice.

Their ship began to turn with painful slowness. Richard watched as more cannons fired with deadly effectiveness at such short range. Men were in the water, some jumping, others blasted to a certain drowning as few were able to swim. There was an enormous splash in the waves dangerously close to the stern of Richard's ship. He took one last look. There was nothing he could do for his men without endangering himself and his family.

Then he saw the longboat, men heaving on the oars as if their lives depended on it. Tully and some of his guards had realised there was no hope of saving the flagship. Richard felt the deck heel under his feet as the wind caught the sails, taking them away from the danger and also out of reach of the men in the longboat.

'Heave to, Captain!' Richard shouted, pointing to the rowing men.

More thunderous booms sounded on the shore and a plume of water rose into the air close by, narrowly missing the longboat. The rowers pulled with renewed energy. The captain had realised what was happening and continued the slow turn, closing the gap in the water between them. Richard shouted to his crewmen.

'Have some ropes over the side, we'll leave the longboat!'

He could now clearly make out the faces of the rowers and was relieved to see Tully amongst them. There was a thump as the longboat struck the hull of the ship and the men scrambled up the side, finding handholds wherever they could. Luke Tully was bleeding from a cut on his head and looked totally exhausted with the effort of their escape.

'I'm sorry, my lord.' He wiped the blood from his brow. 'There were too many of them. I think they were expecting us.' He sounded breathless.

'I'm glad you made it back, Tully. Get someone to take a look at that wound.' Richard stared back at the harbour. One of their ships was on fire, with smoke billowing into the sky.

He called to the captain. 'We need to get underway. Quick as we can. They might pursue us in the *Trinity*. She's a much faster ship than this and can out gun anything in our fleet.'

They were not pursued and he assumed the men defending Southampton were fully occupied by the ships he had been forced to sacrifice. Richard gave the order to set a course for Calais and went below. George was waiting for him in his cabin. Before he could say anything an anguished cry of agony came from the adjacent cabin.

'Isabel.' George scowled at him with bitter accusation in his eyes. 'The baby is coming.'

'My wife is with her?'

'And your daughter. We need to get her ashore, Richard.'

'We can't turn back. I just hope the baby can wait until we get to Calais.'

He went back on deck to find the weather had worsened. A sheet of sea water sluiced over the deck as the bows crashed through a high wave. Richard gripped tightly to the handrail as he made his way to the captain.

'Can we sail any faster?'

The captain frowned as he studied the taut canvas sails. 'The wind is veering. If it stays in our favour, we should reach Calais by nightfall, my lord.'

'Do your best, Captain.' Salty spray lashed at Richard's face as he looked at the unsettled waves ahead. 'We need to get to Calais as soon as we can.' He was talking as much to himself as to the captain. They had lost valuable time in the attempt to retrieve his flagship, as well as many of his best men and several of his largest ships.

The ship heeled as a freshening breeze filled the sails. Richard clung to the wooden rail and wondered how his daughter was coping below decks. He knew he should stay out of the way, as Anne would know what to do. The life of the baby was in God's hands now, as was his own future.

He reached inside his spray-soaked tunic and felt the polished surface of the crucifix he wore around his neck. The fine detail was worn smooth. The silver felt warm to his touch, an amulet for a better future. As the ship ploughed through the heavy dark seas, Richard's lips moved in prayer. He prayed for the life of his grandchild. He prayed for them all.

Night had fallen when the lights of Calais finally appeared on the horizon. The winds had not been kind to them and the old ship was forced to tack up the English Channel, every mile hard won against the angry black sea. Richard sent Tully down below with a message for Isabel, telling her there was not much longer to wait. He stayed on deck, personally overseeing their navigation and keeping watch for Edward's fleet, which would surely come after them from Kent at first light.

Tully returned with a fresh bandage on his head. He was careful to find handholds as he made his way across the wet deck. The ship was still heeled over and lurched violently as they crashed through another heavy wave.

'How is my daughter?' Richard continued looking out to sea, knowing what his wife must be thinking of his actions.

'I could only speak to the countess, my lord. She says we must make haste.' He looked concerned. 'There are complications.'

Richard looked ahead to the lights which were now drawing closer. He'd made this journey many times and knew it wouldn't take long. He was looking forward to getting back to the safety of Calais, the ideal base from which to regroup his forces and plan his next steps with George. The weather was continuing to worsen, with the wind strengthening and rain now adding to the soaking of his clothes from the constant spray, so he was unsurprised to hear the rumble of thunder.

Tully pointed to the shore. 'They're firing at us! Our own cannons are firing at us!'

Richard looked again. He was tired and wet and finding it hard to make sense of Tully's words. Then there was another boom, louder this time and matched with a flash from the guns he had mounted on the high defensive walls. It all made sense in an instant. While he had been sailing around the south coast, Edward's ships had sailed straight across the shortest width of the Channel. Calais was lost.

'Captain, heave to!' Richard shouted at the top of his voice, aware they must stay out of range of the guns. 'Signal the fleet to stand off!'

He turned to Tully. 'I left Baron Wenlock in charge. I persuaded him to switch his loyalty to Edward. It's a fair bet he's responsible for this.'

The guns fired another deafening salvo, as if to confirm he was right. It angered Richard to know he was still paying the men who now fired at them.

Tully agreed. 'We'll have to send a ship under a flag of truce. I'll go with them.' He peered through the rain into the darkness. 'There must still be men loyal to you in our garrison.'

'You'd be risking capture?'

'We don't have time to wait until daylight, my lord.'

Richard knew he had no choice. 'Tell them about my daughter. See if you can find a midwife and will you ask for something to ease her suffering?'

Tully disappeared into the night, already picking the men to go with him. Richard went back below decks. Sea water had found its way through the hatch and was swilling around his ankles as the ship rolled. He hammered on the door of his daughter's cabin.

'Anne?' He could hear Isabel sobbing, even over the noise of the wind howling overhead.

He tried again. 'Anne. It's Richard. We need to talk.'

The door to the cabin opened and Anne appeared, wiping her hands on a cloth. Richard recognised it as one of her petticoats, ripped up for rags. She was cleaning blood from her hands. His daughter's blood. Behind her he saw Isabel crying on the bunk with his other daughter kneeling at her side. The ship lurched again and Anne grabbed his arm to steady herself. He could see all he needed to know in her eyes. He pulled her into the companionway.

Anne closed the cabin door behind her. 'How much longer?'

Richard hardly knew what to say. 'Calais is lost, Anne.' He looked into her tear-stained face. 'I'm sorry it has come to this.'

'Then we must get ashore somewhere else. Now, Richard.' There was a hardness in her voice. 'Do what you can. Before it's too late.' With that she returned to the cabin, closing the door behind her and leaving him standing alone.

Richard went to his own cabin and found George sleeping in his bunk. An empty bottle clattered back and forth on the cabin floor with the roll of the ship. Richard picked it up, then uncorked a bottle from his sea chest and swigged a mouthful of the strong brandy. He took it back to Isabel's cabin and knocked. He could hear groaning from inside as his wife answered and he handed her the bottle. She took it without speaking and closed the door. He had done all he could now, there was nothing to do but wait.

The rain eventually stopped and the wind eased. The guns of Calais had stopped firing once they realised the fleet was staying out of range, their silence strangely adding to the tension. Richard went back to his daughter's cabin. There was no sound from inside and he pushed the door open. Anne was sitting at the end of the bunk holding a small bundle wrapped in white cloth. He realised the cloth was covering the baby's face.

There were tears in her eyes and Anne's dress was smeared with blood. She looked up at him. 'A boy.'

Richard felt overwhelmed with sadness. He didn't know what to say. He looked at his daughters. For a moment he thought Isabel was dead. Her face was so pale and her eyes closed. Then she began sobbing. His daughter Anne just sat with her back against the cabin wall, her eyes wide, looking in horror at her blood-covered hands.

A new dawn lit up the sky as the entire ship's crew stood reverently on the deck. A simple funeral. George stood impassively holding the little body of his son while Richard said a prayer, his voice failing him with emotion. They carefully lowered the weighted bundle into the cold dark waters of the English Channel. Richard didn't look into Anne's eyes, or those of his daughters. He wondered if they would ever forgive him, if all he had put them through could ever be worth the life of his grandson.

Another hour passed before Tully's ship appeared through the early morning sea mist and came alongside, the wooden hulls crunching together as he made the risky transfer. Richard was tired and soaked to the skin. He wiped a wet cloth across his face and tried to focus on what they needed to do.

Tully carried a leather bag. 'You were right, my lord.' He took off his hat and wiped his brow. 'Baron Wenlock asks for your surrender, in the name of the king.' He reached into the bag and produced a small bottle. 'I couldn't find a midwife. They gave me this for your daughter. He also asked me to give you this. He was most insistent I was to make sure that you alone must read it, my lord.'

'Thank you, Tully.' Richard took the note, unfolded it and held it to the light. John Wenlock was warning him. Calais was a trap. The army of Charles of Burgundy was poised to capture him once he was ashore. Wenlock promised he would prove himself loyal when he could. For now he cautioned them most strongly against entering the harbour.

The captain joined them, ready for instructions. Richard turned to him. 'Set a course for Honfleur, Captain. We are going to France.'

Tully looked surprised. He waited until the captain was out of earshot. 'What is there for us in France, my lord?'

Richard carefully folded the letter and tucked it inside his tunic. 'We don't have many options, Tully. I have to speak with King Louis. When we return to England it will be with an army.'

'To put George of Clarence on the throne?' He sounded incredulous.

Richard hesitated before answering. 'Let us see what King Louis has to say.'

He knew Tully wouldn't be the only one to question George's right to rule England. George may be Edward's brother, yet he would never be a leader, could never hold his own against those who would challenge him in parliament. Worst of all, he had already proved he didn't like to take advice. Richard had another plan. He had shared it with no one, not even Anne, as he wasn't even sure he could pull it off.

His thoughts were interrupted by a shout from the lookout. 'Sails ahoy!'

Richard cursed his failing eyesight. He could barely make out the sails of the distant ships and called for Tully to see if they were English. The ships were still too far off to identify. Richard ordered the captain to hold his course and for the men-at-arms to stand by as they closed on the distant ships.

At last Tully was able to make them out. 'It's the king's fleet, my lord.'

Richard cursed his luck. 'Call our men to arms!'

He looked back at his fleet and realised some would make easy targets for Edward's experienced commanders. Worse still, having his family on board meant Richard could not afford to take any risks. The one saving grace of not being able to rescue his flagship meant it would be harder for the enemy to know which ship to find him on.

Cannons were dragged into position and archers climbed high into the rigging, finding good vantage-points. Men-at-arms began strapping on armour and preparing weapons. Gunnery crews carried the heavy cannon balls from below decks and Tully's crossbowmen formed a guard around the access to the cabins. All they could do now was wait.

The wind was in their enemy's favour so he held back to watch as the two fleets closed, hulls ramming hard and cannons immediately firing as soon as targets came in range. Despite their disadvantage of numbers, Edward's ships were attacking with savage determination. One of the square-rigged caravels in Richard's fleet was hit with a shot which brought the main mast crashing to the deck in a splintering of wood. Richard could hear his men yelling as another began billowing smoke and flames as fire arrows found their mark in tar-covered rigging.

Tully stood at Richard's side and pointed to the enemy flagship. 'That's the banner of Sir Anthony Woodville, Earl Rivers.'

Richard cursed again. He'd had his chance to deal with the young earl and now he would pay the price for his outdated sense of chivalry. He decided to throw caution to the wind. 'Captain, bring our guns to bear on the closest ship!'

The deck tilted as the massive canvas sails responded to the change of course and Richard grabbed the handrail. Despite the danger they were in he was not going to let Edward's less experienced fleet pick them off one by one. The breeze freshened and he could taste the salty tang of sea spray. 'Gunners! Fire at will!'

They sailed alongside a sturdy looking carrack flying the royal standard from its mast. Richard's archers and crossbowmen began firing at anyone they could see on deck. Sailors fell dead as arrows and bolts struck them at viciously close range. Then his cannons began booming. The first shot struck the carrack broadside, smashing the heavy timbers and leaving a gaping hole. The second blast was iron shot which shredded the sails. The enemy ship veered away, crippled and no longer part of the battle. Richard looked behind and saw one of his ships being boarded, another on fire and at least one looking as if it was sinking. There was no time to worry about rescuing the survivors.

Then there was a cheer from his men as the Yorkist fleet began to pull back. They had carved his fleet in two and were taking as many ships back to England as they could. Richard was relieved his ship was not among them, although he wondered what fate would befall his captured crews at the hands of Lord Rivers.

Tully was assessing the damage, counting the remaining ships aloud. 'We've lost more than a dozen ships, my lord.'

Richard watched the departing fleet and realised they would return as soon as they could. He called to his captain. 'Put some sea between us while we have the chance.'

As the French coast began to appear on the horizon, so did more masts in the distance. Richard felt a sense of foreboding. The English Channel had always been his element. Now it seemed they would be hunted down before they even had the chance to make landfall. The men on his remaining ships had been at sea too long. They were already running low on fresh water and had only brought food and supplies for a much shorter voyage. Richard needed rest. He called to Tully once more, to identify the approaching fleet.

Tully studied them. 'Merchantmen. I can count at least twenty. They fly the flag of Burgundy, my lord.'

Richard was relieved. 'I'll not have them report our position to Burgundy. We'll take them as a prize.'

It was worth the risk and could solve his problem of how to pay his crews and purchase new supplies during their enforced stay in France. There was no contest as Richard's fleet surrounded the two dozen merchant ships and a couple of unlucky Breton fishing boats. Their crews surrendered without a shot being fired, to suffer the fate of being escorted to Honfleur as booty. Richard sent a fast rider to alert the king of his arrival and changed into dry clothes. He told his crews to sell what they could of the Burgundian cargo, then found a house in the town for his family and had the first uninterrupted sleep since he had left Exmouth.

It had taken nearly four days to reach the king's chateau at Amboise, so Richard was relieved to find the king was still in residence and expecting him.

King Louis greeted him with his usual ebullience. 'Earl Warwick!' The king hugged him like a long lost friend. 'It is so good to see you, safe and well.'

Richard knew his whole future depended on this meeting. 'I am thankful to Your Grace for agreeing to meet at such short notice.' He smiled. 'Events have moved a little faster than expected.'

The king looked behind Richard at his small entourage. 'Your wife, the countess, and your daughters?'

'Safe in Honfleur, together with my fleet.'

The king pulled a face. 'That will never do, I understand the town is full of pirates?'

'You have heard we met some Burgundian merchantmen?'

The king's smile vanished. 'You must release the ships you have seized, Earl Warwick. It would harm our reputation if we are seen to be allowing piracy.' He frowned. 'Matters are difficult enough between France and Burgundy. I must insist!'

Richard was surprised by the unexpected outburst. 'I will send orders to have the ships released, Your Grace, although I fear their cargo has long gone by now.'

'Then you will have to recover it.' The king's tone made it clear he expected no answer.

The king was keen to get down to business and led Richard into his private rooms, where they could not be overheard. The room was untidy, with papers scattered on the table and old ashes in the grate. The king cleared some books from two of the finely carved chairs and gestured for him to sit.

'I was told you had killed King Edward.' There was a mischievous glint in his eye.

Richard shook his head. 'You must not believe all you hear, Your Grace. King Edward is still my friend, despite all he has done.'

'So you believe he should remain on the throne?'

Richard hesitated, then realised the time had come to declare his hand. 'Could I still count on your support if I were to restore King Henry?'

King Louis looked pleased. 'There would be conditions.'

'Name them, Your Grace?'

'Your daughter Anne is still unmarried?'

'Yes, Your Grace. She is fourteen. Almost a woman now.'

'Then I propose a marriage.' He watched Richard's face to judge his reaction. 'To Prince Edward of Lancaster.'

Richard had to think fast. 'Margaret of Anjou would never agree to it.'

The king looked pleased with himself. 'Quite the contrary, Earl Warwick. She has already confirmed her approval.'

'I would have to meet her, to discuss.'

'That can be arranged. She is here, in Amboise.'

'Does Queen Margaret not regard me as her enemy?'

'She does, although like any good daughter, she listens to her father.' The king laughed. 'I have persuaded her father to ensure she understands what is best for their family.'

Richard could see his plan falling into place. One daughter married to the house of York, the other to the house of Lancaster. George would react badly to the news, although as Isabel's husband there would always be an important place for him at court.

He looked at the king, noting the twinkle of satisfaction in the old man's eye. 'You said there are conditions. Are there other conditions?'

'I will provide everything you need to restore King Henry. You must make your peace with Queen Margaret of Anjou.'

'And the Duke of Burgundy?'

'Yes.'

'You surprise me, Your Grace. I thought Charles of Burgundy was your sworn enemy?'

'He is. For now we must keep Burgundy from supporting Edward of York.' He leaned forward. 'Our time will come to deal with the Duke of Burgundy. I will teach him respect for France, and you, Earl Warwick, can become the Prince of Holland and Zeeland.'

✝

Richard made the journey to Angers, capital of Anjou, with as grand a retinue as he could bring together. He rode with his wife, his daughter Anne and her ladies in waiting following behind. Anne had seemed distant towards him since they arrived in France. His daughter Isabel was not well enough to travel and remained in Honfleur with her husband the duke. This suited Richard, as certain aspects of the discussions he expected to have would not bode well with his son-in-law.

Queen Margaret of Anjou had aged well. Richard hadn't been sure what to expect, although he knew she had been living in poverty for some time. He remembered the first time he had seen her. As a fifteen-year-old at her coronation she had left quite an impression on him. Now she was forty years old and looked at him with the same confident gaze, giving no clue to what she might be thinking.

They met in the grand hall of the great castle of Angers, with its imposing high towers and air of slow decline. The queen was dressed in cloth of gold and wearing a coronet which flashed with precious rubies. At her side sat a young man with questioning eyes. Edward of Lancaster was dressed as a prince, although he seemed to lack the bearing of one. As Richard knelt before the queen, waiting for her to speak, he noticed the hem of her dress was worn thin where it had rubbed on the ground.

He could wait no longer. 'Your Highness, I understand King Louis has told you of my intentions?'

Queen Margaret hesitated before responding. 'King Louis sees us as pawns in his game, Earl Warwick.' She spoke in English, with the soft accent of Anjou.

Richard continued to kneel and looked up into her eyes. 'We must remind him that we are more than pawns. I am a knight.' He saw he had her attention. 'And you a queen.'

She did not return his smile. 'An exiled queen. Thanks to you, Earl Warwick, another woman calls herself Queen of England.' There was a note of bitterness in her voice. 'Why did you take up arms against your lawful King?'

Richard had anticipated this. 'I always swore loyalty to King Henry. I took up arms against his corrupt advisors, Your Highness.'

The queen frowned at him. 'I know you kneel before me because King Louis has told you to.'

Richard reached inside his tunic and handed her the gift he had brought. 'I'd like to return this to you, Your Highness.'

Queen Margaret stared at the old silver crucifix in astonishment. 'How did you come by this?'

'I rescued it from the property you had to leave behind in England. I thought it might have some value to you.'

She looked at him differently now. 'This belonged to my mother, Queen Isabella.' Her voice was softer. 'Before that it belonged to my grandmother, the Duchess of Lorraine. I was named Margaret after her.'

'I am pleased to return it to you, Your Highness.' Richard could sense a subtle shift in the way she looked at him. There was now an appraising glint in her eye as she looked again at the old silver crucifix and back at his face.

'You brought this from England with the intention of seeing me?'

'The King of France will help me return King Henry to the throne. He will need you at his side once more, Your Highness.'

Margaret had regained her stern composure. 'And you, Earl Warwick, how do you profit from this reversal of fortunes?'

'I propose a marriage, Your Grace. Richard glanced at Edward of Lancaster, who had been listening impassively. 'My daughter Anne would be married to your son.'

'No!' Her voice sounded shrill.

Richard tried to control his anger. 'My daughter is heiress to a great fortune, Your Grace.'

She glowered at him. 'My son is a royal prince. He will marry a French princess.'

'Your Highness.' Richard felt his plan unravelling. 'You will need to consider this matter carefully.' Despite himself he could hear the threat in his voice.

Margaret calmed herself. 'I sense the hand of King Louis in this?'

Richard looked into her eyes. 'You want to be certain of my commitment to your cause?' He didn't need to wait for her answer. 'Then our families must be bound together through this marriage.'

The wedding would have to wait for a papal dispensation, so a solemnisation was arranged in the gothic cathedral of Angers, with its towering twin spires. Richard escorted his daughter. She wore her wedding dress of cloth of gold, with her long hair combed down as a sign of her purity. Prince Edward was now dressed in a knight's regalia, wearing a coronet on his head and a finely crafted sword low slung on his belt.

King Louis was at the front of the congregation, alongside the portly Duke Rene of Anjou and many French nobles and knights. Queen Margaret sat with Countess Anne and their ladies in waiting. The pipe organ had been destroyed in a fire and never repaired, so Richard had arranged for his personal trumpeters to play a fanfare which echoed around the high ceilinged nave as their procession made its way to the altar.

The betrothal was blessed in French by the Bishop of Anjou and prayers were said in thanks of the union. During the over long sermon Richard stared up at new, circular stained glass windows, built to replace those lost in the fire. They showed Christ of the Apocalypse, with twelve colourful panels radiating from him showing crowned figures playing musical instruments, rejoicing the remade world. That seemed strangely appropriate for the occasion, although he was bemused by the twelve signs of the Zodiac built into the design.

After the ceremony was over Richard finally found himself alone with his wife. He looked at her, realising for the first time in ages how attractive she looked in her new dress. It had been specially made for her stay in Angers with their daughter while he began the preparations for an invasion of England. He could still sense the unfamiliar awkwardness between them which troubled him.

'Anne hardly reacted when I told her she was to be wed to Prince Edward of Lancaster.'

'I prepared her as well as I could.'

'The marriage was far from a certainty.'

'How did you persuade Queen Margaret?'

'I didn't. King Louis used her father's greed and, I suspect, her brother's ambition.'

'And now once again, we need a papal dispensation.'

'King Louis will obtain one. It will give her time to get to know the prince.'

She put her hand on his arm affectionately. 'He is a handsome young man.'

Richard had to agree. 'I see something of his grandfather's spirit.' Then he whispered in her ear, in the way he had used to when only she must hear. 'And his new wife has something of her mother's beauty.'

She looked pleased at the compliment. 'With time, Anne will come to love him.'

'That is my hope. For now I know she will do her duty.'

'And you, Richard, what is your duty now?'

He held her close, for the first time since they had left England. 'My duty is to return King Henry to the throne.'

Anne looked at him with concern in her eyes. 'At what cost?'

'Whatever it takes. I have no other option.'

✝

George reacted badly to the news of Anne's wedding. 'You misled me!' he seemed unconcerned that their conversation could be overheard. 'This always was your plan, wasn't it?'

Richard had expected trouble from his son-in-law. 'King Louis would only support me if we made our peace with Queen Margaret.'

'And what am I supposed to do?'

'You will be next in line to the throne after King Henry and his male heirs.' Richard tried to calm him. There had been rumours of messages from Edward to his brother and Richard needed George's loyalty.

George seemed unimpressed. 'Edward's army is waiting for us. The Burgundian fleet is blockading the Channel. Henry is an imbecile. How can you possibly put him on the throne?'

'Edward has made it easier for us. A serious error of judgement.'

George already knew. 'Henry Percy?'

'Yes. I couldn't believe it when Edward released Henry Percy from the Tower.' His father died fighting for Queen Margaret, now he has restored him to the Earldom of Northamptonshire.'

'Driving your brother John to our side?'

Richard didn't want to share his plan with George just yet. His brother John had finally agreed to help draw Edward north, away from the coast. 'John's army is greater than Edwards. Experienced men, who were loyal to King Henry.'

George still seemed unhappy. 'As soon as we set out from here we'll have to deal with the Burgundy fleet.'

'Take a look at the sky, George. There's a thunderstorm brewing. We have nearly sixty ships safe in the harbour, ready to sail as soon as it passes. No fleet can stay at sea indefinitely. The Burgundian ships will have to run for shelter.'

The storm was worse than Richard expected, so when they set out from Honfleur at the first light of dawn there were no other ships to be seen. As well as the men who escaped with him, he had promised to reinstate Jasper Tudor as Earl of Pembroke, who brought a sizeable army of Lancastrian supporters and mercenaries. Unwilling to risk a landfall in Kent, Richard's fleet sailed to Plymouth and landed unopposed, gathering support from Wales and the West Country as they marched. As they reached London they were greeted with rumours that Edward had fled for Burgundy, taking only his most loyal nobles with him.

Richard wasted no time in freeing the king from the Tower and taking control of Westminster. He was grateful for support from his brother George, who was appointed as Chancellor and helping decide which officials to replace and who should be pardoned. As soon as he was able to he rode north to see his brother John at Pontefract Castle.

'You remind me even more of our father!' Richard hugged his brother warmly.

'And you look well for a fugitive with a price on his head!' There was an edge to John's reply.

Richard took off his cloak and riding gloves. 'I hope you have come to tell me these rumours about Edward are true?'

'Edward has gone, Richard. He escaped in the night with the Duke of Gloucester, William Hastings and Anthony Woodville. We rounded up as many of his men as we could find. Most seem ready to swear allegiance to King Henry.'

'Good. I think you will find King Henry will grant them all a pardon.' Richard was relieved. 'Queen Elizabeth is in sanctuary in Westminster Abbey. She has just given birth to a son.'

John already knew. 'I heard she has named him Edward.'

'Now we have three Edwards to worry about.'

'Where is Edward of Lancaster?'

'Waiting with his mother in France.'

'You've sent word?'

'Of course. They are to sail as soon as he has married my daughter Anne.'

'So now there's no going back?' He looked at Richard as if wondering how much to tell him. 'I hear you are making yourself unpopular in London, Richard. Some men of Kent acting in your name have been over zealous and freed all the prisoners. Not just those loyal to King Henry. Armed gangs control the streets.'

'I'll deal with them. We must have order as soon as we can. You know these things take time.'

His brother frowned. 'Time is the one thing we don't have, Richard. Even now I expect Edward is preparing to return, with an army paid for by Charles of Burgundy.'

'We will be ready for him, John. I've sent men to secure Calais and plan to use it as a base from which to control the Channel and cut off any attempt by Edward to surprise us.'

'There is also the matter of the king.'

'I have restored him, as I promised. He is in what used to be Queen Elizabeth's apartments.'

'You know what they are saying? They are calling him a stuffed woolsack, a shadow on a wall.'

'Then I must remind the people that the king was appointed by God.'

Chapter 26 - Spring 1471

Richard had read the parchment letter from Anne many times and knew every word. He had been frustrated in December when the papal dispensation was granted and he couldn't leave London to see their daughter marry. He consoled himself with the knowledge she had at last become a princess of Lancaster and he would be with his family at Christmas. Then Anne wrote that they would have to wait for the winter storms in the Channel to ease before sailing from France.

The weather finally improved and Richard rode to Dover with a fine carriage and men to escort them back to London. He'd cursed his failing eyesight again as he scanned the sea mist shrouded horizon, for sight of their fleet. His brother John had been right. He needed the people to see Queen Margaret at the king's side, with him accepted as her chief minister. It was the only way to convince them of his legitimacy and commitment to the side of Lancaster. He also missed his wife and knew she would not be finding life easy in the court of Queen Margaret.

After a week of waiting a small caravel arrived from France and the captain handed him Anne's letter. It bore her private seal, although from the formal way she wrote Richard guessed she was concerned someone else might read it. Reading between the lines it seemed Queen Margaret was making more excuses to delay her arrival in England. Anne confirmed that she and their daughter were well, although she gave him no clue about when they would return.

Richard was disappointed and his return to London without the queen added fuel to the rumours that he was falsely representing her interests. He was worried about holding his fragile grip on the country until the queen was back in London. People were openly criticising his alliance with France. The treasury had still to recover from Edward's excesses and was still bankrupt. The streets of London were far from safe, with armed gangs still at liberty.

Then on a bright spring morning, the news he had been dreading finally came. A rider from John's castle in Pontefract had travelled through the night and arrived as Richard was getting dressed for the day. He immediately sent for his brother George, and when he arrived Richard welcomed the Archbishop to his study and went straight to the point.

'Edward is in England with the Duke of Burgundy.' He watched his brother's reaction. 'They landed at Ravenspur in a fleet of ships loaded with mercenaries.'

George frowned, trying to make sense of the news. 'Dear God! We always knew he would come, although now it has happened I fear for us all.' He looked at Richard questioningly. 'Do you know where they are headed?'

Richard nodded. 'He's taken York. He told them he only wanted his dukedom and Sandal Castle back. It seems they threw open the gates to welcome him!'

He was relieved to see his news was clearly a blow for George. Since his return to the ranks of the Lancastrians he had found it difficult to know who he could rely on and was even ready to suspect his own brothers. It had crossed his mind that as Archbishop of York, George was extremely well connected in the old city and could easily have encouraged the people to grant access to Edward.

George was still thinking through the implications of the news. 'What has John done about it? He has quite an army at Pontefract Castle.'

'That's the worst of it.' Richard shook his head. 'John seems to have let him pass.'

'Why would he do that?'

Richard stared out of the window. It looked out over the Thames and a number of boats were already on the water, ferrying people up and down the river, apparently unaware of the impending disaster facing the city. He remembered how staunchly loyal his brother John had been to Edward and his father before him.

'You know, George, I think he turned his face to the wall. John has spent too long fighting for Edward to take him on.'

'So what's our plan?'

'The Duke of Clarence is on his way here with an army. I believe I can persuade John to bring his men from the north, then we'll need as many men as we can find from Kent and Wales and all the able bodied men we can rally here.'

George understood. 'Edward will have three armies to face.'

'It's time to call in all my favours and find out who supports our cause.'

'I think it could prove harder than you expect.' George's face was grim. 'The Lancastrian families have long memories, Richard. More than a few have lost fathers in battles against your armies. Even your own men will find their loyalty tested when they are asked to risk their lives to defend a king they no longer believe in and fight one they helped put on the throne.'

Richard had to resort to threats and generous bribes and promises to raise even half as many men as he would have liked. He waited as long as he dared then set out north with several thousand men from the midlands. As they neared the old walled city of Coventry rumours began to reach him that Edward's army was close by. It seemed a prudent move to withdraw within the city walls until his brother's men arrived or the rumours were proved false. He was settling down for the evening when Tully called for him.

'My lord, you have to come and see this.'

Richard looked at him with a puzzled expression. 'What is it, Tully? Has my brother's army been sighted?'

'You had best come and see for yourself, my lord.'

Richard followed Luke Tully up the stone steps to the top of the city wall to look. Edward's army had come right up to them and was arrayed in battle order outside the city walls. In the centre of the row of mounted knights was the tall, unmistakable figure of Edward, in full armour. To his left was a knight holding high the banner of York. On his right was another carrying the royal standard. Edward's pretence was over. Now he was openly claiming his throne.

For three days Richard resisted the challenge to fight, waiting for either George or his brother John to arrive with reinforcements. Then the York army disappeared as suddenly as it had arrived, followed closely by the appearance at last of John from Pontefract Castle with his army of archers and northern knights. John had also brought his great cannons to add to Richard's artillery. At last they had an army capable of taking London.

They decided to wait in Coventry for the arrival of George, Duke of Clarence, when his messenger rode to the gate under a flag of truce. The duke had joined

Edward with his army of men raised in the cause of Lancaster, every one of them now ready to fight for York. As a final insult, Edward had taken Warwick Castle unopposed and was making it his headquarters. Richard was unable to control his anger and loudly cursed the day he had ever thought George would be a suitable husband for his daughter Isabel. His brother John tried to calm him.

'The Duke of Clarence has offered to broker a peace with Edward.' He held the letter in his hand which could save so many lives and change the future course of events. 'He says he can secure us all a royal pardon, Richard.'

Richard took the letter and ripped it in two. 'There's his answer.' He threw the torn pieces to the floor.

John frowned at his brother and spoke softly, almost to himself. 'I hope we've enough men to take on both Edward and George's armies.'

Richard shook his head. 'My guess is we have no more than twelve or fifteen thousand men between us. I'd have liked twice that many by now. We'll have to manage with what we've got.'

'It's going to be close.'

'That's why we can't waste one more day.' Richard agreed. 'We have to take the initiative and reach London first.'

John looked out of the window at the sky. 'Let us hope the weather holds. I hate marching in the rain.'

They set off late in the morning in full armour and soon had the news that Edward had already taken London unopposed. His army had marched into the city that day to the cheers of the Londoners. Edward had immediately taken King Henry back into custody and set about preparing for war. He was now said to be rallying men to his cause and proclaiming Richard and those who followed his banner as traitors in league with France.

There were also rumours that the Archbishop of York had pledged allegiance to Edward and received a royal pardon. Richard struggled to conceal his disappointment. It would be impossible to take Edward on in London now. He remembered the nightmare of fighting in the streets of the city before, charging down narrow streets, never sure who was friend or enemy. They could only stand any chance if he was certain of the support of the people and by all accounts they had rallied to Edward's cause.

He gathered his commanders in his tent and spread out the map. Well drawn, it showed all the main approaches to the city.

'We must choose where to make our stand.' He saw their tense faces. 'We have more men than them, so let's learn the lessons of St. Albans and meet them on open ground.' He pointed to the map. 'We need enough time to prepare.'

By that evening they arrived in Barnet, about one mile to the north of the city. Lookouts were posted and scouts sent ahead to try to find out where Edward's army had got to. The scouts soon returned with grim news. Edward was already on the outskirts of Barnet with over ten thousand men, taking up position close to a marsh in the valley to the south of their camp. Richard rode to their forward position with Tully and scanned the darkness.

'I can't see a thing!' Richard looked up at the black sky. There was no moon.

'They are out there close by somewhere, my lord.' Tully squinted into the night. 'We could spoil their night's sleep with the guns?'

Richard agreed. 'We've dragged those cannons all this way, let's show them why.'

The first of the guns boomed across the valley with a blinding flash of light, followed by a second, then a third. His gunnery captain, a thick set veteran of the northern sieges, looked into the night. There was no sound from across the valley, just the drifting smell of sulphur in the still air.

'It's no use, my lord. We can't find the range.'

'We've given them something to think about. Keep the guns here and have your crews standing ready at first light.'

The gunnery captain went to tell his men. Richard heard a rider approaching from the rear and turned to see his brother John, who had been overseeing the deployment of his men. He dismounted and joined Richard, peering into the darkness.

'How far away do we think they are?'

Richard turned to him. 'There's no way of telling. Have your lookouts stay sharp and ready to sound the alarm.'

✣

He woke at dawn after a restless night. Strange sounds kept him alert during the night and he lay awake, turning over recent events in his mind. Easter Sunday was normally a day spent in peaceful prayer and for a moment Richard wondered if that offered a chance of reconciliation, then dismissed the thought. They had passed the point of no return. He looked out over the fields of Barnet. They were wreathed in damp, early morning mist, filling the valley with an ethereal, swirling, whiteness that hid everything from sight.

Tully was already dressed in his mail coat and helped Richard strap on his armour.

'They are close, my lord. You can hear their voices in the valley.'

Richard listened. He heard horses neighing, muffled voices and metal objects clanging as men prepared for battle. The early morning mist made sounds seem to travel more clearly, although he found it hard to judge the distance and direction.

'Quickly, then. Let's be ready for them when they come.' He strapped on his sword belt. 'I want you to watch my back, Tully.'

'Don't I always, my lord?' Tully grinned. 'I've been watching your back since you were fifteen!'

Richard looked at Tully and smiled. Tully was the one person whose loyalty he had never questioned. The loss of his brother George to Edward's cause had affected him more deeply than he'd expected. If his brother John also decided to defect to Edward, it would mean the end.

'You do, Tully, and I thank you.' Richard put on his helmet and raised the visor. 'Let's go and finish this!'

Trumpets sounded eerily in the swirling mist as Edward's archers unleashed a storm of arrows, taking Richard's men by surprise. Some were still putting on their armour, others were tending the horses. The arrows struck home to the yells of men who were wounded. Then a salvo of Yorkist bombards roared in the early morning air. Heavy stone balls crashed into the lines of men and horses, breaking bones and crushing heads and deadly iron shot shredded flesh not protected with armour.

Edward's army stormed forward up the slope, closing the gap between the two armies and seemingly oblivious to the deadly arrows of Richard's hastily assembled archers. Richard gave the signal to his gunnery captain and the heavy cannons they had dragged half way across the country unleashed a hail of shot. This time there was no question of the range and each blast cut a swathe through the advancing men.

On Richard's right flank the men-at-arms under the command of his brother-in law the Earl of Oxford pushed back against the Yorkist left, swiftly driving them from the field. Then there was a disaster. The earl's soldiers were caught in a shower of arrows from their own side, confused for Edward's men by their badge of a star that looked like the York badge of a sun with rays. Men fell dead and dying. Others fled in panic.

Richard rallied his men. 'Stand firm!' He shouted, looking for his brother John.

There in the thick of the fighting was his brother's banner, still flying. Close by was another, the banner of the white boar. He was saddened to realise that Richard, Duke of Gloucester, who John had taught to fight at Middleham Castle, was now using those skills against his teacher. The young duke pressed his army forward, followed by the knights on warhorses, charging into the fighting men with sharp pointed lances and swinging broadswords and war axes without mercy. Even as Richard watched, his brother's banner disappeared from view.

'Tully!' Richard shouted, 'We have to help my brother!'

With Tully at his side they hacked and slashed through the press of men towards where he had last seen John's banner. The men of his personal guard fought bravely, cutting a path through the battlefield before they were surrounded by Edward's knights. One was speared by a lance and another had his helmet shattered by a war hammer. Tully narrowly missed a swinging mace, then pulled Richard out of the path of a riderless horse with wild eyes that stamped iron hooves on men in its path.

They had been fighting since dawn and the sun was nearly overhead, burning off the morning mist to reveal the scale of the carnage. Dead and badly wounded men in the red of Warwick lay scattered on the field. Richard spotted the unmistakably tall figure of King Edward, fighting in the thick of the battle, killing and driving all before him.

Richard could see his line was broken through, the hordes of Yorkist soldiers putting an end to his dreams. His men started to run. First one threw down his sword, then another. Those who stood their ground were shown no favour, brutally slain with savage war axes that crushed their plate armour as if it were made of paper.

A soldier limped towards him clutching his red banner of the bear and ragged staff. A hail of arrows flew through the air and the standard bearer realised too late they were aiming at the banner. An arrow thumped into his chest, spinning him round and causing the banner to crash to the ground. A rousing cheer went up from the York archers as they saw the end of the House of Warwick.

As the sun rose to its height the battle was over. Richard looked back to where he had left his horse. If he was quick there was still a chance to escape. He could ride to the coast and find a ship to the safety of Calais. He would have to run. He pulled off the heavy helmet that obscured his view and threw it to the ground. Three knights surrounded him. Richard's blade slashed through the air and wounded one. The other two showed no mercy. Richard sank to his knees, mortally wounded. He pulled off his gauntlets and pressed his hand to the wound. Blood ran through his fingers and he looked to the sky, into the glorious shining sun.

William Shakespeare: King Henry the Sixth
Act V. Scene II

A field of Battle near Barnet.

These eyes, that now are dimmed with death's black veil,
Have been as piercing as the mid-day sun,
To search the secret treasons of the world:
The wrinkles in my brows, now fill'd with blood,
Were likened oft to kingly sepulchres;
For who liv'd king, but I could dig his grave?
And who durst smile when Warwick bent his brow?
Lo! now my glory smear'd in dust and blood;
My parks, my walks, my manors that I had,
Even now forsake me; and, of all my lands
Is nothing left me but my body's length.
Why, what is pomp, rule, reign, but earth and dust?
And, live we how we can, yet die we must.

Epilogue

Luke Tully was wounded in the battle. His life was spared, as were many of the common men who surrendered to the mercy of the king, and he found Richard's body and that of his brother John. They had been stripped of their armour and were taken in a cart to be put on public display at St. Paul's Cathedral. It was important for Edward to prove Richard was really dead, so there they remained for two days in open wooden coffins before George Neville was able to take them on their final journey to join their parents at Bisham Abbey.

Richard's wife Anne returned to Portsmouth from France and was on route to join Queen Margaret and her daughter Anne at Weymouth when she was told of her husband's death at the battle of Barnet. She went instead to Beaulieu Abbey, where she begged for sanctuary.

King Edward effectively ended Lancastrian resistance at the Battle of Tewkesbury in 1471, where those who were executed included the teenage son of Henry VI, Prince Edward. King Henry met an ignominious end in the Tower of London shortly afterwards, allegedly of 'pure displeasure and melancholy'.

Richard Neville's lands were shared between Edward's brothers George, Duke of Clarence and Richard, Duke of Gloucester, as well as other favourites at his court. George was made Earl of Warwick, as well as Earl of Salisbury. Richard, Duke of Gloucester, married Anne Neville in 1472 and her father's illegitimate daughter Margaret became her lady in waiting.

Tully eventually found his way back to the household at Middleham Castle. He was there when the entire estate was granted to Richard, Duke of Gloucester, who made it his main residence, even when he became King of England. This was how Luke Tully found himself wearing the badge of the white boar on a fateful day at Bosworth Field.

Author Notes

It can be a challenge for the reader of historical fiction to understand which events are based on fact and which are pure fiction. I have tried through my extensive research to ensure that all the events, people and places named in this novel are based on historical facts, verifiable from several sources.

The only exceptions are the two people who play important roles in Richard's life, his loyal squire and his mistress. Richard Neville had several squires throughout his life yet their names are lost. There are many accounts of how he surrounded himself with men who would lay down their lives to protect him, so Luke Tully represents them all. I thought I had discovered the name of the mother of Richard's illegitimate daughter Margaret, then found it couldn't be verified, so unlike the biographies where she vanishes into the background, I have been able to suggest the important part she played in Richard's early life.

In the course of the research for this book I enjoyed learning about the lives of people in the fifteenth century and the chance discoveries that bring it all to life. One such 'find' was the exploration of the life of Richard's daughter Margaret. I read that one of her descendants had a certain notoriety and with a little digging I managed to establish the line of descent:

Richard Nevill. By an unknown woman he had issue:

Margaret Neville, She married Sir John Huddleston of Teesdale and had issue:

Joan Huddleston married Antony Fleming and had issue:

Antony Fleming of Rydel, d.1537. He had issue:

William Fleming of Rydel, d.1598. He had issue:

Eleanor Fleming married John Lowther d.1637 and had issue:

Agnes Lowther married Roger Kirkby and had issue:

William Kirkby of Aslack married unknown and had issue:

Eleanor Kirky married Humphrey Senhouse and had issue:

Bridget Senhouse, b.1696 in Deerham and died 1744. She married John Christian (b.1688) and had issue:

Charles Christian, b.1729 and d.1768. He married Anne Dixon (b.1730) and had issue:

Fletcher Christian, b.SEP 25 1764 and d.OCT 3 1793.

(I like to think that some of Richard Neville's character shines through in Fletcher Christian's actions as the anti-hero of the mutiny on the *Bounty*.)

Sources and Further reading

Baumgaertner, Wm. E., Squires, Knights, Barons, Kings: War and Politics in Fifteenth Century England, (Trafford Publishing 2010)

Betham, William, The Baronetage of England: Or The History of the English Baronets (Nabu Press 2012)

Boardman, Andrew, The Medieval Soldier in the Wars of the Roses (Sutton Publishing, 1998)

Castor, Helen, Blood and Roses (Faber & Faber 2005)

Clark, David, Barnet -1471 Death of a Kingmaker (Pen and Sword Military 2007)

Douglas, David & Myers, Alec, English historical documents. [Late Medieval]. 1327 – 1485 (Psychology Press 1995)

Ducios, Charles, The History of Lewis XI, King of France. (Rarebooksclub.com 2013)

Gairdner, James, The Paston letters, 1422-1509 (General Books 2011)

Griffiths, Ralph Alan, The Reign of King Henry VI: The Exercise of Royal Authority, 1422-1461 (Earnest Benn 1981)

Haigh, Philip, The Military Campaigns of the Wars of the Roses (Sutton Publishing 1995)

Hallam, Elizabeth (Ed) The Chronicles of The Wars of The Roses (Weidenfield and Nicolson 1988)

Hicks, Michael, The Wars of the Roses (Yale University Press, 2010)

Hicks, Michael, Warwick the kingmaker (Blackwell Publishing, 1998)

Kendall, Paul Murray, Warwick the kingmaker (W&N 2002)

Kennedy, Elspeth. (Trans.) A Knight's Own Book of Chivalry (University of Pennsylvania Press, 2005)

Newman, Paul B., Daily Life in the Middle Ages (McFarland, 2001)

Norman, A.V.B., The Medieval Soldier (Barnes & Noble Books, 1971)

Pollard A.J., Warwick the kingmaker Politics, Power and Fame (Hambledown Continuum, 2007)

Rodger, N.A.M., The Safeguard of the Sea: A Naval History of Britain 660-1649 (Penguin 2004)

Rose, Anne, Calais: An English Town in France, 1347-1558 (Boydell Press, 2008)

Santiuste, David, Edward IV and The Wars of The Roses (Pen & Sword Books Ltd., 2013)

Saul, Nigel, Chivalry in Medieval England (Harvard University Press, 2011)

Wagner, John A, Encyclopedia of the Wars of the Roses (ABC-CLIO, 2001)

Weir, Alison, Lancaster and York: The Wars of the Roses, (Ballantine Books 1995)

Also by Tony Riches: Queen Sacrifice

10th Century Wales is a country divided, with the kingdom of the south becoming Saxon and the north violently defending the old ways. The inevitable civil war is brutal and savage in this tale of divided loyalty and revenge, treachery and love.

Kings and queens battle for control of the country, with wealth and glory for the victor and death and ruin for the loser. The Bishops of Wales struggle to keep the faith while knights and war lords turn events to advantage and the lives of ordinary people are changed forever by the conflict.

Queen Sacrifice is also a legendary tactic in the ancient game of chess. Russian chess grand master Lakov Neishtadt describes the sacrifice of the queen for higher interests as 'a source of continuing fascination for the chess novice and master alike.'

The narrative faithfully follows every move in the queen sacrifice game, known as 'The Game of the Century' between Donald Byrne and 13-year-old Bobby Fischer in New York on October 17th 1956.

Paperback and eBook available from **Amazon**

Also by Tony Riches: The Shell

Mombasa beach: The dream holiday of a lifetime turns into a nightmare for a young couple. Brutally attacked and kidnapped, she has to battle for survival in one of the remotest and most dangerous areas of north east Kenya.

He has to find and rescue her - before it is too late. Palm trees line an idyllic beach of white coral sand. An Arabian dhow sails on the clear blue waters of the Indian Ocean. Two lovers are ruthlessly torn apart, perhaps forever. Lucy is bound and helpless, taken far from the safety of the world she knows. Unconscious and bleeding, nothing has prepared Steve for what he needs to do.

Lucy's journey is mental as well as physical as she discovers how easily the protective shell of her old world has been stripped away. Everything she took for granted is gone and she has to fight to survive, one day at a time. Whatever happens, she knows her life will never be the same again.

Based on actual events and current news reports, this fast-paced action and adventure novel explores the reality of the tensions between the old tribal ways and life in the new, rapidly developing country of Kenya.

Paperback and eBook available from **Amazon**

7902125R00203

Printed in Great Britain
by Amazon.co.uk, Ltd.,
Marston Gate.